Not the most auspicious start to my guiding career, Crystal admitted to herself.

Conner sat back down, took a grateful swig of the coffee and sighed. "This could have gone better," he said stating the obvious.

"What happens next?" Crystal asked.

"We wait until dawn, see if he turns up, and escort everyone out of here. Hopefully, Philip is waiting for us at the lodge, and we can drive this whole miserable lot back to the city a day early. In the meantime, I suggest we follow everyone's lead and try to get a little shuteye."

Conner's radio crackled with Sam's voice, "We've found the missing man from your group, Conner. He's at the bottom of a cliff. I'm sorry to say this search and rescue operation has become a search and recover."

Conner paled at the news.

"What does 'search and recover' mean?" Crystal asked.

"It means he's dead."

Winter Takes All

by

ML Erdahl

A Seattle Wilderness Mystery,
Book 1

Winter Takes All

Cover Art by *Abigail Owen*

The Wild Rose Press, Inc.
PO Box 708
Adams Basin, NY 14410-0708
Visit us at www.thewildrosepress.com

Publishing History
First Crimson Rose Edition, 2019
Print ISBN 978-1-5092-2678-8
Digital ISBN 978-1-5092-2679-5

A Seattle Wilderness Mystery, Book 1
Published in the United States of America

Dedication

To my wife, Emily,
whose love and support made this book possible.

Chapter One

Through the rhythmically squeaking windshield wipers of her idling car, Crystal Rainey spotted the Space Needle peeking from behind the high rises of downtown. Her parents, who lived a short distance from the iconic landmark, would certainly not approve of what she planned to do. Crystal shot off a quick text.

—*I'm at 312 Beacon Ave. If I don't text back in an hour, send help.*—

She stared at the vista of the city for another moment before shaking her head to snap out of her reverie. *Enough wasting time.* Her one hour was ticking.

It was a foolhardy risk confronting a murder suspect in his own home, but at least her best friend Olivia was aware of where she was.

Turning off her car, she tugged her hood over her head and strode through the pools of light cast by the streetlamps, determined to get the answers she needed. Astonished, Crystal realized it was not even two weeks after New Year's and everything about her had changed, forever.

****

Things had gotten a little out of hand when Olivia had produced the makings for cosmopolitans to ring in the New Year. Typically, the annual shindig consisted of a few drinks coupled with some dancing, but, oh,

1

those cosmos. They had led to an epic two-day hangover. The last time Crystal had overindulged to this magnitude was six years ago, on her hazy twenty-first birthday.

Despite her less than perfect constitution, Crystal managed to drag herself out of bed to catch the bus to work. The Seattle winter did nothing to help her spirits as she stared at the passing landscape. Rain rivulets obscured her vision through the bus window and were a persistent, bleak reminder of the weather which settled over the Pacific Northwest this time of year. To top off her burgeoning poor temperament, the air on the bus was a damp aromatic mixture of wool clad people and their musty belongings.

Seated beside her, an elderly man in a faded three-piece suit gave a soft snore. His scuffed brown leather briefcase rested on his lap, and the last few remaining gray hairs of his comb over flapped in the air current cast by the heat vent mounted under the window.

The bus bounced through a pothole, re-awakening the dull ache in the back of her head and causing the gentleman to sit up straight, glance out the window, and ask, "What's the next stop?"

"Fourth and Stewart," Crystal answered as she continued staring out at the city.

"Thank goodness. I'm glad I didn't oversleep again. Made me late for work last week." The man patted his remaining hair back into place and yawned. "Did you have a good holiday?"

"Fine," Crystal droned. She attempted to put as much disinterest into the one word as she could. She was *really* not in the mood to talk.

"Off to work?" The man was shaking his

grogginess off and refused to pick up on her body language.

"Yes," she confirmed.

"What do you do?"

"Office work. I make copies, file documents…that sort of stuff."

"Oh, do you like it?"

"It pays the bills."

"So, no, you don't like it." He gave her a sympathetic look.

"I hate it," she agreed with a sigh. "My boss is petty, cruel, and vindictive. A perfect trifecta." She made this complaint so often she could barely muster up the energy to feel angry.

"Aww, cheer up. It is a new year after all. Things are meant to change for the better. Well, this is my stop. Good luck with your job."

"It was nice talking to you." She gave a little wave to the man as he gathered his briefcase and toddled off the bus into the rain. Oddly, she did feel better after speaking to the stranger.

This *was* a new year. The season for change and a chance to better her life. Feeling the beginnings of a warm spread of optimism, she drew her phone out of her bag to jot down a few resolutions to help get out of her funk.

Get a better job. Meet a nice guy. Go hiking more often.

This was a comprehensive list of what was incomplete in her life. She was smart enough to find a better job than the hopeless one she had stumbled into after college. It was just a matter of getting herself organized and sorting through the job market. Also, she didn't know why she hadn't met a nice guy. She was in good shape from the hiking she did manage to fit into her life, and her pert nose, chestnut hair, and matching brown eyes had received their share of compliments. She just needed to get herself out there and good things would happen. As to her last resolution, she adored being in the forests of the Pacific Northwest and vowed to spend more time in the wilderness.

Satisfied, she titled her file *New Year's Resolutions*.

An error message popped up on her screen. *Do you want to replace existing file?* That was odd. She renamed her current file *New Year's Resolutions 2* and tapped save.

Opening the original document, she saw it had been written shortly before midnight on December thirty-first of the previous year. No wonder she didn't remember this list. She must have come up with it in last year's tired fog during Olivia's annual celebration. She tapped on the icon of the file and stared at what popped up on the screen.

Get a new job. Meet an awesome guy. Get outside more often.

Something inside Crystal froze, and her mind churned over the implications of what lay on the screen before her. She switched off her phone and lowered it into her bag. Everything around her slowed down, and the noise of the city receded to an odd echo. Here was proof her life was going nowhere.

"Fourth and Pike," the bus driver called. Her stop.

She grabbed her bag and umbrella and strode into the rain. The first step to improving her life was freeing herself from her dead-end office job at Smith, Axford, and Devry.

****

The impetuous departure from her monotonous job had faded into several panic induced days of being unemployed with a laughable bank account. A lucky break, though, had landed Crystal in her present seat, studying the stern-eyed woman who was about to become her new boss. Her last supervisor at Smith, Axford, and Devry had been nothing like the controlled professional across the desk from her, and the stark difference heartened Crystal. Her life was headed in a new and exciting direction, even though she was inwardly freaking out about how unqualified she was for her new position as a wilderness guide.

"Here is your W-9, your health insurance form, this shows the starting wage, and signing this says you won't work for another outdoor adventure company while employed by Emerald City Outfitters."

Crystal snuck a peek at the wage. Relieved, she was pleased to see it was actually a little more than she had earned at Smith, Axford, and Devry.

"You can also work in the store if the wilderness guide time doesn't make forty hours a week," her new boss Amelia informed her. "This is rarely a problem. Our ECO Adventures, as we call them, are extremely popular and are often booked year-round."

Crystal was not excited about working in the store, but she also didn't want her condo foreclosed on, so she could live with some retail work if she got to spend most of her time leading people through the wilderness.

Dutifully filling out the paperwork, Crystal handed it back to Amelia.

"Since this is now in order, let me fill you in on the

details of the outing beginning tomorrow. You'll meet the guests and fellow guide in front of the store at nine a.m. and take the company vans for the hour long drive up to Snoqualmie pass. This will be a beginner level hike, so expect to spend a lot of time helping people in and out of their snowshoes. The other guide knows what to do, and where to go, so follow his lead. Be entertaining and helpful. This particular excursion leads to an alpine chalet, where the group will be staying for two nights, returning Sunday morning. There will be food and sleeping accommodations for you, as well. Any questions?"

"Sounds pretty straightforward. I'll be here tomorrow." Crystal had a million questions, starting with "how do I snowshoe," but this wasn't the time or place.

"Remember. Be on time. Nine a.m. sharp." Amelia gave a stern glance before turning her attention to the top piece of paper in her in-box, dismissing Crystal.

Standing to leave, Crystal attempted to exude casual calm, but her hands clenched in anxiety by her side. She had so little time to purchase the right gear, not to mention learn how to snowshoe.

Buying snowshoes at Emerald City Outfitters was out of the question. She had portrayed herself as an expert, and the jig would be up pretty quickly if her next stop was less than fifty feet from Amelia's office. She would have to go elsewhere to do her shopping.

Heading out of the store and down the stairs to the parking garage, she took a moment to let her mother know what happened. Her mom had been bombarding her with texts and phone calls since Crystal had quit her job. Crystal had been doing her best to dodge them, but now that she had positive news in her life to report, she finally deigned to text her overly curious mother back—*Found new job. Homelessness averted. I'll see you at Sunday brunch. Will tell all when I get there. Love.* Since she had let her mom, and therefore the rest of her family know, even if somewhat cryptically, she hurried to phone Olivia and share the good news.

"Hey, Crys," Olivia answered.

"I got the job!" Crystal shouted a foot from the phone.

Her friend's high-pitched squeal rang out over the speaker, and she waited for it to finish before putting the phone to her ear.

"When do you start?" Olivia asked.

"My first outing starts tomorrow morning if you can believe it."

"How exciting. I'm so happy for you."

"It is exciting, but I'm nervous," Crystal said. She filled her friend in on the snowshoeing details.

"I'm sure you'll be fine. It's hiking in the snow, but with those tennis racket shoes, right?"

"I think there is a little more to it, but that seems to be basically all it is. Still, I'm worried. I need to come off as an expert on all things outdoors to the group, not to mention the other guide."

"What's your plan?"

"First, I've got to get a handle on how to snowshoe. I'm off to get a pair, and then I'll watch a bunch of instructional videos on the internet. I'm also going to look up the names of trees as well as any animals we are likely to see this time of year. I can always fill the time with fun facts, even if I'm not actually an expert."

"Well, why are you talking to me?" Olivia chided. "Get studying, and call me Sunday when you're done. We'll go out to celebrate next week and you can tell me about everything that's been happening in your life."

Crystal grinned as she ended the call. Olivia's unending cheerfulness always helped put her in a good mood and gave her a healthy dose of enthusiasm.

As she approached her doddering Honda, Crystal googled where to buy snowshoes on her phone. Alpine Zone popped up, seven miles away. Hopping in her car, she drove the short distance to the store. The strip mall entrance was underwhelming, but as she entered, a pulse of excitement overcame her. She was buying gear for her very first outdoor guiding trip. Getting directions from the lady at the register, Crystal spotted her quarry, mounted on the back wall, and weaved her way through the aisle.

Stopping, she studied several varieties arrayed before her, trying to decipher a difference. What type of snowshoes would an expert own?

Out of the corner of her eye, she saw a salesman approach. "Can I help you find a pair?"

Crystal swiveled her attention from the display and goggled at the man who had just spoken. He was over six feet tall with the athletically muscled body of an avid outdoorsman. His brilliant blue eyes, artfully tousled dishwater blond hair, and friendly smile captivated her. Forcing herself to tug her gaze from his strong jawline, Crystal found herself once again staring at the snowshoes.

"Can I help you pick out a pair?" the guy repeated.

"Oh, yes," Crystal stammered, blushing. "I'm going snowshoeing for the first time tomorrow, so I need snowshoes and anything else you think might be helpful."

"I'm happy to help…" he trailed off, looking at her.

It took a second for her mind to catch up. She filled in the blank he was looking for, "Crystal."

He pointed to his name tag, "I'm Conner. Let's get you set up, Crystal," he said with an affable smile, causing her insides to melt into a warm glow. Grabbing a snowshoe off the wall, he presented it. "This brand costs a little extra, but gets great reviews, and will never let you down. I own a pair and can vouch for them. They are bigger than most, so they can feel a bit awkward in the beginning, but they are better at keeping you on top of the snow when you hit powder. They also come with trekking poles."

"I'll take them," she said. "I want the best pair." She was supposed to be an experienced wilderness guide, after all.

"You won't regret it. They come in both pink and forest green." Studying her for a second, he said, "I'm taking you for a pink girl."

"Pink, definitely."

"Do you have waterproof boots and gloves?" Conner asked.

"Boots, yes. Gloves, no," she said.

Crystal followed his robust frame through the store, and they picked out fleece-lined gloves to match her snowshoes.

"Do you need sunglasses? Parka?" he asked.

"I've got both of those," she answered.

"I believe you are all set, unless there is anything else you had in mind?"

"Um, you mentioned you snowshoe."

"All the time."

"Can you give me a few pointers?" It would be much more fun to get lessons from this good-looking salesman rather than watching endless videos on the internet.

"I'd be happy to." He motioned for her to take a seat in the boot section. He sat down opposite her on the shoe-fitting stool's black padded seat.

"First, I'm going to show you how to get into them."

He undid the packaging and assisted her with slipping her feet into the bindings and tightening the straps. He had Crystal take the snowshoes off and on a few times by herself and then showed her a few techniques for walking in different types of snow. Soon, he had her tromping around the sales area while describing different ways for climbing and descending hills.

Crystal's pulse jumped as he eased her out of the snowshoes, guiding her legs with his calloused, yet gentle hands. "That's all there is to it. The next step is to get out there and have fun." Crystal prayed her face wasn't turning red from his attention. She took a few conscious, deep, calming breaths as he grabbed her items and carried them to the register to ring her up. "I'm going to give you my card, so if you have any more questions, or need anything else, feel free to give me a call."

"Thank you so much." She gathered her bags and retreated back to her car. Her impromptu lesson with Conner left her feeling immensely relieved. She had a fighting chance of pulling this off.

It wasn't until the drive home that she wondered about the number Conner had given her. Did he give out his card to call him for more outdoor advice, or did he give her his card to call him, call him?

Shaking her head to clear her meandering thoughts, she reminded herself she had better focus on work. She had a lifetime of snowshoeing to fake, which was going to take all of the free time she had.

Parking in her condo's garage, Crystal carried her purchases upstairs and settled down to use her time as productively as possible before she led her first tour group into the forest. Crystal opened the internet to brush up on her wilderness knowledge. Before long, she had memorized how to identify different types of fir trees by their needles, scrolled past a hundred adorable pictures of snowshoe hares, and refreshed herself on first aid. Time passed by at a rapid clip as she sank deep into her research and was shocked to find it was almost ten o'clock by the time she pried herself away from her computer.

Stretching her hands above her head and yawning, she acknowledged she could do this for months and still only be scraping the surface of what an expert guide needed to learn. Nevertheless, she was confident she had a solid base of knowledge to entertain and teach the group. Desperate to feel rested on the first day at her new job, she forced herself to head to bed.

Overstimulated, her brain refused to shut down. Every time sleep encroached, she would try to identify imaginary animal tracks or species of evergreens, thwarting her ability to fall into a deep sleep. As she tossed and turned, an odd concept struck her. For the first time in her life, and despite her anxiety, she couldn't wait to get up and go to work. Eventually, exhaustion overtook her stimulated consciousness and drove her into a restless slumber.

****

Her alarm startled her awake at six-thirty a.m. She roused herself out of bed, spurred on by her cat, Elf, who never let her miss feeding him. After dishing out his breakfast, she gave him a few pets and assured him Mrs. McReady would be by to feed him and clean his box. Nerves at starting her new job had stolen her own appetite, but she forced herself to eat a light breakfast of jam and toast. Her morning ritual cried out that she brew a cup of coffee to help overcome the night's insomnia, but the acid in her stomach overruled the idea and she toughed the morning out without her usual caffeine.

After freshening up, she began the arduous task of dressing for mountain weather. First up, was the snug base layer of thermal pants and t-shirt. Next, she pulled a fleece-lined purple sweater over her head and slid into a pair of polar snow pants. Finally, she tugged on her waterproof down jacket, her new matching pink gloves, and an ear covering wool hat. Wrapping a light brown scarf her sister had knitted around her neck, she checked herself out in the bedroom mirror. After a few minor adjustments to straighten her clothing, she saw a woman dressed for the part of an intrepid wilderness guide looking back at her. The anticipation of beginning her new job caused sweat to blossom on her palms. Ignoring her fretting, she slung her backpack over her shoulder, grabbed her snowshoes and poles, wrestled everything out the door, and took the stairs to the garage.

Settling all of her equipment in the backseat, she whispered a quick prayer and turned the key in the ignition. Thankfully, her capricious car started, and despite the morning's crowded streets, she made good time to Emerald City Outfitters. Parking in the employee section, she glanced at the time on her phone. It was thirty minutes before the scheduled meeting time, but after Amelia's warning regarding tardiness, she'd rather be way too early than a second late.

Leaving her snowshoeing gear in the car, she walked to the front of the store where the tours met to see if anyone had arrived. Not a soul was present, so she sat down on a nearby stone bench to wait. Despite the stress leading up to this morning, Crystal discovered her anxiety settling and her impatience taking over as she waited for the group to show up. The morning's chill seeped through her many layers of clothing and she clutched her arms around her body. She stood, stamping her feet for warmth. Spotting a Starbucks across the street, Crystal found herself regretting the decision to pass on coffee. Checking her phone again, she determined there was plenty of time to grab a quick latte to help perk her up and fight off the chill. She bustled across the street and put in her order. When the barista finished making her drink, she slipped off her gloves to wrap her hands around the hot cup. Taking an open table, she nibbled on a croissant she hadn't been able to pass up, and took a few sips of her coffee, enjoying the warmth of the cafe. Glancing at the clock on the wall, she saw the meeting time was almost upon her.

Strolling back across the street, with half of a croissant and latte in hand, she could see several people casually gathered in a circle at the top of the steps. As she began mounting the stairs, their friendly and excited conversation energized her more than the caffeine. They were looking forward to the day's adventure, and Crystal was going to be part of the experience. Oddly, one of the voices was familiar, and as she crested the steps she wracked her brain to place it. One woman spotted her coffee cup, grabbed the man next to her, and separated from the group, passing Crystal as they continued on toward Starbucks. With their departure, Crystal was able to catch a glimpse inside the crowd. She froze, recognizing the face belonging to the familiar voice. It was Conner, the handsome snowshoe salesman, who happened to know Crystal had never been snowshoeing in her life.

Her instincts screamed for her to run, and she considered hurrying by the crowd and back to the safety of her car. With him in the group, there was no way she was going to be able to bluff being an expert guide.

Her panicked plan to abandon her new job was thwarted when Conner spotted her.

"Well, why didn't you say you already had a snowshoeing trip planned?" His lopsided grin at her presence didn't make what was about to happen any easier.

"Uhhh." Crystal wracked her brain, but it wasn't providing her with a good answer to his simple question.

"Crystal, right?" he asked, as more people walked up the steps to join the group. "We'll be leaving in fifteen minutes. We're waiting for the last few stragglers and the other guide to join us. Then, we'll be ready to go." He spoke loud enough to make this statement an announcement to everyone.

Crystal stepped close, grabbed his arm, and dragged him aside. *"I'm* the other guide," she whispered. A newly formed pit in her stomach snatched her breath, and she could barely hear her own words. Any second, he would leave and inform Amelia she was a fraud. How did she ever think she could pull this off? Maybe she could grovel for her old job back.

An odd expression of anxiety crossed over Conner's face. He opened his mouth to speak but closed it with a snap.

Crystal ventured a small bluff. "I'm sure Amelia told you I was an inexperienced guide."

"Oh, yeah, she did," he agreed. Crystal's heart unfroze, and she began to breath again until he continued speaking, "But she also said you were an experienced snowshoer."

Crystal clasped her hands together, pleading. "I know you could go straight to Amelia, but please don't. You have no idea how much this means to me. From the moment Amelia said I had the job, I've done nothing but research this hike we're going on."

His steady gaze took her in for a long moment, before he nodded. "You got it. I'll even cover for you, but you need to do something for me," Conner whispered.

"Anything."

"You can't tell her I work for another outdoor company."

Crystal's mind flashed back to the initial paperwork she had filled out. They weren't supposed to be working for competitors.

"Hey, lovebirds! Are we going, or not?" called a

sizable middle-aged man.

Crystal returned Conner's smile, and he winked. They shifted their attention back to the gathering. Four more people had joined the group during their whispered conversation, and the two who had split off earlier were hurrying back with coffee cups in their hands.

"Well, it looks like everyone has arrived," Conner called out. "My name is Conner, and this is Crystal." She gave a little wave to the attentive crowd. "We'll be your guides."

The man who had called her and Conner lovebirds spoke from where he sat on the bench Crystal had perched on earlier. "I'm Philip Calvert, and everyone on this trip works at my company, Calvert and Associates. We are an architectural firm, the best in Seattle. I sprang for this little excursion as a celebration for completing the new science building at the University of Washington. We're snowshoeing with you throughout the day, and plan on toasting our grand accomplishment at this quaint chalet tonight." He was a bulky man sporting a balding scalp surrounded by a fringe of hair. His muscular arms screamed ex-athlete, rather than architect, but if he had been, he had since surrendered to the ravages of fast food. His mouth was set in a perpetual sneer, and he folded his hands on his belly as if he were the King of England resting on his throne.

"This is my wife." He lifted his hand from where it rested and waved in the direction of the woman next to him. "Madeleine."

"Hi," Madeleine muttered, staring at the coffee shop. Like any other Seattleite, her caffeine addiction was probably urging her to get her own cup for the trip. She was thin and pale, with sharp features that Crystal placed in her mid-fifties. Her face was pinched in a state of perpetual worry, and streaks of gray contrasted starkly with her black hair. Despite her outward indifference, the woman's eyes tightened in annoyance when her husband called out her name.

Well, don't they seem like a happy couple.

"The two people beside me are Bree and Justin, our new intern and the company's junior associate," Philip continued, unconcerned by the icy demeanor emanating from his wife.

Bree gave a little wave of her hand, flashed a perfect smile, and gave a bright "Hi." Her cheer came across as forced after Philip's imperious tone. Bree was younger than Crystal, in her early twenties. She had luxurious blond hair, sharp blue eyes, and a curvaceous figure Crystal couldn't help but envy.

Standing next to her, Justin was a lanky man in his early thirties. He had a square jaw, emphasized by a well-groomed goatee. He, too, waved, and a broad smile lit up his face.

"I'm Georgia, the office manager." Crystal spotted a woman with steely gray hair poking out from beneath her yellow wool hat and a deep smile creasing her face.

The couple bearing two coffee cups from their completed coffee run, spoke next. "I'm Ryan, and this is my wife Alice. We're senior associates." Their fair skin and reddish-brown hair reminded Crystal of her brother-in-law, who professed to be of pure Irish descent.

"And I'm Gary. The other senior associate." Turning, she spotted a fit-looking, forty-something, man standing in the back. His rodent-like features pinched down into a sneer. "Like the boss asked, are we gonna get this show on the road or what, babe?"

Crystal blinked. She couldn't ever remember being called "babe" by a virtual stranger in her life. "Yes, we are."

The need to continue the conversation was ended by Conner speaking up. "As you know, we're going up to Snoqualmie Pass to start our hike at the ski resort. I know you are looking forward to a walk through the majestic winter forest to our lodgings, the incomparable Baranhof Chalet. If the forecast is correct we will get sun today and snow tonight, which will allow for amazing views along the way. That's enough talk. It's time to go have some fun."

Chapter Two

Built in a large A-frame style, the chalet was designed for handling the winter's snowstorms. The steep pitched roof had sloughed the snow onto either side in deep pillowy drifts, and warm lights glowed in the windows as dusk was beginning to settle on the snowshoers. A plume of white smoke from the chimney promised a warm fire was already crackling to greet the guests.

The group stopped under the large covered porch marking the front entrance. Long cedar planks made up both the floor and the ceiling, while recessed lighting cast welcoming pools of light over them. The sullen energy between their charges had made the snowy trek to the chalet less memorable than it should have been. If it hadn't been for Conner's deep well of cheerfulness, it would have been an eight-way bicker-fest all the way in.

"Ok, folks, take off your gear here, and Crystal and I will stow it for you," Conner announced. "Inside you'll find your hostess, Roxie. She will see you to your rooms and provide a dinner you won't soon forget."

"I read there was wine on this trip," Madeleine pronounced. "Where can I get a glass?" Others murmured agreement.

"Roxie will be able to assist you with

refreshments," Conner announced. He doffed his pack and snowshoes in seconds. Crystal blessed her practice as she was the second out of her gear and helped a few of the others who got hung up on the straps.

Conner sidled near her and murmured, "Why don't you store the snowshoes and poles in the utility shed?" He nodded toward a small outbuilding, to the side of the entryway. "I'll carry their packs upstairs. We'll be sleeping and eating in the basement. The clients aren't paying to hang out with us. This gives them a chance to cut loose a little without feeling self-conscious. Take the stairway to the left of the foyer, pick the room you like, and I'll be down in a bit."

"You got it." Crystal gave him a jaunty half-wave, half-salute. However, she was a little crestfallen to hear they would be in the basement. Other than Philip's boorishness ruining what was otherwise a majestic snowshoe hike, she had been enjoying the experience so much, it seemed natural to be heading inside for wine and dinner, before retiring to a plush room.

However, this was actually a job, she reminded herself. She opened up the utility shed and found pegs studding the walls. She slipped the snowshoes onto them, leaned the poles against a wall, and shut the door. She took a moment before entering the chalet to fight back a prodigious yawn, blinking away the exhaustion of the day.

Turning her back on the shed and snow adorned forest, Crystal stepped through the front door and into a grand entryway. She spotted the stairway to her left leading to the basement accommodations but couldn't resist pausing to look around the rest of the chalet.

The ceiling stretched high above her in a sharp

peak, opening up a vast room. Before her were three wide wooden steps ending in a spacious landing occupied by an intricately carved table bearing several open bottles of wine. The crackle from a wood fire filled the air, casting merry shadows across the ceiling. Large windows behind her held incredible views of the snowy wonderland, still visible in the spreading winter gloom. The chatter of voices transferred her attention from the woodland scene to the people.

Philip leered at his blonde intern Bree and thrust an overflowing glass of red wine into her hands. The young woman gingerly accepted it, glancing over at Justin and shuffling her feet, in an attempt to circle around her boss's girth. Philip jammed an arm against a wall to prevent her from excusing herself and leaned forward to whisper in her ear. Ryan and Alice stood in the opposite corner, the married couple speaking in hushed tones and casting angry glances at Philip. Madeleine stood in front of the fireplace, swigging an equally full glass of white wine, while glaring at her husband and Bree. The office manager Georgia and the other senior associate Gary were nowhere to be seen.

Footsteps from down a hallway to the right caught her attention and Conner appeared around the corner. He was followed by a portly woman, who Crystal assumed could only be Roxie.

"Hello, everyone," Roxie said with a warm southern drawl. "I see ya'll found the wine. There are hors d'oeuvres in the dining area for those of you who are peckish. Conner has deposited your bags in your respective suites if you feel like freshenin' up. I'll be in the kitchen if there's anything else you need."

Conner joined Crystal, and together they headed

down to the dimly lit basement, leaving their charges in Roxie's care.

The warmth of the chalet, after a day spent in the snow, was making her head swim. "I think I'm going to lie down for a bit," Crystal told Conner.

Spotting a light in a small bedroom, Crystal made a beeline through the common area to the unoccupied room, shut the door, and threw her pack in a corner. The room was spartan, featuring only a single bed, a small dresser, and a nightstand with a battered lamp. Kicking off her boots and flopping on the bed, she closed her eyes, planning on a short nap before dinner. The previous night's sleeplessness and the exhaustion of the day's excursions held other plans for her though, and she tumbled into a deep slumber.

****

Crystal woke to the sound of glass shattering. Her sleep-addled mind jumped to the conclusion that Elf had knocked a glass off the counter. He liked to do annoying things in the middle of the night. Then voices rising in anger helped her recall where she was. It was impossible to make out what was being said, since several people were yelling at once. Fumbling for her phone, she checked the time. Her screen illuminated when she found the right button, 1:34 a.m.

She groaned, rolled over, and attempted to go back to sleep, but the continued shouting kept her awake. Should she do something? What was her responsibility in this situation? Footsteps from upstairs were followed by something heavy crashing to the floor above her head. Instantly, she jumped from her bed and opened the door. Emerging, she was grateful to see Conner stumbling from his room, too. His hair was sticking up in the back and his half-mast eyes betrayed his grogginess.

"What do you think we should do?" Crystal asked.

Conner cocked his head to one side and listened. Everything was quiet. Then a door slammed.

"We better get presentable and see what the heck is going on up there," Conner grumbled as he ran his hand through his hair, attempting to tame his cowlick.

Laughing as it flipped back to the exact same position as before, Crystal attempted to comb her own locks into place with her fingers. "Yours is looking as good as mine, Sleeping Beauty."

Conner flashed her a sleepy grin. The self-confident way he stood with his messy hair and pajamas, coupled with the easy way he took her teasing, made her heart dance a little faster.

She had crashed fully dressed with the sole exceptions of her boots and jacket, so she headed to the bathroom to get her unruly hair tamed, while Conner ducked back into his room. Halfway there, the sound of a poorly muffled engine roaring to life startled her. Was that a snowmobile? She shook the rest of the sleep from her head, gave up on her hair, and tightened the laces on her boots. It was a bad situation if one of those maniacs was taking off on a snowmobile in the middle of the night. More shouting and doors slamming carried to their quarters, and Conner reemerged from his room, tugging on his jacket as they mounted the stairs together.

Halfway up, Crystal entered a scene of chaos. The ornate table on the landing had been knocked over. Broken wine glasses sat amid a crimson pool in the middle of the floor. She fretted it was blood until she got closer and recognized from the cherry and plum scents it could only be wine.

Standing in the middle of the debris, Bree stared out the panoramic window at the darkness with tears streaming down her face as Georgia consoled her. Thumping down the stairs in his winter boots and jacket, Justin flew past everyone and out the front door.

"What's going on?" Conner had started to ask, but he was gone before Conner could complete the sentence, leaving the words hanging in the air. Conner sighed as he and Crystal crested the last few stairs. Disarray continued to fill her eyes. A hallway leading to the guest rooms extended eight feet before turning left. The two bedroom doors visible from her vantage point were thrown open, and more glistening glass lay shattered at the end of the hall.

"What is going on up here?" Conner repeated the question to the weeping Bree.

A different voice answered as Alice emerged from one of the bedrooms. "Philip started a fight with everyone. Like usual."

"I could have sworn the noise I heard was a snowmobile starting up," Crystal interjected.

"It was. After Philip was done carrying on, he shouted about getting out of here. He kept screaming that he wasn't able to stand being hassled by a bunch of thankless parasites. So Philip had the brilliant idea to head into the darkness, drunk, on a snowmobile," Alice deadpanned.

"Do you think everyone will be ok?" asked Bree from the window.

"What do you mean by 'everyone'?" Conner's brows shot up in concern.

"After Philip took off, Madeleine, Ryan, Gary, and now Justin have all gone after him. He'd had a lot to drink, and I think they're afraid he'll get into a wreck," Georgia filled them in, while patting Bree on the arm.

Conner groaned. "This is serious. There are more than a million acres in the Snoqualmie National Forest and daybreak is still six hours away this time of year. To be safe, I'm going to notify search and rescue." He turned his back on the women and hustled downstairs.

"Let's get this glass cleaned up before someone hurts themselves," Crystal suggested. She wanted to emulate Conner's example and start taking charge of the situation. Alice rolled her eyes at the suggestion of cleaning and disappeared back into her room.

Ignoring the woman's reaction, Crystal passed through the main room by the fireplace and ducked into the kitchen. Behind the pantry door, she found a broom and a mop. As she handed over the broom to a waiting Georgia, Conner returned encumbered with his gear and a small radio in his hand. Clicking the side of the radio he said, "Conner Oakes, ECO Adventures to King County search and rescue."

A raspy voice answered from the other end, "KC SAR here. What is your situation?"

"I have several guests who have left the Baranhof Chalet two miles from the recreation parking area."

"We have GPS coordinates on the location. How many guests are missing and how long have they been lost?"

"Five guests have been missing for approximately five to fifteen minutes. One was on a snowmobile, and four on foot. I'm going to try and round them up if they are in the immediate vicinity, but I wanted you to be aware of the situation."

"Thank you for the update, Conner. Be safe."

"I know what I'm doing, Sam. You trained me in search and rescue, right? If I get lost you have no one to blame but yourself," Conner said, a wry grin on his face.

"Roger that, Conner."

Conner slipped the radio into his pack and motioned Crystal aside, leaving Bree and Georgia to start sweeping up the shattered glass.

"I'm sure you overheard. I'm heading out to retrieve our guests. Your job is to keep everyone else here. I tried waking Roxie, but I don't think it worked."

"What happens if you don't come back?" Crystal tapped her hands on her legs in anxiety.

"I'll be fine. I volunteer with search and rescue all the time and know how to be safe. However, if anything else happens, Roxie has another radio. Call Sam at Search and Rescue and he'll know what to do."

Crystal nodded as Conner zipped up his parka and headed down the first flight of stairs to the front door. As he threw it open, Crystal could see fat flakes of snow falling in the darkness. Conner shut the door behind him and Crystal braced herself before turning back to face the rest of the scene.

Alice reemerged from her room, having donned her winter jacket and boots.

"Alice, you can't go out in the dark," Crystal cautioned. "It's dangerous."

The woman scowled at Crystal's warning. "Which is exactly why I'm going out. My husband is out there trying to make sure our travesty of a boss is safe. I'm going looking for him."

"Search and rescue has been notified, and they are taking the proper steps to ensure everyone's safety." Crystal was proud of her professional tone, sounding as if she were actually in control.

"I don't give a damn. Ryan is out there and could be in trouble," Alice's voice was still calm, but Crystal could swear it trembled as she spoke. With a quick step, Alice shoved past Crystal toward the front door. Crystal caught hold of a handful of jacket, but Alice yanked her arm free, darted down the stairs, and threw open the door. She halted in the entrance because her husband was only twenty feet away, struggling toward the chalet through the falling snow. His feet sank to mid-thigh with every step he took. He grimaced as he levered his body up for a labored stride and staggered before windmilling to catch his balance.

Alice cried out at the site of him and plunged into the snow to greet him. She sank to her waist and struggled as Ryan slogged toward her.

"I should have grabbed my snowshoes," Ryan chided himself. "I don't think I made it fifty yards before I was exhausted, so I turned around and headed back. Idiotic thing to do." He wrapped his wife in an embrace as they met together in the snow.

"I'm so relieved you're safe," she murmured and clung to him. She buried her face in his shoulder as he cradled her head in one hand.

They assisted each other the last few steps to the chalet, snow still swirling down in the night. Crystal noted how fast it was piling up and worry began to clench her heart.

"I'll make something hot to warm you up," Crystal said as they passed her. Looking into the night and seeing nothing, she gently shut the door and leaned her back against it. Closing her eyes, she let out a deep sigh, and took a moment to wish Conner back safely.

Crystal walked into the kitchen as Alice and Ryan settled themselves at the nearby dining room table. She spotted a coffee maker flanked by two canisters labeled regular and decaf. As she started a pot of decaf brewing, Alice and Ryan leaned into each other, talking in low tones. Curious, she poured two cups and approached them quietly, hoping to "accidentally" overhear some of the conversation. However, Alice sat up as she neared and pulled away from her husband, patted his hands and announced, "I'm so glad you're ok."

Ryan followed his wife's eyes and leaned back, preening. "Me, too. It was dark and frightening with the snow coming down like it is, but I wasn't going to let anyone freeze to death without trying to save them, even though the person in question is Philip."

Unable to keep her piqued curiosity under control anymore, Crystal blurted, "What happened tonight?"

"Oh, nothing out of the ordinary for Calvert and Associates," Alice answered.

Crystal stared at them a second longer, urging them to elaborate.

"We're a little dysfunctional," added Ryan. "You may have noticed."

"I heard shouting and something large hitting the floor," Crystal prodded them.

"It was probably the wine table. Philip shoved it over in a rage on his way out. The shouting was standard Philip and Madeleine marital communication, and then I think it was Philip and Bree arguing later.

Like I said, we're not the most well-adjusted." The whole time Ryan spoke, his wife glowered at him. Even Crystal could read the message Alice was attempting to communicate. *Shut up.* Taking his wife's unspoken hint, he clammed up, grabbed his coffee, raised it to his lips, and stared out the same dark window Bree had returned to peering through.

Crystal studied their stony faces, gave up, poured a cup of coffee for Bree and started in her direction. Georgia took the entire scene in from a nearby couch.

Seeing Crystal's reflection approach in the darkened window she was trying to peer through, Bree turned. Her eyes were red rimmed, but at least she had stopped crying.

"Here you go," Crystal soothed. "Don't worry. Conner's out there. He's trained in search and rescue. He'll bring them all back safely."

"Do you think so?" Bree worried.

"I know so. He's as experienced as they come." Crystal didn't know this to be precisely true, but didn't want to say anything to further upset the distraught young woman. "Do you know what touched off the arguments leading to this?" Crystal asked in a soft tone.

Bree started for a second, before answering, "Madeleine and Philip were shouting earlier in the night," she hesitated. "I don't know what it was about this time, but she made him sleep on the couch," Bree pointed to where Georgia currently sat.

Georgia, who had been listening in the whole time, nodded in agreement.

"You're sorta new, sweetie," Georgia said to Bree. "If you stick around with us long enough, you'll learn to expect half of these outings we're forced to do end up like this. Philip has done them for years. 'Team Building,' he calls them. I think it's been his way of canoodling with the female staff. However, Madeleine has started coming along on these retreats to put a stop to that."

Bree flushed, and glanced at the ground.

"Alice and Ryan said Philip argued with you, too," Crystal mentioned.

Bree opened her mouth to speak, but the front door burst open and voices echoed in the spacious room from the doorstep. Crystal and Bree both stepped over to look down the stairs to the entrance.

Conner stood outside the door, ushering Justin, Gary, and Madeleine inside. It reminded Crystal of a sheepdog herding a flock of sheep into the barn. Snowshoes and poles lay scattered and Crystal rushed downstairs to help.

The three members of the tour group passed her as they hurried up the steps from the entryway, sloughing off more snow as they struggled out of their winter coats.

"I'll put away the gear. Come inside," Crystal urged Conner.

"Thanks, Crystal." He followed the others as Crystal stashed the gear in the shed.

After she secured the shed door, she retreated back into the warmth of the chalet and headed upstairs to find Conner and the other three seated at the table with Ryan and Alice. Bree was pouring a cup of coffee from the pot and placed it in front of Justin, who was rubbing his hands and blowing on them. Justin smiled up at Bree, which she returned with interest.

Conner spotted Crystal as she approached the table,

"I was explaining to everyone, we weren't able to locate Philip. It looks like he did take the snowmobile."

"Do you think he'll be ok?" Bree asked. The poor girl blanched when she spotted an anxious Madeleine staring at her.

"I hope so," Conner answered. "Madeleine said he's used snowmobiles in the past. He should know how to safely operate one. As long as he doesn't get lost in the dark, there's a lodge near the parking lot. They'll put him up for the rest of the night."

"Well, I for one am going to get a few hours of sleep," Justin announced as he stood from the table. "Philip has ruined enough of my night. I'm sure he's raiding the mini fridge at whatever passes for the presidential suite in the lodge right now, and laughing to himself for getting such a good reaction out of us."

As if that were a general announcement, everyone got out of their chairs, filed from the dining room, and down the hall to the guest suites. They entered their respective rooms, but Conner and Crystal exchanged a wry glance as Madeleine popped back out long enough to grab an undamaged bottle of wine.

"I'm going to notify Sam at SAR," Conner stood as well, making his way back to his pack and extracting the radio.

Crystal listened to Sam being brought up to speed as she fetched Conner a cup of decaf.

Not the most auspicious start to my guiding career, Crystal admitted to herself.

Conner sat back down, took a grateful swig of the coffee and sighed. "This could have gone better," he said stating the obvious.

"What happens next?" Crystal asked.

"We wait until dawn, see if he turns up, and escort everyone out of here. Hopefully, Philip is waiting for us at the lodge, and we can drive this whole miserable lot back to the city a day early. In the meantime, I suggest we follow everyone's lead and try to get a little shuteye."

Conner's radio crackled with Sam's voice, "We've found the missing man from your group, Conner. He's at the bottom of a cliff. I'm sorry to say this search and rescue operation has become a search and recover."

Conner paled at the news.

"What does 'search and recover' mean?" Crystal asked.

"It means he's dead."

Chapter Three

Crystal's eyes widened in shock and her hands flew to her mouth. "What are we going to do," she whispered through her fingers.

"There's nothing we can do now. Let our guests try and get some sleep and I'll break it to them in the morning. Given the circumstances, we'll cut the trip short and head back as early as we can." Exhaling a deep breath and wishing her goodnight, Conner stood and headed downstairs.

Crystal sat at the table, thinking. What had driven Philip Calvert into the snowy wilderness in January? His wife and employees were hiding information with their half-answers and whispered conversations. Crystal's curiosity got the better of her and she decided to snoop around before heading back to bed. The mountain chalet was decorated with natural materials shaped into artwork. Mounted above the fireplace, a cross section of an ancient tree had been polished to a high gleam. Bare wooden branches were displayed in vases alongside geodes and fossils on floating shelves mounted throughout the entire main room. Down the hallway, the doors were all closed with the exception of the last, which stood ajar. Crystal could hear movement and murmuring inside several of them as she tip-toed to the open doorway.

The room reflected the rest of the turmoil in the

chalet. Clothes were strewn about, which Crystal assumed had been flung by a hasty would-be-rescuer. The same decorative theme carried throughout the chalet into this room, and Crystal admired the polished and shaped pieces of wood and stone mounted on the walls. However, one of the shelves had been knocked to the ground and several geodes and fossils sat amidst the remainder of what she presumed had once been a blown glass vase. All of the debris had been swept into a corner with the comforter from the bed, which lay crumpled on the ground next to the pile. Was this the large thump that had finally spurred her and Conner into action? She stared at the mess, trying to make sense of it. Exasperated, she shrugged her shoulders and headed downstairs to her room. She lay awake, fretting about a man dying on her first outing, and listened as the wind whistled overhead.

****

Knock, knock, knock.

"It's almost dawn." Conner's voice called through the door.

"I'm up," she mumbled. Her lids drooped closed, and she forced them open with concerted effort.

She couldn't believe she'd fallen asleep, but once the adrenaline of earlier wore off, her whole body had shut down.

Forcing herself to hurry, she managed to get ready in twenty minutes. She could hear Conner upstairs, knocking on doors and rousing the occupants.

Still clad in a flannel, rose-print nightgown, Roxie stumbled out of her room. "It's a might early to be getting up for breakfast. What's our boy Conner up to?"

Lowering her voice, Crystal filled her in. "One of

our guests swiped the snowmobile last night and drove it off a cliff." Outside, a keening howl of wind shook the chalet.

"For real? Was it the rat-faced one, Jerry...? Or was it Gary? He looks like he would steal gruel from a starving orphan."

"It was Philip."

"Now, why would he go and steal the snowmobile? If he paid for this entire excursion, he must be loaded," Roxie cocked her head in puzzlement.

Crystal gave a hasty synopsis of the night's escapades.

"Did I really sleep through the whole ruckus?"

"Umm...Yes."

"You didn't think to wake me?"

"Conner tried, and I didn't think you would have wanted to be woken up for all of the craziness."

"This sounds like the most entertaining night up here all winter long, and you let me sleep through it?" Roxie complained. "I'm going upstairs to see if they fight some more."

Without bothering to change out of her nightgown, Roxie hurried upstairs, eager to catch some of the action. Crystal grabbed her pack and followed. Glancing down the hall from the top of the stairs, she spotted a door creak open and Bree quick step back to the room where the shelf had been knocked over the previous night.

The door to the room she had left was gently closed by a person on the other side. Crystal hadn't seen this particular sight since college, when people had snuck back to their dorm rooms after a night of fun.

Leaving the hallway behind her, she headed to the

kitchen to hear Roxie berating Conner. "It is so incredibly dull up here and you let me miss it all. I'm madder than a wet hen..." she griped.

"I'm surprised you could even sleep through the ruckus," Conner answered. "I pounded on your door and shouted for you to get up."

"You know I'm a deep sleeper. It's okay to shake me if it's worth it," protested Roxie.

"I hate to tell you this, but you also just missed Bree sneaking back to her room," Crystal added.

"Oooh...An evening of fighting followed by a night of hanky-panky. Reminds me of my youth," Roxie chattered as she began preparing pancakes and bacon.

"I want to get the group back to the city." Conner groused. "We don't have time for breakfast."

"Of course you have a few minutes for breakfast." Roxie brusquely assured him. "You might be able to hike out on an empty stomach Mr. Wilderness, but I guarantee these other people need some proper nourishment to get home."

Ryan and Alice appeared out of their room as the first pancakes were lifted from the griddle. They dropped down in their seats as two plates were laid before them, brimming with syrup and bacon. A pot of coffee and orange juice were added to the table as they both dug in.

Conner frowned, but Crystal could tell he was bowing to the inevitable. She snatched the next two plates for both of them and shoved one into his hands.

Together, they ate in the kitchen as the rest of the guests joined the table. Madeleine waved off the pancakes and bacon, but helped herself to a cup of coffee. From the tightness around her eyes, Crystal guessed she had put a decent dent in the chalet's wine cellar.

Bree's puffy eyes betrayed a tale of a different sort of rough night. She had attempted to use concealer to hide the signs, but she had been crying again recently. She nibbled at a pancake, but set aside her fork after a few small bites. Chewing in silence, Justin watched her, worried.

"I hear it was an adventurous night." Roxie circled the table, topping off coffee mugs.

"You could certainly say that," Gary piped up. "Our boss treats us to a luxurious winter escape, and it sounds like everyone still couldn't help but argue with him. Drove him right into a snowstorm."

Madeleine glared at him, but it was Alice who responded. "You can stop kissing Philip's ass, Gary. He isn't here to listen to it, so save it for later."

Ryan snorted at his wife's comment, but everyone else shifted in their seats at the words. Roxie acted disinterested, but Crystal could tell from the way she leaned toward the table how hard she was straining to hear.

"If everyone is finished, I need to break some bad news to you," Conner cut in. Roxie gave him a little elbow jab to shut him up, but he ignored it.

"They were getting going again, and you had to go and break it up," Roxie muttered.

"Last night, Search and Rescue found Philip."

"Thank God!" Madeleine set down her coffee mug. "How's he doing?"

"I am deeply saddened to say Philip perished last night when the snowmobile he was driving went over a cliff. Search and Rescue is coordinating a team to recover his body, but it sounds like it's treacherous conditions and it may take time to ensure the rescue team's safety."

Like the hush created by a fresh snowfall, silence fell on the table, which only caused Roxie's whisper to reverberate all the louder. "When you told me he had gone over a cliff, Crystal, you didn't mention he bought the farm."

Madeleine drew a trembling breath. "Our last words were a stupid argument."

A fresh wail from the wind rattled the damper in the fireplace. Tears coursed down Bree's face and Justin put his arm around her.

"What does this mean for the business?" Gary asked. "Are we going to be ok?"

"Are you even human, Gary." Alice rolled her eyes. "Madeleine runs the company now. Let's give her a moment to get over her husband's death. Maybe she can organize a new life plan over a second cup of coffee."

"No second cups of coffee," Conner interrupted. "Let's get you all home this morning."

A burst of wind and the patter of snow smacking the windows cut him short. Frowning, he headed downstairs and threw open the front door. The full fury of the wind whistling through the forest caught them all by surprise. Nearby, a splintering crack was followed by a muffled thump.

"Did a tree just fall over?" Georgia's eyes were wide.

Conner shut the front door and rejoined them. "It appears Mother Nature has come up with a new plan.

We can't hike out in this. There's a good chance one of us could get hurt by a falling branch or tree. We'll have to wait it out, so get comfortable."

The news was too much for Madeleine, who thrust herself back from the table, and with shuddering sobs, fled the room.

Madeleine's door slammed, and Georgia stood, her eyes wet with unshed tears. "I better go check on her." The soft spoken woman hurried down the hallway.

"I suppose I better go, too." Gary gave a heavy sigh, and downed the dregs of his coffee. Grabbing the carafe, he topped off his cup and followed after the two women with reluctant footsteps.

At his departure, the remaining members of Calvert and Associates gave up on breakfast and again retreated to their rooms, murmuring in sympathetic whispers. Conner headed downstairs to get an update from Sam on the status of the storm. Crystal spent the day helping Roxie tidy up after breakfast and the mess left from the night before. They made sandwiches for lunch, which the guests retrieved for themselves when the mood struck. The windstorm continued unabated, and as dusk settled, Crystal located Conner in the shed, checking the snowshoes.

"What's the latest news on the weather?"

Sighing, Conner set a hex key wrench to the side. "As I'm sure you guessed from the setting sun, we're going to be here overnight. This storm rolled in earlier than expected, and it looks like it will pass pretty quickly, but not until after dark. I'm just killing time in here. Let's head downstairs and see if we can find something to eat."

The day before, Crystal had crashed so hard, she

hadn't bothered to explore the dim quarters set aside for the staff. Now, the lights had been turned on, and she was able to take in her surroundings. The basement stairs opened up into a lounge area occupied by a battered old floral print sofa and two plaid recliners. In one corner was a bookshelf populated with a sparse assortment of tattered paperbacks. Sea green carpet and faded yellow walls jarred Crystal's senses and it took her a second to process the whole scene.

Conner chuckled. "I don't believe this basement has been updated since the late 1980s. I think the carpeting and paint choices would have been trendy back then. One of our fellow guides, Suzy, who often leads groups here, disagrees and thinks whoever decorated it was simply color blind. Whatever the case, until the storm passes, this will remain home, sweet home." The layout reminded Crystal of her dorm in college, with various bedrooms surrounding a shared common area. "You can see our stylish kitchenette over there, and this here is our living room. There isn't a TV because we aren't meant to be overheard by our clients." Wandering over to the bookshelf, he swept his hand in a grand gesture. "However, take a look at these choices; "The Two Towers", "The Pirate's Love", and "Computer Coding for Dummies." With selections as fine as these for entertainment, who could ask for anything more?"

"This may be the height of luxury," she agreed with a smile. "However, I can't help but wonder what's for dinner? I could go for a bite to eat." The moment of silence after she spoke was punctuated by her grumbling stomach. Crystal mentally cringed. Not the sexiest move in front of Conner.

"Sounds like your stomach votes in favor of eating. Mine, too. Let's go see what's in the fridge." Conner gave a wide smile. "With Roxie as the cook, you are in for a treat." Stripping off his parka, he tossed it on the sofa. Crystal followed, finding herself enjoying the feeling of exploring her surroundings with Conner.

The kitchenette was from the same time period as the living room. Linoleum with a hodgepodge pattern of variously shaded brown squares was peeling away from where it met the base of beige cabinetry. An off-white fridge and microwave appeared to be newer than their surroundings, but the avocado colored two-burner stove made Crystal laugh out loud.

"This place is pretty great, right? Give it another two decades and it'll be converted into a museum," Conner joked. "Let's see what's for dinner."

Crystal opened the fridge, and Conner flung open the cupboard.

"Roxie is the best." Conner presented a jar of cheese pimento spread and butter crackers. "She always stocks some of my favorites."

In the fridge, Crystal discovered two ready-to-microwave plates of homemade fried chicken, mashed potatoes, and biscuits.

"How long have you known her?" Crystal asked.

"She was the hostess for the first overnight tour I ever took out, and I've been doing this for six years." Conner spread cheese on a cracker and handed it to Crystal. "She's the only hostess who thinks of the guides. Some places have top ramen and cold cereal waiting for you, but you'll never be treated like the help when Roxie's in charge."

"Umm, how does she get here?" Crystal asked

tactfully, peeling the plastic wrap off the top of the plates. Roxie's bulk hinted she didn't do a lot of strenuous hiking.

"The snowmobile Philip took last night is what she uses to transport herself and supplies to the chalet. She comes in via a trail leading from the opposite direction of where we arrived. She came in yesterday and got everything set up." Conner opened the microwave and popped the dishes in. He covered them with a large bowl he pulled from the second cupboard and started the microwave. "If I know Roxie, you should check the back of the fridge. You're missing the best part."

Crystal reopened the fridge door she had closed a moment before, and sure enough, in the back were two huge pieces of pecan pie resting on individual plates. Her mouth watering, she took them out and placed them on the small countertop to come to room temperature.

The microwave beeped twice, and Conner grabbed their meal. Crystal found the silverware drawer, while Conner poured them each a glass of water.

"Unlike the guests, there is no wine for us, unfortunately," he remarked. "We're not allowed to drink when we're working."

They both sat down and dug in. Even microwaved, the food was delicious. The chicken was moist, the mashed potatoes were creamy, and the biscuits were flaky. Crystal was ravenous and had to slow herself from eating too fast, so as to not outpace Conner. In between bites, they gushed about how wonderful the food was. Crystal didn't know her well, but Roxie was rapidly becoming one of her favorite people. Finally, they both leaned back from the table with sighs of satisfaction.

Conner broke the after-dinner languor. "Why did you tell Amelia you were an experienced snowshoer?" He interrupted before she had a chance to answer. "I'll answer my own question. To get the job, of course." His warm eyes and slight upturn of his lips showed he wasn't angered by her deception.

"There's more to it," Crystal answered with a frown. "Have you ever worked a regular nine to five office job?"

"No, I haven't." He leaned forward to listen.

"It's amazing how hard it is. Not physically, of course, but mentally. After several years of pushing paper and following dress codes, I stopped and wondered, why am I doing this? I was never going to be in the fancy glass offices. I wasn't going to fly to Tokyo to close the next business deal. At best, I was going to manage ten people doing the same tedious job I had done after decades of service. I had to get out, so I may have exaggerated on my résumé."

"I guess I can't relate. In college, I earned a forestry degree. With a last name like Oakes, how could I not study forestry?" Conner smiled at what was obviously an old joke. "After school, I launched straight into the guide biz. This is all I know, but I love it and you will, too."

"You think so?"

"You have the right spirit. I can see the joy in your expression when you are out there. Attitude is by far the most important thing. The skills will come with experience."

Tears sprang to her eyes. She tilted her head back to hold them in, but a few leaked out.

Conner widened his own eyes, concerned he had

upset her, but Crystal smiled and fanned her tears away. "I guess all of this happened so fast. It's been more stress and anxiety than I think I realized, quitting my old job. I've changed a lot in my life, and I think it all caught up to me right now. Not to mention someone dying on my first outing." Crystal dabbed at her tears with her sleeve and composed herself with a deep breath. "And why do you have two jobs with competing companies?" she asked, trying to direct the attention away from herself.

"Again, the answer is simple," Conner said. "Money. My dream is to own a houseboat on Lake Union."

"For real? A houseboat sounds wonderful. From time to time, I've imagined what it would be like to live on the Lake."

"It's always been a dream for Maggie and me." His eyes lost some of their focus, and a wistful look crossed his face.

Maggie? Who's Maggie? She plastered on a smile as Conner described the views of the Fourth of July fireworks from the houseboats, but her freshly blooming heart wilted. Of course, Conner had a girlfriend. Crystal imagined Maggie to be blond, beautiful and perfect, an ideal match for the rugged outdoorsman.

Conner extracted his phone from his pocket and opened his pictures while he spoke.

"Here's Maggie and me at the beach this summer." He handed her his phone.

There was Conner with his head pressed next to a dripping wet, tongue-lolling black lab.

Maggie was a dog. Her heart started pumping again

and her gaze left the screen to focus on Conner's grin.

"I didn't know you had a dog." Crystal blurted. As soon as the words tumbled from her mouth, she could feel a warming sensation coloring her cheeks.

"Oh, yeah, I've had Maggie for three years. Living on a houseboat would mean unlimited swimming. Black lab heaven."

Crystal smiled back, but her blushing reaction to his relationship status had laid everything out in front of him. Embarrassment still heated her cheeks, but her chagrin was replaced by a wonderful thought. From the look on his face, Conner cared that she was interested in him. The only reason for him to care about her interest in him was if he was interested in her.

Heavy footfalls thumped down the stairs, and Roxie descended into the basement. "I do hope y'all enjoyed the fried chicken." She spoke with her usual slow soft inland southern drawl.

"It was amazing," Crystal gushed and Conner echoed the praise.

Sitting down next to them, Roxie sighed in contentment and gestured at her feet. "I'm so happy to finally be able to take a load off. My dogs sure are barkin'."

"Roxie, you can drop the act," Conner said. Crystal was confused until Roxie spoke again.

"Conner, you know I like to stay in character when I'm hosting," Roxie said without a trace of the South in her speech. "I almost slipped last weekend."

Crystal must have continued to look confused, because Roxie clarified.

"I was an actress in my twenties, mostly local theater stuff. Sometimes, I like to play around with accents and mannerisms. I was messing around and having myself some fun, but people always adored the southern drawl. Every time I used the accent, the comment cards were full of praise for my southern hospitality. It's all for show, though. I'm actually from Vancouver, Canada."

"I still think you should try a British accent one of these times," Conner insisted.

"I never could perfect my highbrow British. I sound more like a chimney sweep than an elegant hostess. Anyway, enough chatter. Conner, you got the stuff?" she asked.

Conner grinned and walked over to his pack. He produced two chocolate bars and set them on the table in front of her. Sugar free was written in bold lettering on both of them.

"I hope these meet your high standards," he said.

"I have diabetes," Roxie informed Crystal, "and I miss my chocolate something fierce. Our dear boy, Conner, took it upon himself to find me a substitute. So far, all of the sugar free chocolate bars have fallen far short of my old favorites."

Roxie unwrapped the first one labeled Swiss Delight and broke off a square. She popped it in her mouth and closed her eyes.

A few seconds later, she opened them. "Nice try, but not good enough."

"I have a good feeling about this next one," Conner said. "The Pike Place Market chocolatier swore it is the best sugar free chocolate to be had."

"I'll be the judge," Roxie said, and tore off the wrapper.

She broke off a chunk and placed it in her mouth.

Closing her eyes again, she fell silent, while Conner and Crystal watched in anticipation.

Without opening her eyes, or saying a word, she broke off another square and added it to the first.

After a seemingly long stretch of time, she cracked her eyelids, gave a sly look at Conner, and teased, "I reckon this might have been the worst piece of chocolate I have ever tasted, so I had to check. Now, I can confirm. It is indeed the worst ever."

Conner threw his head back, laughing. "So bad you had to try another piece?" he joked.

Roxie nodded with a mischievous twinkle. "I'll take this one for more testing to see if I can figure out what's wrong with it, but you can keep the first chocolate bar."

"Maybe I'll get it right next time." Conner smiled.

"Well, I'm off to bed. The guests are all wined, dined, and probably making another holy hell mess, but I'll deal with it tomorrow."

"Good night, Roxie," Crystal said with a wave and a smile.

"You too, hon," Roxie said. "Sleep tight." She rose ponderously, made her way to her bedroom, and closed the door.

"Now it is time for Roxie's pie de resistance," Conner announced. He retrieved the pieces of pie from where Crystal had left them on the counter and handed her one of the enormous slices. A crimped light brown pastry edge held up a perfectly shaped wedge topped with roasted pecans. Crystal lifted her fork, cut off the point of the pie and tasted.

"Oh, wow," she murmured through a mouthful. The buttery crust melted on her tongue and the gooey richness overwhelmed her taste buds. The crunch of the pecan topping made for a delightful counterpoint to the rest of the melt-in-your-mouth goodness. "This is the most amazing pecan pie I have ever had."

"I wasn't lying," Conner exulted. "However, I caution against eating all of it. I finished my piece last time and the sugar high kept me up until two a.m. It made the trip out the next morning a little rough."

"Good advice. When I first spotted this gigantic piece, I couldn't imagine how I would eat it all. After my first bite, I didn't know if I could stop."

They each finished half of their slices, before finding the will to put their forks down. "Be right back." Conner stood and stepped over to his pack. After a little rummaging around, he presented two small Tupperware containers.

"I was a boy scout, and their motto is 'be prepared'. I don't think this is precisely what they had in mind, but Roxie was cooking tonight and that means leftovers."

He handed a container to Crystal, and they each transferred the remainder of their dessert.

"I'll clean up and make us a pot of hot tea, if you want to shower first," Conner offered.

Crystal thanked him and ducked into her room. She opened her pack and pulled out her night clothes and toiletry bag. She stepped back out, spotted Conner placing a kettle on the stove, and crossed to the bathroom.

It was clean, even if it was dated. The pale yellow tiles were consistent with the decor, but the rose wallpaper clashed no matter what decade you were in. However, the scent of bleach lingered in the air, so

Crystal was confident the bathroom was clean enough to enjoy a shower. She did her best to be quick, wanting to ensure there was plenty of hot water for Conner. Toweling off, she changed into the clothes she had packed to sleep in; a pair of gray sweat pants, a purple thermal long sleeve t-shirt, and purple wool socks. A glance in the mirror made Crystal catch herself. Reconsidering, since she was going to spend time talking and drinking tea with Conner, she pulled her top over her head, put her bra back on, followed by her thermal t-shirt. Comfort would have to wait until she made it back to her room alone. She tied her hair in a loose pony tail and took one more quick glance at the mirror, nodding to herself in satisfaction. Back in the common area of the kitchenette, Conner had washed the dishes and stacked them in the drying rack. A tea pot rested in the middle of the table, a paper tea tag dangling down the side, along with two chipped white mugs.

Conner glanced up at her from one of the armchairs where he was reading the battered copy of *The Pirate's Love*. "This isn't my usual genre, but I've been here often enough that I've read the other books. I always figured pirates lived interesting lives, but I never knew there were so many opportunities to meet beautiful women while terrorizing the seven seas." He held the cover up, which depicted a shirtless man, his muscular arms encircling a buxom redhead on the deck of a ship.

"You never know when a chance for love might present itself." Her mind fixated on Conner, and in particular how forward her comment could be taken. Heat suffused her cheeks, and she ducked back in her room with her toiletry bag and the clothes she had worn that day in her hands. She shut the door behind her and bit down on her knuckles to shut herself up.

"Well, in that case, I better shower," Conner said through her door. The tone of his voice was good humored and didn't seem to carry any innuendo, but Crystal still sank to the bed, flopped backward, and threw her arm over her face. She listened to his bedroom door open, and then close, as he crossed to the bathroom.

She removed her phone from her pack to check if she had any bars. She didn't, which wasn't a huge surprise, so she put her phone on standby. She had been hoping she could text Olivia to get advice, but she would have to figure out the situation with Conner on her own. She remembered a breathing exercise from a yoga class she had taken, closed her eyes, and cleared her mind. The flush cooled from her cheeks as she imagined clouds passing in a blue sky.

She listened to Conner leave the bathroom and cross back to his bedroom. Composing herself, she left the safety of her room.

A minute later, Conner joined her wearing pajama pants and a white t-shirt with the panda logo from the World Wildlife Fund. The t-shirt wasn't fair, making him even more likable. He was handsome, strong, tall, witty, and also liked animals. She had no idea why he hadn't been snatched up by some amazing woman.

Crystal poured them each a cup of tea as Conner sat down opposite her.

"It's chamomile," he said. "I always drink hot tea on winter nights, and I also find a cup of this in particular helps me sleep."

"It's a nice touch." Crystal smiled. "I would

usually go for hot cocoa, but after Roxie's pie, my teeth ache from sugar."

"So, tell me. How are you enjoying your first couple of days being a wilderness guide? I mean, other than a guy dying, of course."

"Other than the guy dying, I couldn't get enough. The beautiful forest and the powdery snow was everything I dreamed it would be. I imagined the group we led out would be more filled with joy to be on an adventure, though."

"They usually are," he reassured her. "This lot was quite surly, especially Philip. He didn't seem to be too popular with his staff, or even his wife."

"You're not kidding. As my mother says, 'If looks could kill, he'd be six feet under, pushing up posies.' It makes me wonder if any of our guests had anything to do with his demise."

"At the very least, it seems like they drove him into the winter wilderness at night. Well, they may not have liked him, but I'm having a good time with you," Conner said. "The last guide who was here with me was a real health nut. He got upset when I ate a candy bar on the trail. I asked why he was mad and he said, 'As guides, we should be setting an example by treating our bodies like temples.' I told him to mind his own business and let me eat in peace. He was so mad, he wouldn't speak to me the rest of the trip. After the hike, he asked the office not to be booked with me anymore."

"Are you serious?"

"Serious as a heart attack. The next trip, they paired him with Suzy for a climb up Mount Rainier, and she has a temper like a sailor with a two week rash. I warned her if she wanted to keep the peace during the climb, she should avoid packing any junk food. However, being Suzy, she took it in a different direction. Rumor has it, they had a few unpleasant exchanges on the hike to base camp. Since I had already warned her regarding him, she'd come prepared by packing some non-essential items. Instead of accommodating him, she thought it would be fun to incite him, just for kicks. She started handing out miniature candy bars at every break to the climbers. To drive it all home, she produced a piece of cake out of her pack and ate it in front of him when they summited. I'm still not sure how she managed to get it all the way up there without smashing it. He quit the second they got back."

"Sounds like you don't want to get on Suzy's bad side."

"I don't want you to get the wrong impression of Suzy. She's smart, tough, and as loyal of a friend as you will ever want. However, that guy was as judgmental and condescending as they come, and there was no way she was going to stand for his attitude without dishing some back in turn."

"I don't think I'm ready for Mt. Rainier," Crystal murmured. "This all happened so fast, I'm not sure what sort of outings I can expect."

"Pretty much anything you can imagine. In the winter we do mostly snowshoeing and skiing, both downhill and cross country. Ethan even takes people ice climbing, but he broke his leg the last time he was out. In the spring and summer, it's hiking for all levels; from kindergartners around small lakes to summiting Mt. Rainier. We also go white water rafting, canoeing, kayaking, paddle boarding, scuba diving, camping, and rock climbing. When you get more time, or more to the point, when Amelia has time, she'll assess your comfort and skill level in each activity, and match you to the classes you'll guide."

"I have some experience hiking, camping, and canoeing, but I've never done the other stuff. I was going to do my best to learn on the fly and bluff my way through when I needed to. In fact, when Amelia called and asked me if I could snowshoe and whether I could lead a group out this weekend, I told her of course I knew how to snowshoe and would be happy to start immediately. I couldn't believe what I was saying." The memory caused Crystal to cringe and bury her face in her hands. After a moment, she raised her head. "I had never been snowshoeing in my life, which you obviously know. I must have been convincing enough, because Amelia sounded pleased and relieved."

"I bet she was. She had hired a guide from another outfit, but his employer was desperate enough during the middle of ski season to give him a big raise, so he backed out on Amelia at the last second. As a rule, ECO adventures always sends two guides out for safety reasons, and she didn't want to cancel on this group. Looking back, it might have been better if we had canceled on Calvert and Associates, but I'm happy you got your foot in the door."

"Trust me when I say, for the person that went through that experience, it was a roller coaster. When the stars aligned to deliver this job opportunity to me, I was convinced I was going to get it. Then Amelia informed me she had hired a more experienced guide instead of me. The next day I sat down in front of my laptop, determined to find a job as a wilderness guide. I wasn't ready to give up on something that had so much potential to bring me happiness. My logic was if the person Amelia had hired had left another job, then that company needed to hire a guide, right? I had great intentions of sending off my résumé to every wilderness guide company, but I just couldn't find the gumption to get started. I attempted to improve my mood with my ritual of powdered doughnuts and mediocre TV. After a movie involving a jealous wife who murdered her philandering and abusive husband—which considering tonight, seemed a little on the nose—I forced myself to stop my pity party, and get back to my computer. I googled *wilderness guide companies Seattle*, and wrote down the top ten. I searched through the pages to see if any had help wanted ads in their employment links, but nothing had leapt out. I forwarded my résumé to Blue Sky Adventures, more out of stubbornness than any real hope. I gave one last check of my email, to see if they had responded, when I found another email from Emerald City Outfitters in my inbox." Crystal's heart picked up speed as she relived the moment. "I couldn't imagine why Amelia had emailed me again."

"What did it say?" Conner asked.

"*Dear Crystal. The position has reopened. Please call me ASAP if you are still interested. Amelia.* Nothing more to it."

"Sounds like her. Short and to the point."

"I just don't know why the woman can't call. I really need to set up my email to give alerts on my phone to avoid this situation, but I get so tired of hearing "ding" every time I get a message. I called her back at once, and she offered me the position. I was trying to play it cool, but I could hear the excitement in my own voice when I accepted. After I hung up, I was so excited, I did a quick pirouette and a little dance."

"I wish I had been there to see your victory celebration," Conner said with a grin that lit up his entire face.

"It isn't meant to be shared in public. I can't believe I'm even telling you about it. Afterward, I scrubbed the powdered sugar from the corner of my mouth, rushed around to change out of my pajamas, and threw on a dark knit sweater that said, I'm a wilderness guide and a professional at the same time."

"Sounds like a good sweater."

"It's my best one. I drove the short distance to Emerald City Outfitters to fill out the paperwork with Amelia, and afterward I went directly to the closest place to shop for snowshoes, where I met you."

"No wonder you asked so many questions."

"Asking you questions is not all I did. When I got home, I was all business. I clipped the tags from my shoes, blew the dust from my boots and practiced slipping in and out of the snowshoes for an hour or so. I wanted to familiarize myself with the sensation of how they felt, so I hiked around my apartment with them on until my cantankerous downstairs neighbor called to complain about the noise. Not wanting to upset her, especially after she had agreed to watch my cat, I stripped off my snowshoes. The hardest part for me was that these shiny new snowshoes did not belong to an experienced wilderness guide. I took a few stickers, which I had nabbed for free from Alpine Zone, peeled them and placed them on the small open spaces of each snowshoe. I even scratched some paint off and worked the binding straps until they appeared at least a little worn. Every fiber in my being cringed at defacing something so new, but I was willing to try anything. For this to work, I figured I needed to do everything I could think of to fool the other guide so they wouldn't report back to Amelia."

Conner leaned back in his chair with a warm smile after her retelling. "I'm not sure who was more surprised, you or me, when we realized we were co-guides on this trip. You did everything you could to get ready in a short amount of time, I'll give you that much. And don't worry about the other guides. We try and look out for each other. In fact, if you want, I'll teach you some basics in our spare time to bring you up to speed and make sure you don't go out feeling too inexperienced."

Crystal flashed him her brightest smile. "You would do that for me? I don't know how I can thank you enough." *Spending her spare time with Conner?* Crystal could not believe her luck.

The mood was spoiled by a man shouting upstairs. A woman's voice answered, followed by a slamming door. They listened for a few long moments, both desperately afraid of a repeat of the previous night, but after a blessed amount of calm, they returned to their conversation.

Conner grimaced. "Like I said, most people have the time of their lives up here. I wish your first trip wasn't this particular group."

"Don't worry about me." Crystal sipped her tea. "Despite the craziness, and the aforementioned death, I'm having a great time at my new job, and you're telling me it only gets better. I'm thrilled."

"Well, Miss Thrilled, I suggest hitting the hay. We

have to get up early to prepare the gear prior to heading back, so set your alarm for six. It's not all snowy walks and pecan pie."

"I knew there had to be a reason they paid us for this. Right now, I feel like I owe Emerald City Outfitters."

Conner winked as he finished his tea, "Don't tell Amelia. It won't do us any favors when we negotiate our raises. Sleep tight, Crystal. I'll see you in the morning."

Crystal wished him the same, as he retired to his room. She finished her tea and carried the teapot to the kitchenette. Following his advice, she padded to her room to get some sleep.

Chapter Four

Conner and Crystal led the group out of the forest and into the parking lot. A light snowfall persisted, and it would have been magical, if not for the previous night's tragedy. Instead, the transcendental quiet delivered by fresh snow only reflected everyone's dour mood as they had trooped along in silence.

A white SUV, with a red stripe and "Search and Rescue" emblazoned on its side in blue, was parked next to the ECO Adventures vans. Conner shucked his snowshoes as a short heavily muscled man, topped with a shock of red hair and matching bushy beard, stepped out to meet them.

Crystal joined Conner, leaving the rest of the group to struggle with their bindings.

"Morning, Sam. This is Crystal, our new guide." Conner shook the man's hand.

"Pleased to meet you, Crystal." Sam shook her hand in turn, his voice the low raspy growl she recognized from Conner's radio. The rest of the group gathered around them as they managed to strip off their gear. "Now that the storm has passed, we should be able to recover Philip. We have a GPS location where he fell, and a climbing team is heading there now."

"Last night's heavy snowfall isn't going to make this any easier," Conner added.

"We'll back out if it isn't safe. Are you going to

join us?"

"I am. I also need to figure out how to get Roxie down to the trailhead. Crystal, can you squeeze everyone into your van and get them back into town?"

"Sure thing," Crystal assured him.

The group gathered their gear in silence. Justin and Gary half-heartedly offered to help the climbing team, but Sam informed them they weren't trained for the work, and would be more of a liability than an asset. Crystal packed the snowshoe gear in the back of the van and the remaining party climbed in with her.

In the review mirror, Bree's shoulders shook with quiet sobs, while the rest sat in shock.

Beside her, Madeleine didn't utter a single syllable. The newly widowed woman was not even blinking as tears streamed down her cheeks, staring out the window at the forest as Crystal drove them down the pass. They wound their way to lower elevations. The snow switched to rain, and they passed the rest of the ride in the silence of their mourning.

****

Crystal maneuvered into the parking garage, and as the group piled out, she set her thoughts on planning how to handle the next few moments.

Finding paper and a pen in the glove box, she approached the group as they retrieved their packs from the back of the van. Crystal broke the long silence, "If you will all write your phone numbers down, we'll contact you as soon as they've recovered Philip."

Georgia jotted down her number, but Gary took one look at the piece of paper and began grousing. "We already gave you our information with the waivers and emergency contacts we filled out. Look it up. What was the point of filling out your company's stupid mountain of paperwork for this debacle if you're just going to ask for it again?" He stormed off, and the others trailed after him. Crystal stood alone in the parking garage, not sure what to do next, but figured the gear had to go inside the store. She grabbed as many pairs of snowshoes as she could carry and hauled them toward the entrance.

Making her way to the information desk, she breathed a sigh of relief when she spotted Lisa, the store's assistant manager. Her short frizzy blond hair, sweet face, and calm manner of speaking made it easy to overlook the fact she was hardy enough to sprint up Mt. Rainier before breakfast.

"Welcome back from your first outing. Let me show you where all of this goes." Lisa grabbed half of the snowshoes and led her to the back of the store through a door labeled service.

As they laid the snowshoes on an empty counter, Lisa asked, "How did your first guiding trip go?"

"Not great." Crystal recounted the night as Lisa followed her back to the van to grab the last of the gear.

"Wow...Is Conner still up at the pass, then?"

Crystal nodded as they laid out the rest of the gear in the service department. She was going to ask what to do next, when Amelia strode into the room, clutching a piece of paper.

"I got off the phone with Conner a little while ago," she said in a reproving tone. "I figured you would be back by now. I did not think it necessary to state in the job description that you were to come back with all of the guests."

Caught off guard, Crystal spluttered out a few

unhelpful words, "Umm, yeah…but…"

Lisa rode to her rescue. "She can hardly be at fault when someone gets it in their head to take off into a snowstorm in the middle of the night, Amelia."

Taking a deep breath, Amelia reined her temper short. "You are correct, of course," she sighed, surprising Crystal. She had expected a vicious assault of demeaning words much like her former boss, Darcy, inflicted on her staff, and was stunned to see Amelia accept Lisa's correction in stride.

"From my conversation with Conner, it does sound like you did everything properly. However, I do know there will be repercussions from this unfortunate disaster, so we better be ready," Amelia warned. "Crystal, why don't you go home and get some rest. I'll make sure you're notified if any news comes in. With everything going on, I made a copy of the company's contact information so you can keep in touch." She handed the sheet of paper to Crystal.

Crystal took the offered list, grabbed her pack and snowshoes, took the stairs to her car, and tossed her equipment in the back seat. Her family's Sunday brunch was scheduled to start in a little over an hour, and rather than head to her condo to freshen up, she pointed her car in the direction of her parents' home. They deserved an update on her life, and Crystal didn't feel like sitting alone in her apartment with only Elf for company.

The Rainey Sunday brunches had been part of her life for years. After she and her sister, Heather, had moved out, it became a way to keep the family in touch with each other as life's responsibilities tugged them in separate directions. Unfortunately, as her sister's life unfolded into wedded bliss and motherhood, it had evolved to become more and more a family forum to discuss what was wrong with Crystal's life and relationships. Despite the familial nagging, she still loved seeing everyone and couldn't wait to witness their expressions when she shocked them with her recent drastic change in career.

The rain had stopped, but the deep gray clouds in the sky promised it would start again at any moment. Thankful for the brief respite from the weather, she drove the few miles to the venerable Queen Anne neighborhood which surveyed downtown Seattle from a dignified perch atop a hill of the same name. Parking in front of the Victorian home her parents had owned her entire life, she took a moment to bask in the comfort of returning somewhere so familiar. Slender ornate spindles lined the wrap-around covered porch. Gingerbread trim stretched the length of the roof line and two small round rooms, reminiscent of little towers, flanked either side of the house. Those had been her and her sister's bedrooms growing up, and they had both pretended to be Rapunzel for hours on end, dangling their hair out of the windows and calling for Prince Charming to come rescue them. Across the street, lay a sprawling cemetery. Crystal had played amongst the tombstones as a child and had never once considered it odd, until Olivia teased her, insisting Crystal was a little touched in the head because of it. A few rain drops spattered against her windshield, urging her to get moving before it began in earnest.

She switched off her engine and was startled when it rattled a few extra times before stopping. Chalking it up to one more thing her car did to cause her stress, she dashed through the rain to the front door, flinging it open.

"Hello?" she called out.

"Crystal," her mother called back. "We're in the kitchen."

Crystal hung her coat on the peg by the door which had been hers since childhood. Bingo, her parents' feisty Yorkshire terrier, raced out to greet her with welcoming barks. She bent down to rub his shoulders the special way he liked, causing him to flop on his side in pleasure. She gave his head a pat. "Let's go boy, I'll get you a treat."

Bingo's eyes flared open at his favorite word and he led her to the kitchen, sitting on the ground below the countertop where his doggie cookie jar was kept.

"Hi, Mom. Hi, Dad," she said as she fished a small bone shaped treat out of the jar and handed it to the eager terrier. Bingo raced out of the room with his prize clenched between his teeth, streaking toward his bed on the living room couch.

"Hi pumpkin," Her dad greeted her with a smile from the sink as he scrubbed a mixing bowl.

Her mother slid a tin of muffins into the oven, set the timer for twenty minutes and spun to face her.

"I can't believe you quit your job without talking to us first."

"There wasn't time for a family meeting, Mom. It was more of a spur of the moment thing," Crystal sighed. She had hoped the interrogation wasn't going to start right out of the gate.

"Spur of the moment? Well, at least you have another job already. Is it another downtown office position doing business deals?"

"I don't do business deals, Mom. I never have. I've only ever been an assistant to those who manage the deals. Well, actually, I'm not even an assistant anymore."

Before her mother could open her mouth, her father interceded, speaking in the reasoned tone he had mastered after years of marriage. "Why don't we have a cup of coffee and you can tell us everything?" He had always been the only one who could derail Crystal's mother when the inquisition train left the station.

Crystal took the cue and grabbed the carafe which had been filled in anticipation of brunch. Her dad was setting out three mugs next to the cream and sugar.

As everyone settled into their seat, Crystal took charge of the situation rather than have the story pried out of her by leading questions from her parents.

"I am now a wilderness guide for Emerald City Outfitters and a man died on my first outing." She hadn't meant to spill all of the news at once, but the stress must have been boiling nearer the surface than she had thought.

Silence filled the room as her parents absorbed the news. Finally, her mom spoke. "How did all of this happen?" Her mother reached forward and grabbed her daughter's hand.

Gathering comfort from her mother's grasp, Crystal took a deep breath. "It's easiest if I start from the beginning." She began by retelling the story of how she quit her job at Smith, Axford, and Devry.

"I was commuting on the bus to work, when I decided to write my New Year's resolutions. They were the wake up call I needed that my life was going nowhere, and I knew right then I had to make a change, even if I didn't mean for it to happen that exact morning. I walked into work, soaked to the bone in our typical January rain, planning on making the best of it until I found something better."

Her parents may be skeptical, but quitting her old job was one of her life's glorious moments. "It started because I was too preoccupied to use my umbrella." She sat upright, relishing reliving the scene as she shared it with her parents.

****

"Wow, nice hair. Why didn't you use your umbrella?" Erica had said from behind the receptionist's desk, bedecked in her favorite bulky red sweater.

"What?" Crystal had touched a damp strand of her chestnut hair.

"Why didn't you use your umbrella? You're soaked."

"Oh, yeah." Crystal peered down at the unopened object-in-question in her hand, forcing her racing mind to focus. The clock on the wall above Erica's head showed three minutes to get to her desk before the work day started. "I'll be right back." She made a beeline for the nearby restroom.

Glancing in the mirror, she shuddered at her reflection. No wonder Erica had been taken aback. Her shoulder length hair was plastered to her head and her mascara had run down her face, giving a raccoon-like mask to her brown eyes.

Olivia burst through the bathroom door. "Oh, my god! Erica told me you looked like a drowned rat, and she was not exaggerating. She said you were in desperate need of this." Brandishing a makeup remover towelette, Olivia thrust it into Crystal's hand. Unfolding the towelette, Crystal began to swipe at the mess the rain had made.

Olivia studied Crystal as she worked, pointing out anything that was missed.

When Crystal paused to examine herself, Olivia muttered, "It'll have to do." With a firm tug of Crystal's hand, she pulled her to the hand dryer. "Put your head under here. You can't show up to work looking like this. Darcy will write you up."

Crystal bent at the waist while Olivia kept clicking the button to keep the air blowing. After a minute of running her fingers through her hair to comb out the tangles under the heat, Crystal straightened and banged her head on the underside of the dryer. "Ouch." She rubbed the sore spot for a few frantic seconds. Catching a glance of her reflection, she produced a brush from her bag to tame the worst of the mess.

"Ok, you've gotta get going," Olivia warned. "I clocked in already, but you were supposed to be at your desk five minutes ago."

Crystal grimaced, stuffed her brush back into her bag, and hastened after Olivia. Hurrying down the hallway, they passed the glass-enclosed offices of the company's high powered brokerage dealers and made their way to the cubicles in the back of the firm. They split up, heading to their respective work stations, but Crystal froze in her tracks as she made the last turn. Standing next to her desk was her boss, the loathsome Darcy Bray.

If you took a bunch of large pumpkins, stacked them on top of each other, and draped the slimy stuff from inside on the top for hair, you would have a pretty fair facsimile of Darcy. She even had an orangish hue to her skin.

"Hello, Crystal," she sneered. "Running a little late today, aren't we? For your information, Smith, Axford and Devry did not become a Fortune 500 company by letting people set their own hours."

"I'm sorry, Darcy. According to the clock, I'm only five minutes late to my desk. I was here on time, but I was in the restroom." Crystal put her best pleasant tone into her words. However, whenever she attempted to come across as contrite, Olivia said she always sounded irritated. Apparently this was true, because Darcy's face flushed from her standard orange to splotchy red.

"I'm going to have to write you up for this," she lamented in her most facetious of voices. "I believe this to be your second write up, if I'm not mistaken?"

Of all things, the first one was for eating a cupcake at her desk. Company policy stated food was only allowed in the break room. Crystal smiled to herself. It had been the most delectable chocolate cupcake with cappuccino buttercream frosting she had ever tasted, but the most delicious part had been breaking the company's ridiculous rules.

"Well?" Darcy growled when Crystal didn't answer.

"Well, what?" Crystal snapped back.

Like meerkats in the African wild, her coworkers, including Olivia, popped their heads above their cubicle walls; they sensed trouble.

An unexpected anger constricted Crystal's chest and throat. A vision of a life unfulfilled and the dread of forty more years with Darcy Bray as her boss, flashed through her head and ignited a spark. The New Year's resolutions she had just written pulsed in the back of her mind, urging the next words from her mouth.

"I'm not putting up with this anymore. I've had enough." Her voice was distant, not sounding like her at all. "I quit."

Crystal had circled past Darcy, snatched the picture of Elf from on top of her desk, and had stuffed it in her bag. Whirling, she had stormed past a shocked Darcy.

"You kick ass!" A disembodied voice had called from behind a cubicle wall. Crystal smiled. The supporting cheer had been Olivia, rooting her on from the safety of her meerkat den.

Crystal had strode by the glass offices, past Erica's desk, through the frosted glass doors of Smith, Axford and Devry, and back out into the rain.

****

"I had always dreamed of going out in a blaze of glory, but never thought I would have the guts to actually go through with it. I never realized how unhappy my job made me until that day."

"How are you going to afford your fancy condo on a wilderness guide salary?" her mother broke in.

"If you must know, I make more at this job than I did at Smith, Axford and Devry." It wasn't as if she expected her parents to gush over her new job, but she had hoped for less skepticism.

"Well, I think it's a wonderful idea." Her father surprised her with his announcement. "Adventure and fun rather than sitting in an office? It's quite the career change. I wish I'd had the guts to do something amazing like that when I was your age."

A flash of warmth washed over her from the

unexpected praise. His words also caused her mother to lean back in her chair with a thoughtful frown.

"But what happened on your first outing. You said someone died." Her father gave her a sympathetic look, studying her closely.

"It wasn't anything I did." Crystal could hear her voice rise in a defensive tone. "The guy left in middle of the night and died in an accident." She launched into the saga of the last few days. By the time she was describing the final details of the drive back to the city without Philip, they were eating her mother's apple cinnamon muffins.

Her parents stared at her with stunned expressions.

"Do you like the boy, Conner?" her mother ventured.

"Mom!" Crystal cried. "I quit my job, found a new one in a completely different field, led a group of people into the snowy mountains, and one of them didn't come back. The one thing you have taken away from everything I've just shared is whether or not I like Conner?" He was the exact type of man she was looking for, but she wasn't willing to share that information with her parents, yet.

"Well, ever since you broke up with Todd, we've been worried for you." Her mother put up her hands in a placating motion.

"Todd smelled like poop. All the time," Crystal groused.

"I suppose he did," her mother agreed. "He couldn't help it if he worked at the sewer treatment facility, but I must say it is nice not having to open the windows when we have brunch. Speaking of brunch, your sister and her family will be here any minute."

"What are we having?" asked Crystal.

"French toast and sausage. Do you mind slicing the bread?"

Crystal found two loaves in the pantry and drew the bread knife from the block on the counter. Her father started cracking eggs as her mother put the skillets on the stove. Bingo waited underfoot for morsels to either fall or be handed to him.

As the first piece of bread hit the griddle, the front door opened, and her sister's family trooped inside.

"Hi Nana! Hi Papa!" Her nephew, Joshua, raced in at top toddler speed. Bingo whined and retreated, but Crystal scooped him up to the safety of her arms. He was not a fan of the rambunctious toddler's attention.

"Aunt Crystal," Joshua shouted and threw his arms around her legs. Cradling Bingo in one arm, Crystal used her other to hug her nephew back. Her younger sister, Heather, and her husband, Nick, followed their energetic son into the kitchen leading their daughter Tabitha between them, who clutched their pinkies in her tiny hands.

Both of Crystal's parents dropped what they were doing and proceeded to hug and kiss their grandson, while her sister joined her at the stove to help with brunch.

"Hi, Crys." Heather gave Crystal a little hug.

"Morning, Sis," she replied and hugged her back. "What's new with the Donnelly Family?"

"Not a whole lot. Joshua learned the word 'ass' in kindergarten from one of his classmates."

"Ass," he echoed in glee. He proceeded to race around the kitchen singing, "Ass! Ass! Ass!"

"We couldn't be more proud." Nick gave a wry

smile as he watched his son's antics.

Crystal's mother lifted Tabitha up and proceeded to make barnyard sounds while tickling her belly. Her squeals of laughter filled the house as brunch sizzled in the skillet.

"What's new with you?" her sister asked while laying out sausage on a second skillet.

Crystal couldn't muster the stamina to go through it all in detail again, so she gave a five minute synopsis of her life.

"Dang, sis," her sister said in mock consternation. "You know, you could text or at least update your Facebook page."

"I've been a little too busy, not to mention in the middle of nowhere with zero cell service, so you get to find out the old fashioned way."

"Well, next time send me a quick text when you're back in cellphone range—*Quit job, got new one. Guy died in wilderness.* I'll piece it together from there."

Crystal laughed and agreed to tell her about any more major life changes.

The two sisters transferred the French toast to a platter and carried it to the table where their father was sitting, sipping his coffee and watching everything with a paternal smile.

Nick retrieved the highchair for Tabitha and a booster seat for Joshua from where they were stored in the den closet, and they all sat down to enjoy the meal. Bingo curled up on Crystal's lap under the table and slept as the family chatted away. Her mind couldn't seem to enjoy the moment, though. Her attention kept returning to Conner in the snow-laden mountains attempting to retrieve Philip's body, and hoping he was safe.

****

Crystal opened the front door to her condo, exhausted with the day's events. Elf, her fluffy ragdoll raced out to greet her, weaving around her legs, as she tossed her pack on the couch. She'd left her snowshoes and poles in the back seat of her car since she hoped she would be out again soon. As she hung her coat up, Elf sprinted into the kitchen, jumped on the counter, and meowed from his eating spot.

"Didn't Mrs. McReady take good care of you?" she asked him. In response, she received several loud yowls followed by impatient flicks of his ears and bushy tail. From the empty cans in the trash, she could tell her cat had been fed a more than generous amount in her absence. However, there was no way to placate him rather than give in, so she dished out a little extra food.

"You're such a greedy monster," she cooed, as he wolfed it down. The safest time to pet her feisty cat was when he was distracted with eating, so she took advantage of the moment, running her hands through his silky coat.

Crystal had picked Elf out of the cat room at the Humane Society where he had been nothing but purrs and affectionate head-butts, seeming the prototypical docile ragdoll. Shortly after she had ensconced him in her condo, his true nature had come out, and he had revealed he wasn't averse to the occasional swat of his claws if he was annoyed with your attentions. He had received his name, Evil Little Feline, from her father, who had rubbed his ears and received a scratch on his hand in return for his effort. The name had been shortened to Elf, and Crystal was always left debating how and when it was safe to cuddle her pet.

She spent the afternoon unpacking her bag and taking a hot bath. She texted Olivia the short version of everything that had happened on the snowshoe trip and promised to get together with her friend soon to share the details.

Entering her new coworkers' phone numbers into her cell phone contacts tempted Crystal to call Amelia to see if any news about the recovery had come in. However, her new boss was not the sort of woman to forget a promise like calling if anything was reported.

The tragedy of her first trip as a guide made her acutely aware she had a tremendous amount to learn. Sitting at her dining room table, Crystal opened her laptop and started researching what had become a relevant topic in her life, search and rescue techniques. She learned about orienteering with a GPS in the forest, as well as the old fashioned style of using a map and a compass to get to a pre-determined location. The day passed with still no word. As the sun set, Crystal gave up on researching and stretched out on the couch to distract herself by downloading the new murder mystery from her favorite author to her tablet. Elf settled on the back of the couch and curled into a kitty-ball for a nap on the cat-themed Christmas quilt her mother had handmade. Silhouettes of Santa hat bedecked felines played amongst cutouts of stockings and Christmas trees. She made a mental note to put the quilt away in her closet where the rest of her decorations were, but she and Elf liked it too much to consider packing it up for another week or two.

She had only made it through the first few pages of the book when her phone rang, and Conner's name appeared on the screen. Crystal answered on the first ring.

"Conner! Did you find him?"

Conner's serious tone broke the news before she comprehended his words. "We recovered him an hour ago. It's official. He's busy trying to barter his way through the pearly gates."

She sat upright. Elf swatted at her hair, but thankfully missed skin. "What do you think happened?"

"It looks like he drove the snowmobile off the cliff we passed on the way up, the one overlooking Mount Rainier. He must have missed it in the dark and plunged right over the side. The Sheriff's Office is investigating and sent his body to the Seattle medical examiner for an autopsy. By the way, the Sheriff in charge of the accident wants to talk to everyone who was at the chalet, so I gave him your number. He said he's going to contact you soon and wants a rundown on the snowshoe hike into the chalet and the following night. As far as the SAR team can conclude, though, it looks like he hit his head on the way down and never woke up."

"That's awful."

"The Sheriff's department is contacting Madeleine now to let her know Philip's body was recovered, but the newspaper reporters from the Seattle Times were here, and I expect the whole story will be in the paper tomorrow." Sam's unmistakable voice rumbled in the background and Conner shouted away from the phone, "I'll be right there." He must have raised his phone to speak to her again, because his voice came through sharp and clear. "Hey, Crystal, I'll be in touch. Sam wants me to help him fill out the report."

"I'll talk to you soon," Crystal hung up.

Crystal stared at her phone. A small part of her had hoped they would rescue him from the snow, maybe hurt, but through some miracle, alive. Her mind flashed to pity for Madeleine. Even though her marriage to Philip had been strained, she was going through an awful time, and if the finality of this news was hitting Crystal as hard as it was, she couldn't imagine what it would do to Madeleine. It was also awful to admit, even to herself, but what Crystal worried about most was what this meant for her new job.

Chapter Five

Crystal gave Elf a pet goodbye on her way out the door. All of the ECO guides had been notified they had a ten o'clock mandatory meeting at the store this morning. Outside, the temperature had dropped below freezing, but the rain was gone for the first time in days. Since she had an hour to get to the meeting, she opted to walk in the crisp winter air. Dodging the icy patches on the sidewalks, she made it with time to spare and headed to the customer service desk to ask Lisa if she had any news.

Lisa's back was to Crystal as she tagged a small pile of wool gloves with a sale sticker behind the counter. "Good morning," Crystal greeted over the clicking noise of the price gun.

Lisa pivoted from the pile of merchandise and her face lit up with a warm smile. "How are you doing?"

"I'm fine. Do you know what the guide meeting is about this morning? I mean, I'm sure it has to do with Philip's death, but what exactly are we meeting to talk about?"

"To be honest, I'm not sure. Amelia had a long discussion with a woman in a fancy suit yesterday evening and has been in a dark mood ever since."

Two more people joined them at the customer service desk. A compact athletic woman with short sandy hair and a thoughtful frown stood next to a lean man with a mop of dark curls, his right leg in a cast, and balancing on a pair of crutches.

"What's up, Lisa?" the blond woman asked.

"I was just telling Crystal, I have no idea," Lisa said.

"I can't believe Amelia made me come in on my day off," she grumbled. "Bunch of B.S."

"You must be Suzy and Ethan," Crystal ventured.

"Sure are. You must be Crystal." Ethan extended a hand from his crutch, and Crystal shook it.

Suzy shook her hand, too. "Amelia let us know you were going to be joining our group. Conner texted us last night and shared a little of what happened on your first snowshoe hike."

"Yes, I did," Conner said as he approached the group from behind. "Amelia is in the break room and wants us to join her."

Lisa said goodbye to everyone and they followed Conner.

Amelia was standing in the center of the room, pouring over a handful of paperwork. Looking up and seeing the group enter, she set the papers down and asked them to take a seat.

Everyone drew out a chair, Ethan a little awkwardly as he propped his broken leg on a second chair. Crystal was pleased when Conner passed a couple of empty seats to sit next to her.

"I believe everyone here knows the gist of what happened last night." Several murmurs of assent greeted Amelia's statement. "Then I'll get right to the heart of the matter. Even though it seems the Sheriff's Office has hinted they don't have any reason to believe ECO Adventures did anything improper, our insurance company has suspended our coverage until the conclusion of the investigation. I've been arguing with them since yesterday afternoon, but I don't think it helped when the death of Philip Calvert made front page news this morning."

"Can they do that on a whim?" Ethan asked.

"A man died on one of our trips, so it's hardly a whim. Our policy says they can suspend coverage in the event of gross negligence. I've tried reasoning with them, but they won't budge."

"Bunch of insurance peckers," Suzy muttered.

Amelia shot a quick glare at Suzy, but continued, "The obvious and unfortunate side effect of our insurance being suspended is we cannot take groups out for tours. Ethan, you'll remain on disability, but even with you on the shelf, I don't have forty hours a week in the store to parcel out to the three of you."

Sweat broke out on Crystal's palms, and the same panic from when she had quit Smith, Axford, and Devry returned. She didn't have much of a savings account to see her through an extended pay cut. Her voice trembled as she asked, "Did the Sheriff's department or insurance company give any indication of how long this will take?"

"The detective in charge of the investigation said it shouldn't take long. An accident investigation typically closes within a couple of weeks," Amelia informed them. "In the meantime, I'll send you a schedule later tonight with your shifts. I'm going to meet with the remainder of the staff this afternoon and see if they want to take any paid or unpaid vacation time and, if we are lucky, everyone can get a few more hours."

The group stood up, thanked Amelia, and left the

break room. As they made their way out of the store, Conner leaned close to Crystal. "If you have time, do you want to join me at the Starbucks across the street? I have an idea."

"It seems I have an abundance of free time," Crystal said with a droll smile.

"Good, because I need you if this plan is going to work."

Crystal liked the idea of being part of whatever Conner was cooking up, so she made her way to the coffee shop with him.

Crystal ordered her standard latte. Conner added a mocha to the order, picking up the tab for both Crystal and him.

"Thanks, but you didn't have to pay for me."

"It's my pleasure."

"Let's hear this plan of yours." Crystal sipped her latte and studied Conner's face. Deep bags under his eyes betrayed how tired he was. Crystal reminded herself he had been working with Search and Rescue late into the evening and hadn't got much sleep.

He took a long sip of coffee and filled her in. "My cousin, Holly, works for the Seattle Police Department. The King County Sheriff's Office may be doing the investigation, but they use the local police resources. One thing I've learned from my cousin is law enforcement gossips about active investigations among themselves, so she'll likely know what's going on."

Crystal's phone chimed, and the notification declared it was a text from Olivia.

"Go ahead and check it." Conner politely averted his attention to stare at the line of people, while sipping his drink.

Crystal glanced at her phone—*Saw the front page of the paper. Conner is a hunk.*

Crystal's cheeks reddened and she closed the message in haste.

"Everything ok? You look a little upset," Conner asked.

"Oh, me? I'm fine. Did you see the Seattle Times, yet?"

"Not yet, but I see there's one for sale over there." Conner left the table.

Crystal took the opportunity to type a quick message back to her friend—*With him right now. Will call later.*

Conner set the paper in front of her as she clicked her phone screen off.

The front page showed Conner bedecked in his red winter parka, centered in the photo, composed and speaking to Sam next to an ambulance. The snow swirled around them as people scrambled in the background. Crystal couldn't help but blush again, because Olivia's text sprang to mind. Conner *was* a hunk.

The headline atop the picture declared, "Body of Lost Man Recovered." She skimmed the caption below the scene. "The body of Philip Calvert was recovered yesterday evening after he fell during an ECO Adventures snowshoe hike."

Another flush overtook her, but now from irritation. "This headline is obnoxious. It makes it sound like he fell off a cliff while hiking with us." She folded the paper and tossed it on a nearby empty table in disgust.

"If I didn't know better, I'd think the same thing.

All the more reason to help me out," he said.

"What's the plan?"

Steepling his fingers in front of his chest, Conner met her eyes. "My cousin won't come over if I ask her out of the blue. She's savvy enough to know I'll work her for information about Philip's death. She's a huge gossip, but she also knows she's not supposed to discuss ongoing investigations with anyone outside the force. However, if I ask her to dinner to meet my new girlfriend, I know she'll come. Once Holly's at dinner, I can get her talking."

Crystal crossed her arms in front of her. If Conner had a new girlfriend he wanted to introduce to his cousin, Crystal didn't see why she needed to be there.

"I can tell you aren't keen on playing the part of my girlfriend," Conner said, taking in her darkening expression.

"Wait. *I'm* your girlfriend? I mean *the* girlfriend?" Olivia was right. When it came to understanding men, Crystal was thicker than a brick.

"Well, yeah," Conner was a little off balance by her reversal in attitude.

"Oh, I can be your girlfriend." The words rolled out of her mouth, bursting with eagerness, and Crystal gave herself a mental face palm.

"Keep your phone nearby, because I'm going to see if she can come over tonight. I'm not convinced this investigation is going to be over in a short period of time, and we need to figure out what this means for our jobs."

****

Crystal scrutinized her lipstick in the rearview mirror. Conner had texted her an hour after they had

81

left the coffee shop to tell her dinner was on at his place. His cousin, deputy Holly Wilkins, was going to be there at six to join them when she got off her shift. Crystal had put on her favorite red silk top and matched it with a black mid-length skirt. She had topped it all off with a pair of diamond stud earrings and a hint of jasmine perfume. If she was going to play the part of a girlfriend meeting family, she was going to do her best to make Conner consider her for a permanent role.

She finished touching up her make-up and checked the clock on her phone. Conner had asked her to come over a half hour early to help set up and she was right on time. She climbed out of her car and walked the short distance to his apartment building. He lived in Georgetown, which had once been the industrial heart of Seattle, but had since become an artists' haven. The brick buildings loomed in an ominous fashion, but the streets were clean and the pedestrians were mostly twenty-somethings heading out into the freezing evening in trendy clothes, intent on enjoying a night out.

She approached the front door and thumbed the button labeled 201 Oakes.

Excited barks competed with Conner's voice as he answered over the intercom. "Come on up, Crystal. Maggie, behave yourself."

The front door buzzed and she tugged it open. Weathered wooden steps led her to the second floor. The door to Conner's apartment was ajar and she tapped her knuckles on its surface as she entered. Maggie dashed toward her, and Crystal cringed, not wanting some of her best clothes to be ruined. However, Maggie pulled up short and sat, wagging her tail with enough vigor to thump either side of the hallway.

"Good girl," Conner praised her. He emerged from the kitchen in blue jeans and a t-shirt, a hand towel thrown over his shoulder. "She has so much energy, I had to train her to sit when greeting guests. Jumping was cute when she was young. However, it became a lot less so when she grew to her full size."

Crystal held her hand out for Maggie to sniff, "Who's a pretty girl and a good dog?" she asked the quivering lab. Maggie licked her hand before shoving her head into Crystal's palm, begging for a pet. Crystal obliged, giving Maggie a good head rub.

"I'm happy you two get along so well. Maggie doesn't like just anyone."

"You're just being nice," Crystal murmured while rubbing Maggie's ears.

"No, I'm serious. She's a rescue from a puppy mill. She has trust issues with most people."

"Well, I think she's a wonderful dog." Crystal gave Maggie a few more rubs on her shoulders as the lab wiggled in joy. "How's dinner going?"

"Great, so far. You look beautiful, by the way." Crystal glanced up from Maggie to see him giving her an appreciative look.

She blushed, "Thanks. I figured it made sense to dress up a little, if I'm going to make this believable."

"Well, you nailed it. I just put the lasagna in the oven a moment ago, but if you don't mind setting the table, it would be a big help. But first, the grand tour." He gestured to the large main area, "Kitchen, dining room, and living room here. Bedroom and bathroom there," he pointed to two doors at the other end of the apartment. The kitchen was open to the dining room and living room. A round oak table sat underneath a chandelier in the dining area, and a tattered sofa facing a small flat screen television atop an entertainment center made up the entirety of the living room. The furniture throughout was of high quality, but dated and well worn. It was the exact apartment Crystal would expect of a man renting to save for a home. Framed pictures of nature scenes, friends, and family were the only decorations.

In particular, two larger framed photos flanked the television and Crystal approached to get a better look. One showed Conner amidst a snowy field and the other was of a black bear, standing in the middle of a stream, and catching a leaping salmon in its jaws.

"The first one is at the summit of Mount Rainier. The other I took in the Olympics, during the salmon run last fall."

"They're amazing." Crystal said in awe.

"Well, get used to it, because this is going to be your life now, Crystal."

Gazing into his eyes, she could see they were brimming with kindness and excitement. "It is my life, isn't it? It's hard to believe, since I've only led one group out before we were suspended."

"It'll be a thing of the past, soon, and you'll be back out in the wild before you know it. It's a crazy life, but you'll never look back."

"I hope this all works out. I'd hate to go back to an office job to make ends meet after I got a taste of this life," she waved at the two photos.

"We're going to find out more tonight. I'm off to change into something nicer for dinner. The dishes are in the cabinets and the silverware is in the top drawer. I'll be out in a second," he made his way to the bedroom and shut the door.

Crystal found plates as well as an unmatched set of salad bowls. A little more searching turned up the silverware and glasses, and she began setting the table for three. Maggie followed her between the kitchen and dining room, her tail thumping on the cabinets in the narrow space as they made their way back and forth. She was putting out the last wine glass when Conner reemerged. He had on a maroon pullover sweater and Khaki slacks.

"You look handsome," Crystal told him and she meant it.

"Thanks. It's my go-to fancy outfit."

"What's the plan?"

"Plan for what?"

"To get this information from Holly."

"You'll see."

"What do you mean? How should I ask? When should I ask? After dinner?"

"Relax and be yourself. You'll know when to ask."

Crystal gave him her best glare. His advice was not helpful at all.

The intercom on the wall called out, and Maggie jumped up to bark several times.

Conner pressed the button and cracked his front door.

Chapter Six

"It smells great in here," Holly stepped into the apartment in full uniform. Maggie rushed up and sat next to her, waving her tail with the same vigor she had shown Crystal. Holly dropped to one knee and grabbed Maggie in a hug, who licked the policewoman's ear in excitement.

"Hey, Cuz," Conner greeted her from the kitchen.

"Hey, Conner. You must be Crystal," Holly stood and held out her hand.

"I am. Nice to meet you, Holly," Crystal took her hand and shook it.

"Conner, you've been holding out on me," Holly complained. "He hasn't once mentioned you, and now he invites me to come and meet you."

"I haven't mentioned Crystal, because you're nosy," Conner explained. "And you ask too many questions."

"Well, I'm a cop. It's what I do," Holly chuckled. She stripped off her coat and gun belt and hung them in a small coat closet next to the front door.

"White or red?" Conner asked.

"I'll have a splash of white," Holly answered. "I just got off three twelve hour shifts and if I drink too much, I'm going to fall asleep at the dinner table."

Conner pulled a bottle of chardonnay out of his fridge and uncorked it along with a merlot which had been sitting on the counter. He poured a little white for Holly, and raised a questioning eyebrow at Crystal.

"Red for me," Crystal answered. Conner poured them each a glass and set the bottles on the table. Holly sat down and Crystal took the chair next to her as Conner busied himself in the kitchen.

"How did you two meet?" Holly asked.

"At work. I'm a guide, too," Crystal said.

"Were you on the trip with Conner when Philip Calvert snuffed it?"

"I was." Crystal sensed this was the opportunity. "Any word on how the case is going?"

"Sorry, I'm not supposed to speak on active investigations," Holly apologized.

Crystal sneaked a peek at Conner to see if he was ready to invoke this plan of his, but he ignored them as he put a loaf of garlic bread in the oven next to the lasagna.

Holly sipped her wine until only a small amount was left. Grabbing the bottle, she added a little more to her glass. "How long have you two been seeing each other?"

"Not too long," Crystal was reluctant to lie to Conner's cousin. "I only started at ECO Adventures a few days ago, but we met at his other job." This was not a lie, she told herself.

"I still can't believe Conner managed to take all those camping trips we took as children and turn it into a career." A slight smile lit up Holly's face as she reminisced.

"It's nice your families spent so much time together," Crystal said. "My family camped and hiked a lot, but it was only my parents, my sister, and me."

Holly shot a glance at Conner.

"Holly's parents raised me," Conner said. "My father split before I was born, and my mother became addicted to drugs. She lost custody of me when I was one, and Holly's parents took over from there."

"I didn't know. I'm so sorry."

"Nothing to be sorry about. My aunt and uncle are my parents and Holly is my sister. It's how I feel."

"I didn't mean to overshare." Holly sipped her wine.

"Don't worry." Conner gave a casual wave.

Crystal's soul ached for the young Conner. Maggie must have sensed her distress, because she lay her head in Crystal's lap and focused her soulful eyes up at her. Crystal stroked the dog's head, and the feeling of the velvety fur helped ease her worry.

"Well, Crystal has Maggie's approval, that's for sure." Holly smiled, taking in the lab. "Nice to see she has come to like you."

Her words made Crystal's heart swell. Crystal trusted animals and their instincts, and Maggie's affection made her feel accepted.

"Dinner's ready," Conner announced as he took the lasagna and garlic bread out of the oven. "Sweetie, would you mind making the salad?"

It took Crystal a second to realize she was "sweetie," and shot up from her seat. She found the pre-made salad kit in the fridge. Conner handed her a salad bowl, and she opened the various pouches, using tongs from the utensil holder to toss the ingredients together.

"Do you know if any of the employees didn't like Philip," asked Holly from the table.

Crystal glanced over at Conner's cousin, who was

now sipping a little red wine from her glass.

"I think the real question is, did any of his employees actually like him?" Crystal answered.

"Makes sense."

"What makes sense?"

"Nothing. Not my circus, not my monkeys. Sometimes, I can't turn my brain off from work."

Conner continued to ignore the obvious opening and set the lasagna and garlic bread on the dining room table. Crystal added the Caesar salad, and sat next to Holly. Conner topped off the three wine glasses and sat down with the two women.

"Tell me about Conner when he was young." This was not only a good question to keep up their boyfriend-girlfriend story, but Crystal wanted to know more about him.

"Oh, he was constantly outside. He slept half of his nights in a tent in the yard and the other half planning outdoor adventures." Holly flashed Conner an accusatory glare. "Do you remember the time you persuaded me to look for garter snakes under some old logs?"

"I remember." Conner started dishing out the lasagna. "We found one and I dared you to pick it up. Crystal, you should have seen it. She grabbed it by the tail. Now, normally they are unaggressive, but she spooked it enough to turn mean."

"The damn thing bit me," Holly grabbed a piece of garlic bread and added it to her plate. "I'm still mad at you, and I still don't like snakes." She took a swig from her wine glass as if to wash the incident from her memory.

"What details do you remember from the night at

the chalet?" Holly asked, setting her wine glass down and picking up her fork.

Crystal paused for a second at the unexpected change in direction of the conversation. "We were downstairs in the basement when it all happened." She started recounting the chaotic night as they dug into their lasagna.

Holly nodded as she ate, sipping her wine. When Crystal arrived at the part when she heard something hit the floor, Holly interrupted.

"The noise you heard was probably Philip. Someone smacked him on the head and knocked him out. The thump was likely him hitting the floor," she said. "The medical examiner determined he had a wicked concussion prior to his death."

The news set her aback. "Are you sure?"

"I shouldn't have said anything. Forget I did. Please, continue."

Crystal finished recounting the tale as they ate, Conner filling in bits and pieces of the story. By the time she was done, they had finished eating and Conner poured the last of the merlot in their glasses.

"How did he look when Search and Rescue found him?" Holly asked Conner.

"Pretty darn awful," Conner said. "He was battered and bruised, but he had just fallen off a forty foot cliff with a snowmobile along for the ride, so we weren't shocked by the state he was in."

Holly nodded. "I wouldn't count on this being done anytime soon. From what the ME's assistant told me, Philip appears to have suffered severe blunt force trauma to his head prior to his death. The detective in charge is looking into foul play."

"Couldn't he have hit his head going over the cliff?" Crystal pressed. She half-expected Holly to clam up again, but she tossed back the last of her wine and answered.

"Nahh…the head wound was inflicted well before he died. Rumor is they think he was dumped over the cliff."

"How long do investigations like this last?" Crystal asked, concerned.

"Tough to say. We're talking murder investigation, and they typically last months, but it takes what it takes. Often, it depends if anyone talks. Another problem with this case is it's been non-stop snowing in the mountains, so accessibility to the crime scene is an issue."

Crystal's hopes sank, and she exchanged a worried look with Conner. She didn't have months worth of savings and the part time job in the store was not enough to cover her bills.

It was up to them to pry any additional information out of Holly. However, Conner's cousin wasn't paying any attention to the conversation, but was instead eyeing the bottom of her wine glass. Glancing up, Holly groused, "For cryin' out loud, Conner, I said I only wanted a little wine."

"Well, I didn't tell you to keep drinking," he protested.

"I can't drive like this. As I'm sure you can imagine, getting a DUI in a police cruiser is frowned upon by the department."

"You know you can sleep on the couch if you need to."

"That's Maggie's bed and she woofs in her sleep,"

Holly grumbled. The long shifts, the pasta, and the wine were all hitting Conner's cousin like a ton of bricks. Her eyelids drooped and she swayed as she got to her feet.

Crystal could tell the evening was winding down and stood to clear the table. Conner helped her and soon the dishes were cleared.

Crystal grabbed her coat, while Holly hauled some blankets from a closet.

"It was very nice to meet you, Holly," Crystal called out.

"It was great meeting you too, Crystal. I see why Conner likes you. You two are good together." Holly waved from the living room, where Maggie sat watching the policewoman.

Holly's words were something for her to ponder. She hoped Conner would think about them, too.

"I'll walk you to your car," Conner offered. "It's getting late, and the neighborhood can get a little sketchy as the evening gets on."

"Thanks."

While Conner helped her on with her coat, Holly stretched out on the couch and tugged the blankets over her. Maggie leapt up and flopped down next to her with a contented sigh. Holly threw her arm around the lab, hugging tight.

She and Conner left the apartment and descended the stairs. They started in the direction of her car, parked a block away, and she was pleased to feel Conner place his hand on her lower back.

"The news from Holly could have been better," Conner said.

"You can say that again. I don't think I can wait

months for this to be solved."

"Maybe we'll get lucky and someone will confess," Conner mused.

"I think if they are willing to commit murder, they won't confess simply because it would be convenient for us if they did."

Conner sighed, "I suppose you're right. Well, at least one good thing happened this evening."

"What's that?"

"My cousin approves of you, and it's pretty rare for her to like someone I introduce to her. Whenever I've gone against her advice, I've always regretted it. Frankly, it's given me a bit of a complex. I know we were pretending tonight, but…"

"Well, Holly is a cop," she nudged her shoulder against his and gave a mischievous smile, "and they *are* known to have good instincts."

A smile tugged at the corner of his lips. "Too true. I don't see how we can't go on a date, now."

A surge of adrenaline coursed through Crystal and giddiness transitioned into exuberance. Her whirling emotions were wreaking havoc, and she found herself fighting back a ridiculous urge to giggle. Her internal roller coaster ride must have been evident, because Conner was eyeing her with trepidation. Taking a deep breath to clear her unruly mind, she managed to respond with an earnest, "I'd like that."

He broke into a relieved smile. "Great. I'll plan something and call you."

Tiny wings took flight in her stomach, and the first vibrant spark of a new relationship forced the fear and anxiety of the investigation out of her thoughts.

"I look forward to it." Crystal willed her voice to

be calm, but her tone betrayed her excitement. Even though the last few relationships in her life had ended in disaster, something told her Conner was different. Maybe it was because he had already shown he could be trusted by not telling Amelia about her lack of experience, but a little voice inside her head insisted she could depend on him. Leaning in close, she rested her head on his shoulder as they took the last few steps to her car.

Conner whistled as he took in her battered blue Honda, "Wow, she's a beaut."

"It gets me from point A to point B. Well, most of the time," she amended.

Swinging open her door, he helped her into her seat. Wishing him good night, she twisted the key and winced at the loud whine her car made, but at least it started on the first try. She peeked in her rearview mirror. A grinning Conner waved as she drove away.

Chapter Seven

After dishing out a dollop of canned cat food for Elf's breakfast, Crystal opened her laptop. She suspected Amelia would have already sent out the updated work schedule. Sure enough, an email was in her inbox awaiting her attention. According to it, she didn't work today, but had a shift tomorrow morning. She examined the upcoming two weeks and did some quick math. It averaged out to sixteen hours per week. She did some further calculations, compared the amount to her budget, and did not like the number she came up with. If the hours didn't improve, her savings would stretch to a little over a month, but only if she tightened her spending.

Maybe someone will confess or the detectives will get to the bottom of this fast. Recognizing the same wishful thinking she had corrected Conner on the previous night, she grimaced.

She made her breakfast and switched on the TV to see if Philip Calvert's death had made the news, when her phone rang. The number was not one her phone recognized, but she accepted the call anyway.

"Hello?"

"Good morning, am I speaking with Crystal Rainey?" the man on the other end sounded young, but spoke with an official air.

"This is she."

"Hi, Ms. Rainey. I'm Sergeant Tyler Prescott with the criminal investigation division. I'm in charge of the Philip Calvert case. I was wondering if you could come to the local downtown Seattle PD station today and answer some questions."

"Of course." Crystal was thrilled. The Sheriff's department was already working on Philip's death.

"Can you meet me in an hour?"

"I'll be there."

Crystal tossed on a white knit sweater and pair of black jeans. A quick couple passes with her brush to tame her morning hair and she trotted out of her condominium complex. She was more than happy to do anything to hurry this to a close and get back to working full time.

With her new sense of fiscal responsibility, she avoided the bus fare or parking fees by walking the mile to the station in a light drizzle. It didn't seem like much, but, at this point, every dollar counted.

Twenty minutes later, she pushed open the door to the station. A harassed looking deputy took a moment between phone calls and informed her to wait in the lobby, until the sergeant was available. She took a seat far away from several frightening looking individuals. In particular, she avoided making eye contact with the guy covered in face tattoos muttering plans to himself about raising bail money. Crystal had decided to move closer to the deputy answering the phones when a young man in the dark green top and khaki slacks of a King County Sheriff marched down the hallway to greet her. To her surprise, Roxie was walking beside him.

The Sheriff stepped forward, offering his hand.

"Crystal, thanks for coming down. I'm Deputy Prescott." His tone was bursting with cheerful enthusiasm as they shook hands. "The local PD is lending me a room down the hall." He waved in the direction he had come from, and smacked his hand against the wall.

Roxie rolled her eyes and mouthed, "I'll wait for you."

Nonplussed, the deputy turned on his heel and led Crystal to the room he had indicated. They took a seat across from each other, and she waited as he arranged a small recorder and blank legal pad on the table. He wrote her name on the top and underlined it twice.

"Ok, let's begin. What can you tell me of the snowshoe trip and the ensuing events the night of Philip's death in the Baranhof Chalet? I need you to go into every minuscule detail you can remember. The slightest clue can break open a case to a trained professional such as myself."

His words had the opposite effect they were meant to convey. His blatant attempt to reassure her while simultaneously touting his investigative skills made her look at him askance, but it's not like she could ask for a different detective. "I'm happy to do anything I can to help solve the case. My fellow guide, Conner Oakes, and I met the staff of Calvert and Associates outside of the Emerald City Outfitters store. We had finished introductions and I had just grabbed my gear from my car and headed to the loading zone." Crystal let herself fall deep into the fateful day's memory.

****

At the loading zone, two ECO Adventures emblazoned white vans had awaited. Crystal had

97

opened the double doors, and tossed her equipment next to a massive backpack, and had begun stowing more packs as they were being handed to her by the milling crowd. Finishing, she had stepped back and slammed the rear doors shut. Out of the corner of her eye, she spotted through the rear window of the second van a variety of snowshoes stacked to the roof. The chattering group had split up between the two vans and were funneling through the side doors. As soon as the last person had stepped through, she and Conner each slid their respective doors shut.

"Follow me. I'll try not to run too many yellow lights," Conner called out over the hood of the van.

"You think I have a problem running yellow lights? Try and shake me."

"Challenge accepted!" he shouted back as he slung himself into his driver's seat and shut his door.

However, Conner didn't get a chance to test her driving moxie through the streets, as they cruised through several green lights before merging onto the freeway heading for the mountains.

After setting her van's cruise control at the speed limit, Crystal directed her attention to the four passengers in the van.

"We are on our way. As Conner mentioned back at the store, my name is Crystal. Does anyone have any questions about our excursion?"

"What is the chalet like?" Bree leaned forward.

"This will be my first time guiding this snowshoe trip," Crystal confessed. It was her first time guiding anyone, anywhere, but they didn't know that, and her credibility would be shot if she mentioned her inexperience. "You'll have to ask Conner when we reach the summit." The road ahead of her started climbing, and the van's engine growled to keep up with the cruise control setting.

Bree sat back, disappointed, and Crystal took it upon herself to pick up the mood.

"However, I hear the hike is enchanting. If we are lucky, we may see a snowshoe hare or even a mountain goat. They frequent the area, and people have reported seeing them within the last few weeks." Crystal had the Northwest Conservation web page to thank for the information. "I also know you'll be greeted with a meal, prepared by an on-site chef, when we arrive at the chalet."

At her words, the passengers interest perked up, and the mood loosened as conversation flowed.

"Do you know if the rooms have views?"

"Is there a fireplace?"

"What are we having for dinner? I'm hoping for steak and baked potato."

Cheerful conversation filled the van. Crystal answered the questions, as best she could, but there wasn't a whole lot more she could add to their speculation. The scenery helped build the anticipation, as snow patches alongside the road grew into higher drifts as they ascended and small waterfalls decorated with ice flashed by, drawing appreciative murmurs.

Despite the overall excited tone in the van, Crystal glanced in the rearview mirror and couldn't help noticing Philip ogling his intern, Bree. She kept scooting closer to Justin, uncomfortable under her boss's gaze. Most of all, disgust flashed in Madeleine's eyes, as she witnessed her husband's lecherous stare.

****

"Interesting." The deputy jotted down Philip, Bree, and Madeleine in a triangle on his empty tablet under Crystal's name and connected the names with bold lines. After a moment of staring at his diagram, he morphed the lines into arrows by adding points to the ends. "Go on. This is exactly what I need to get to the bottom of what happened."

After ten minutes of recounting, Crystal was a little disturbed to see that the Sheriff had just written his first notes, but she didn't let it deter her from digging into the recesses of her memory. "It was an uncomfortable hour, but thankfully the ride ended when we made it to the pass."

****

They had pulled into the lot designated for tour busses and vans. Parking in the spot next to Conner, she opened the door, and hopped out. Her feet crunched down into a pile of icy snow, and she had taken a moment to savor the feeling imparted by pure mountain air.

Shivers coursed over her skin as the shock of stepping from the heated van into the freezing temperatures of the mountain pass sent her nervous system reeling. Drawing a deep breath, she contemplated the snow covered mountainside, savoring the moment before exhaling. The sun peeked out from behind a cloud bank, and the snowy slope sparkled in the wan Northwest winter rays. Her shoulders relaxed, and she became cognizant of the fact she had been taking shallow breaths as far back as she could remember. She sighed as tension fled her body.

Crystal took a second to appreciate every choice she had made which had led her to this moment.

"Ok, folks," Conner said, swinging open the double doors at the backs of both vehicles. "Let's get your snowshoes and head to the trailhead." The passengers clambered out of the vans and waddled side to side on the treacherous footing. Their footsteps crackled in the frozen pieces of ice and sand which had been churned up throughout the parking lot by snow chains. Their unsteady movement reminded her so much of penguins, Crystal had to fight back a smile. Conner began asking their foot sizes and passed out different color coded snowshoes, based on what was called out.

"Wait to put them on until the trailhead," he cautioned. "Believe it or not, it's easier to walk with your boots in this mess."

Crystal started unloading the packs while Conner continued handing out snowshoes. She took them out, one by one, the owner of each stepping forward to take it from her hands. Once each person collected their gear, they made their way across the parking lot to where a trailhead sign poked above a snow drift.

Conner joined Crystal, and she hauled out her own backpack and snowshoes.

"Just so you know, shoe size doesn't matter." He whispered the words so only she could hear. "The right snowshoes are actually based on a recommended weight range. I just estimate how heavy people are, but ask their shoe size to distract them from the fact that I'm sizing them up."

"You have a future as a carnival side show."

"That's my back up plan in life. By the way, our van ride was so tame, I didn't get a chance to test out your racing skills. You want to race up the mountain, instead?" He gave a roguish grin.

"Good luck keeping up with me," she answered. "If you hike like you drive, I'll be sipping hot cocoa and warming my toes next to the fire, by the time you get there."

"Loser makes the hot cocoa?"

"Deal!"

"As much as I like having cocoa made for me, it's probably best if we don't ditch our tour to race ahead in the snow," he said with mock thoughtfulness. He stretched past her and grabbed the last enormous backpack. He slung it over his broad shoulders with an easy shrug and grabbed his own well-worn snowshoes and poles.

Laughing, she shut the doors and locked the vans as Conner herded the group across the parking lot. Following him, she cinched the straps on her pack. Joining everyone at the start of the trail, she listened as Conner began explaining the procedure to fasten into the snowshoes. "Loosen the top two bindings by flipping them open. Slide your boots in and ratchet the bindings to adjust the fit. They should feel firm and tight, but don't cut off the circulation. We don't want to lose any feet out here. I've been trained to amputate a foot in the event of an emergency, but I hate it every time I have to do it." The crowd gave appreciative chuckles, and they all stooped to fumble with the straps.

Crystal started taking mental notes on Conner's skill of injecting humor and excitement into the timbre of his voice to keep the mood cheerful. She wanted to emulate him when it was her turn to speak.

She found herself smiling, caught up in the fun. Thankful for her practice at home, she slipped into her own snowshoes in moments. Looking up, she spotted Ryan struggling, so she knelt in the snow and helped him wiggle his boot into the fitting. He fastened the clasps shut, and grunted in satisfaction. Seeing Alice standing next to him fighting with her strap, Crystal slid over and helped her fasten the bindings. Alice nodded her thanks, before they both took their first awkward steps toward the front of the group, where Conner was handing out poles.

"How do you extend these things?"

Turning, she spotted Gary fiddling with his snowshoeing poles.

"You flip the lever here, pull it out to a comfortable distance for you, and then close the lever again to lock the pole into place."

"It looks like we're ready to go," Conner announced from the front. He was quick stepping through the snow in his snowshoes, tightening people's straps, and checking their gear.

"I have all the necessary equipment for a winter hike. If you need anything, it's on my back. Extra food, water, heat sources, first aid....You will also find you'll run out of oxygen faster here, since we are at four thousand feet. If you feel fatigued, or short-of-breath, let Crystal or me know, and we'll take a break."

Conner stepped behind her and, under the guise of tightening her backpack straps, he whispered in her ear, "This hike coming up is what makes our job worth it. Enjoy yourself, because we get to see things on a daily basis that many people never see in their lifetime. I'm going to have you take the back of the group and keep an eye out for anyone struggling."

Crystal nodded her head as he circled back around

her and took the lead.

"Away, we go," he called out, starting up a short incline before merging onto a flat trail with two machine grooves cut into the snow. Two cross country skiers shot by, utilizing the grooves, breathing hard.

"This is the part of the trail we start on," Conner explained. "It's a groomed trail, maintained by the ski lodge, which we'll be sharing with cross country skiers. If you see one coming, say skier out loud to warn the rest of our party, and step to the side away from the grooves. We'll follow this track for almost a mile, until we turn off onto an unmaintained trail. The snowshoes earn their keep on the ungroomed section. Without them your feet would plunge deep into the pristine snow. This tougher portion of the hike is less than half of a mile, but it is by far the most magnificent. I'll let Mother Nature speak for herself, but I daresay you will remember it for the rest of your life."

With his grand pronouncement, Conner led the group after the disappearing cross-country skiers. Philip tracked after Conner, his bulk only an inch shorter than Conner's six-foot two frame. Philip's perpetual scowling face was followed by his lanky wife, Madeleine, her serious expression more suited to heading off to war. Every other face, though, was lit up with bright eyes and eager grins. The entire party trailed after Conner, occasionally stumbling when they stepped on their opposite shoe, as they struggled to master the mechanics.

The sounds of the Interstate and parking lot faded with every step and were soon replaced by packed snow crunching under their steps. Snow-laden evergreen boughs dipped to the ground on all sides, creating an arched pathway before them. Crystal's eyes watered in the cold, and her mind awoke as the frosty air stimulated her better than any double espresso ever could. The reality of the situation struck home, rocking her to the core. This wasn't a regular excursion into the outdoors. She was making a living doing what most people considered an exciting adventure.

"How long have you been a guide?" Her reverie was broken by the woman in front of her, Georgia, who had glanced over her shoulder to speak.

"Not long," Crystal evaded.

"I can't believe you get paid to do this," the woman gushed. "If I wasn't nearing retirement, I'd quit my job to try and take yours."

"I was thinking the exact same thing as you are. I can't believe I get paid to do this, either."

"I've lived my whole life in this area, and I've never done anything like this before. I feel like I've been missing out for years."

"Me too," Crystal answered. A quizzical look flashed across Georgia's face at the comment, but she didn't pursue the odd statement. Crystal chastised herself. She needed to come down from the elation of the moment and start remembering she was supposed to be the experienced co-leader of this trip.

They made quick time through the forest on the maintained trail, before stopping in front of an unblemished sheet of deep, white powder which veered off their current trek and wound its way up a hill, the path encroached on all sides by snow bedecked branches.

"Now, it's time for the fun to begin," Conner called out. "This is going to be a lot more strenuous than the level trail we were on, so the pace is going to be much slower. I'll blaze the trail, and I suggest you follow me, stepping in the packed snow of my footsteps. It will make it a much easier ascent than sinking into the snow on your own."

Conner struck off, his feet plunging at least a foot into the powder, as he powered his way up the hill. Remembering the lessons he had taught her when she had purchased her snowshoes, Crystal heeded how he drove the front of his foot into the slope first, leaving a make-shift series of stairs behind him. The subsequent hikers followed his directions and stepped in his tracks. As she lifted her shoes off the groomed trail and into the steps packed by the others, Crystal's foot still sank a few extra inches. She tugged her shoe to free it from the hole it was in and lunged forward to the next shoe-print. After a few more steps, her quadriceps burned and a sheen of sweat blossomed between her skin and her thermal under-layer. Her breath gusted out and coalesced in the freezing air before her. Glancing up the trail, she was awestruck as Conner wrenched his snowshoe out of another deep hole. His heavy pack didn't even slow him, while he chatted with Philip and Madeleine. The group wended their way up the hill, and people began panting as the exertion took hold.

This trail was only several arm spans wide, and they entered a winter scene from a fairy tale. Branches covered in snow created a fluffy cocoon surrounding them on all sides. Crystal brushed a few as she hiked, and snow powder danced through the air as it descended.

Her ears detected a soft trickle of water before she heard the gasps of amazement. The entire group ahead of her had stopped and were swiveling to the left and right of the trail. Madeleine set her pack down and drew out a monstrous camera. Crystal caught up to the gathering and sighed in appreciation as she took in the scene. A small creek, who's running water was moving fast enough to avoid freezing, passed under the trail. Large rocks, topped by precarious piles of snow, dotted the center of the creek, and icicles glistened alongside the banks in the daylight. No one made a sound for a moment, and the soft burble of the water passing only enhanced the tranquility of the snowy landscape.

"It reminds me of a Robert Frost poem," Crystal said in a hushed tone. The quiet forest somehow made it improper to raise her voice to normal speaking level.

Her memory stretched to remember the lines she had read many years ago in one of her countless English literature classes, when Conner's deep voice called out:

"Whose woods these are I think I know.
His house is in the village though;
He will not see me stopping here
To watch his woods fill up with snow."

"The exact one I was thinking of." She threw him a smile.

"My favorite poem." He shot a grin back.

"Damn it all to hell," Madeleine muttered, ruining the serenity of the moment. She had extended a collapsible tripod and mounted her lens-heavy camera. Once it was placed in the snow, the weight kept sinking the front leg deeper than the others.

The reverie was broken by her swearing, and the others took their phones out for pictures, videos, and selfies. With his snowshoes, Conner packed a small circle of snow around Madeleine, and she managed to level her camera, barking at anyone who dared interfere with her shot. Crystal jumped in to help Bree, who was holding her phone out for a selfie with Justin, and snapped several photos of the two scrunching their faces together, mugging for the shot.

****

"Interesting." The officer drew a line from Bree's name to a blank space below and wrote in Justin. Circling it twice, he began tapping his pen against the tablet and chewing his bottom lip.

After a few seconds of watching him stare at his note, Crystal spoke up, "Would you like me to continue?"

He glanced up from his ball and stick diagram. "Please do. This is helpful."

****

Once the picture taking slowed down, Conner had spoken up. "We have a short way to go before a stunning vista, and then it's a brief distance to the chalet. I promise this hill lasts only a little longer before the hike levels out. Let's keep moving, because the daylight ends early this time of year."

Even though the remaining uphill hike was only a tenth of a mile, which Gary volunteered while obsessively checking his fitness tracker, it was still enough to spike Crystal's heart rate. Philip, in particular, was struggling. Crystal worried as she took in his florid face and gasping breaths. She found herself starting to recall the CPR steps she had learned in her first aid class. Visions of attempting chest compressions on Philip, and him sinking deeper into the snow with each thrust, filled her mind. She opened her mouth to call out for a break, when Conner spoke first. "We made it to the lookout."

One by one, the tour group crested the hill.

"Wow!"

"Look at the view!"

The exclamations made Crystal have to check herself to not urge Georgia to hurry. The older woman was content to proceed at her slow and steady pace. After a virtual eternity, they joined the others at the viewpoint. She couldn't help but gasp, along with the rest of the crowd, at the sight sprawling out from the plateau they had summited. The rocky edges of a sheer cliff gave them an unobstructed panorama of the alpine wilderness.

Conner caught her attention, raised an eyebrow, and gave a little nod in the direction of the view. She nodded back. It was time for more of her home research to pay off. She began her first wilderness guide speech.

"As I am sure you know, we are looking at Mount Rainier, the highest mountain in the Cascades. It is 14,410 feet high and is large enough to generate its own weather patterns. It's an active volcano that is currently dormant, as is most of the Cascade Mountain range. You can see the swell of the old crater at the top. The sole exception is the mountain you can make out in the distance, Mount St. Helens, which blew her top in 1980, sending mud flows and ash clouds out to the land around her. Mt. St. Helens is still active, having occasional earthquakes and even an ash cloud, when the mood strikes her."

"Trust a woman to blow her top, when the pressure gets too much," Gary snickered.

Crystal was satisfied when at least three members

of the group rolled their eyes at his comment. It took all of her effort, but she restrained herself from doing the same.

Almost everyone started snapping pictures with their phones while Madeleine wrestled her camera back out of her pack and knelt in the snow to steady herself.

"Mount Rainier has twenty-five named glaciers and numerous snowfields cascading down its slopes. Approximately ten thousand people attempt to climb it each year, but only half succeed."

"Why don't they make it?" Georgia asked.

"Unpredictable weather and conditioning. Like I mentioned, the mountain can make its own weather and I think after our little climb, we can all agree snow travel is more difficult than it seems."

"No shit," Philip agreed. Some of the redness had faded from his face and he had his breathing mostly under control.

As they admired the view, several grayish birds lit in trees next to them and began studying the hikers.

"These friendly birds are Gray Jays, also known as camp robbers." Crystal remembered seeing them on a web page for birders of the northwest. Cameras swiveled to zoom in on their avian interlopers. "They'll beg for food every chance they get. Don't feed them though, because it makes them dependent on us. If that happens, and they can't find people, they'll starve."

Ignoring her warning, Philip tossed trail mix in the snow, laughing as the birds swarmed down to scoop up the food. "It reminds me of you, Ryan," he barked. "Always going after crumbs, when there is real food to be had."

"Good one, Philip," Gary guffawed.

Ryan stepped forward, his brow furrowed and his hands clenched into fists by his side. His wife, Alice, seized his arm and started whispering in his ear, casting a fierce glare at their boss and his lackey.

Justin leaned near Bree and stage-whispered, "Gary is such a kiss-ass."

****

"Did any of them come to blows over this exchange?" the deputy interrupted. He scribbled down Ryan and Alice on his sheet and drew lines back to Philip's name.

"No, Conner broke it up. He stepped in between them and calmed them down."

"How did he do that? Sounds like they were pretty worked up."

Crystal thought back to the admirable way Conner had risen to the occasion and defused the situation. "He handled it with calm professionalism."

****

"Don't feed the wildlife, sir. It's a criminal offense and carries a two-thousand dollar fine or thirty days in jail." Conner announced the threat matter-of-factly, while physically stepping between the feuding men.

"I'm only throwing some peanuts to a few hungry birds, son. No need to get all worked up," he patted Conner on the shoulder with a smirk.

Philip tossed a sneer at Ryan, before he started off on the trail, leaving the others behind.

"Ok, everyone," Conner did his best to interject some enthusiasm into the tense crowd. "It's only a short distance to the chalet and dinner."

The group stirred, coming out of their stasis. Ryan tugged his arm from his wife's grasp and stomped after their boss. Alice narrowed her eyes and frowned after the pair.

Conner glanced at Crystal and rolled his eyes at the departing group, before turning his gaze back to her.

Crystal mouthed "wow" while raising her brows. He gave her a what-can-you-do shrug, and they headed out to finish the hike to their night's lodging.

****

The Sheriff continued nodding through her story, but lost interest as Crystal retold what happened in the chalet. He cut her off halfway through. "This is consistent with what your friend, Roxie, told me. All of this is very interesting. I appreciate you taking the time to come down and share."

"Do you have any questions for me?" She had imagined being grilled by a hardened investigator digging for clues in her story, not a bunch of names scribbled on a sheet with lines connecting them.

"Nope. This is a lot to go on, but I may call you if I need anything further." He gave a patronizing smile and stood up, indicating the questioning was at an end.

Crystal stood, too, and let herself be led out. Roxie was still waiting for her in the lobby.

"Hi, Roxie," Crystal said.

"Crystal." Roxie delivered her southern charm in full force. "How've you been keeping yourself?" Crystal felt a glow of affection for the hostess. The woman was nothing if not committed to her role.

Sergeant Prescott left them both after another round of vigorous handshakes and retreated down the hallway with his legal pad and recorder clutched in his hand.

"You know, when it's only you and me, you don't

have to use the accent," Crystal reminded her.

"I know," she remarked, all trace of the South gone. "But I used it with the Sheriff, so it's the right thing to be consistent in front of him. No need to go and confuse the young man. Do you want to get a bite at the cafe across the street and catch up?"

"Sounds great."

They crossed the street together in the light rain and found a table in the corner.

"Perfect for people watching." Roxie sighed, relaxing into her seat. "Look at those old timers over there." Crystal followed Roxie's nod to a table circled by five Navy veterans with baseball caps denoting the ships they had served on. They laughed and cracked jokes with the waitress who was topping off their coffee mugs. "Don't they look like they're having a blast? I bet they do this almost every single day, and they are still having the time of their life. Aren't people the best?"

Crystal smiled at the site of the happy exchanges between the men, when a thought struck her. "Roxie, how did you get back down from the chalet?"

"Conner drove another snowmobile up to me the morning after you all left. He snowshoed back to rejoin Search and Rescue after I stuffed more food in him. The boy was fit on starving himself in his hurry to get back out there."

"Do you live in the city?" Crystal asked.

"I have a little place in the central district. I typically have Monday through Thursday off from my hostess duties, and when the young Sergeant called me, I headed down to give my two cents," Roxie offered. "As my mother used to say, 'He's as green as Aunt

Gertrude's gravy.' Aunt Gertie didn't get the family cooking gene. Anyway, since I heard from Connor that it looked like Philip had been killed, I decided to ask the friendly sheriff how many murder cases he's investigated."

"I don't think I want to know…" Crystal groaned.

"You guessed it. Zero." She slapped her palm on the table for emphasis. "He was assigned the case when it was thought to be an accident investigation. The other homicide detectives are swamped, so he gets to learn on the job by trying to solve Philip's murder."

"I was a little surprised when he didn't ask me any follow up questions."

"Which is why I waited for you. After he questioned me, I figured you wouldn't be long."

"He's never going to get to the bottom of this, is he?" Crystal moaned. "I'm going to end up living with my parents. I'll have to sleep in the basement with the furnace since my mother converted my old bedroom into her sewing room. I can't believe the detective urged me to go into every last detail and his notes looked like two dimensional tinker toys stuck together by an unimaginative child."

The waitress stopped by and took their orders. Roxie asked for a Denver omelet, but Crystal only got a cup of tea. Eating out was certainly not in her budget.

"The grapevine told me your tours were suspended," Roxie sympathized.

"Don't you work for ECO Adventures, too?"

"Me? No. I work for this rich fella, Baranhof, who owns nice properties in the woods. He rents them out to tour companies, the general public, and corporate…watcha call 'ems - retreats."

"Do you like it?"

"It's usually a good job. Except when you get a batch of crazies like this last group. They drank fourteen bottles of wine, broke four crystal glasses, smashed up a room, and they even stole some towels. C'mon, we're not some cheap roadside motel for Pete's sake."

"Don't forget, it looks like someone killed their boss while they were there," Crystal reminded her.

"Well, at least they had the decency to haul that mess out of my chalet."

"Did you see any blood? Anything you can remember standing out as suspicious?" Crystal pressed.

"Nothing unless you count smashed wine glasses and shelves," Roxie grumped.

"The shelves could have been knocked over in a struggle."

Roxie didn't even acknowledge Crystal's musing. "The shelves had a delightful little art collection. There was a blown glass vase, a trilobite fossil, and a geode. You know, the rocks with lots of sparkling purple crystals inside? They dinged the hardwood floors something fierce when they hit the ground. Bunch of animals. I can tell you one thing, they are not getting their deposit back."

"Wasn't it Bree staying in the room with the smashed shelves?" Crystal asked.

"The young, good looking girl?"

"Yeah, her," Crystal reflected. "Probably Justin was there, too."

"Maybe a lover's quarrel? A mystery for our Sheriff to solve," Roxie groused.

"Maybe he's better than we think."

Roxie snorted as her omelet was delivered. "After the questioning we just sat through, I'm not counting on it, sweetheart."

Chapter Eight

Flopping on the couch next to her, Olivia tossed a pillow at her friend. Holding up her hand, she started ticking her fingers off. "You walk out on Darcy, tell her what you think of her on your way out the door, and text me that I'm supposed to pretend to be your former boss if I get a call for a reference. By the way, Amelia from Emerald City Outfitters did call and Erica transferred her to me. I described your superior work ethic, your punctuality, your wonderful personality, and how I was considering giving you a promotion before you left. I think she totally bought it." After the brief interruption of herself, Olivia began ticking her fingers again. "Turns out it's for a wilderness guide position, and now you say a guy up and got himself murdered on your first trip."

Crystal had sent a few texts, trying to explain the events from the previous week of her life, when Olivia had eventually said all of this was too momentous to not discuss in person and offered to come to Crystal's condo to make them dinner. Upon her arrival, Crystal had given her a rundown of everything from the case becoming a drawn-out murder investigation to Conner asking her on a date. After Olivia had finished ticking off the highlights, she stood and busied herself in the kitchen, preparing tomato soup and grilled cheese sandwiches.

"Thanks for covering for me and being my reference. I couldn't have done any of this without your help or Erica's," Crystal said.

"You're totally welcome, but what you just told me does not even come close to everything. Start from when you told Darcy to stuff it."

"I kind of lost my mind for a bit. I took off into the rain and walked all the way back here. It's all kind of a fog."

"That's interesting and all, but how did you even find the job in the first place? Was it posted on the internet and you searched wilderness guide instead of office assistant? How does this even happen?" Olivia fired off the questions without a single breath in between.

"I'll start at the beginning, just after I walked out on Darcy. When I got home, my body was wrung out from the adrenaline rush of quitting and the miserable wet walk in the rain. I decided to take a hot bath to calm down and get warm."

Crystal stood up from the couch and looked out the large window overlooking the city. On a clear day, she could see all the way to Lake Union and Elliot Bay. Today, she could only see the tops of the nearby buildings and trees further down the hill. Only a short distance from downtown Seattle, the Capitol Hill neighborhood was pricey, but had a vibrant pulse Crystal cherished.

"It took a while, but the chill finally worked out of me. I threw on my favorite sweats and…"

"You still have your Minnie Mouse sweatshirt and pink sweat pants? They're so faded, you can't even make out Minnie anymore."

"The very same. I won't part with those until they fall off of me. After my bath, I was feeling celebratory, so I made that gourmet cocoa mix my mom gave me for Christmas. I settled down on the couch and toasted myself for finally quitting."

Crystal turned from her window to see Olivia slide the sandwiches into the pan. Elf perched on the back of the couch, watching Olivia work.

Crystal walked over to her cat and stroked between his ears. Elf gave a languorous blink of happiness at the head rub. As she withdrew her hand, he swiped at her with his claws.

"Dang it," Crystal complained as she examined the scratch. "What was that for?" It was a rhetorical question and he gave her a lazy stare in answer.

"That cat of yours is a menace." Olivia pointed the spatula at the offending feline. Elf began to purr in satisfaction and looked up hopefully at Crystal.

Crystal glared at her pet and decided to ignore his obvious plea for further attention. One scratch a day was enough for her, thank you very much. "As I sipped my cocoa, I felt like life was going to work out. My new year was off to a wild start, but I was excited that a change was happening. I had rid myself of a soul-draining job. What exhilarating future awaited? With my life unfolding before me and a million things to accomplish, I did what any other sensible person in my position would do. I fell asleep on the couch."

Olivia stirred the soup warming on the burner. "This doesn't sound like you at all. Usually when things get out of control, you start to panic."

Crystal shot her friend a glare. "That's not true."

Olivia arched an eyebrow in response.

Crystal snorted. "I was having a great nap, when I was woke by the sound of the mail coming through the slot." She nodded at her door. "I pushed Elf off of me and went to go get it. Most of it was junk, but at the bottom of the pile was my power bill. That's when it all struck home. I have a power bill, a cable bill, a phone bill, a mortgage for my condo and absolutely no way to pay for any of them."

"Now, this sounds like the Crystal I know," Olivia interjected. "You never do anything too wild or too crazy without a good freak out."

Crystal nodded. "I want to argue with you, but the panic attack was in full force." Simply recalling the moment sent shivers rippling over her skin. "Worst case scenarios kept replaying on a constant loop of stress. I would have to sell my condo, move in with my parents, and start all over. The humiliation of losing everything had me on the brink of tears. The walls of my condo were closing in like a prison, and I felt a burning desire to escape. The stress made me want to throw up. If I hadn't left for a walk, I probably would have."

"So your great solution to life's problems was to walk back into the rainstorm?" Olivia smirked at her friend.

"Don't knock it. It paid off in a big way. This time, though, I was wearing a set of rain gear I had bought at the Emerald City Outfitters summer sale. I wandered down the hill to Lake Union, wracking my brain for solutions. I didn't want to go back to office work, which is the only thing I was qualified to do. Going back to school was off the table. I don't have enough money for a month's worth of bills, much less another degree. I love my parents, but there is no way I wanted to move back in with them. That's when it struck me."

"What?"

"My rain gear was leaking."

"Really? That's the revelation?" Olivia groaned.

"That's when I remembered something you said."

"Well, I do give great advice. What did I say?"

"You told me about how you always liked buying clothes at Emerald City Outfitters because they would exchange anything, no questions asked."

Olivia pointed the spatula at herself. "So in a way, I'm responsible for you getting your job. Gosh, I'm such an awesome friend. What would you do without me?"

"I would have eaten crow, apologized to Darcy, and been back in my old cubicle next to you." Instead, Crystal had left the lake, following the wake of the bell-ringing South Lake Union Trolley, nick-named the SLUT by the locals. "Maybe it wasn't the most important item on my current life to-do list, but at least it was something productive. I went to return my faulty rain gear."

****

Crystal always adored visiting the Emerald City Outfitters store. Broad wooden steps led to a modern log cabin facade, while a small man-made waterfall cascaded among fir trees lining the sides of the steps. The water rumbled loud enough to drown out the constant noise of the city. She crested the stairs atop the large landing marking the entrance of the store, and stopped under the covered entryway. Stripping off her leaking rain gear, she approached the ten-foot tall wooden front door. A design, carved to look like a tree limb, traveled from the top to the bottom, curling out at waist level to form a handle. She tugged, awed as always by how effortless it was to open such an expansive door.

The store was too enormous to take in with one glance. A crowd was milling throughout, searching through racks of clothes and trying on outdoor equipment. The winter sports section had been relocated to the front for the season, while the hiking and camping gear had been consigned to the back of the store until the snow melted. The ski and snowboard section to her right was packed with shoppers, as people took advantage of both an after Christmas sale and the recent heavy snowfall in the mountains.

Glancing around, she spotted the customer service desk located in a corner next to the registers. She worked her way through the crowd of shoppers and walked to the counter.

****

"When I got to the store, I handed over my rain gear to the assistant manager, Lisa, who went to find me a new set. I was bored, so I started looking around. That's when I saw it."

"What? It better be good this time."

"A bulletin board. It had all sorts of skiing, snowboarding, and snowshoe classes offered at different mountain resorts. However, tucked away in the corner was a help wanted ad. I still have the picture on my phone." Crystal picked up her phone, tapped the screen a few times and presented it to Olivia.

Help Wanted

Wilderness guide to take tour groups on local hikes and other outdoor activities. Knowledge of flora, fauna, first aid, and orienteering required. Experience a plus.

Email résumé to hr@ecoinc.com

"Fate was hand delivering me a dream job in restitution for dealing with Darcy Bray for several wretched years. I considered ripping the ad down to prevent anyone else from seeing it. Then Lisa spoke behind me and I jumped a mile high."

"What did she say?"

"She asked if I was going to apply. Before I knew it, I had said that I would. She was so encouraging. She said all of the other guides say it's a phenomenal job and that she'd have taken it in a heartbeat, but can't be gone overnight or her husband would have a heart attack the first day from taking care of the kids alone."

"That's a pretty awesome endorsement."

"You can see why I went for it."

"You quit your job, went for a walk, and found a job opening posted by a wilderness guide outfit? This is some serious serendipity at play." Olivia stared at Crystal in awe.

"I can't believe it's a job. They pay me to go on adventures. I didn't have the position yet, though." Crystal pointed at the grilled cheese in the pan. "You better flip those or they'll burn."

Olivia gave the sandwiches a quick turn. "How did you even get considered for the job? You've sat in a cubicle next to me for your entire professional career."

"I won't lie. There was a good amount of bluffing on my résumé, but I'm not completely unqualified. The second I got home, I powered off my phone to avoid distractions and began to transform my résumé from mild-mannered office worker to bad-ass wilderness guide. I've hiked hundreds of miles in the national parks and forests surrounding Seattle, so it's not like

I've never been outside before. I also volunteered with the Washington Trail Association a few summers ago to help fix the washouts on the hike to Lake Serene."

"That doesn't really make you qualified."

"This is where the aforementioned bluffing comes into play. I had to look up which is which, but flora are plants and fauna are animals. I also looked into orienteering. Turns out, it's navigating with a map and compass. I added all of these to my résumé, and have been spending my free time reading about them on the internet."

Olivia slid the sandwiches onto plates and ladled the soup into a pair of bowls. "I can see you finagling that, but first aid? That sounds pretty important."

"You don't remember? Really?"

"Remember what?"

"We're both certified, you dingbat. When I broke up with Todd, you called me to say that you had passed a sign outside a fire station offering free CPR and first aid classes. Your logic was that if it was taught at a fire station, it must be taught by hunky firemen like in the calendars. Your advice was that a hot date from a fire fighter would wipe my memory of what's-his-name."

They sat down at the table with their dinner. Olivia cocked her head to the side as the memory came back. "I remember now. Yeah…that didn't work out like I thought."

"Well, it was taught by a firefighter, but *she* wasn't our type. I did get a wallet sized card stating that I had passed CPR and first aid classes to the satisfaction of Katherine Harris of the Seattle Fire Department. It's a good thing, because Emerald City Outfitters needed to make copies for their records before I started work."

Crystal took a big bite of her sandwich. The tangy Pike Place Market cheese that Olivia used always made it a treat.

"I told you the classes were going to pay off big time. Not the way I meant, but aren't you glad you learned CPR and first aid now?"

"I wouldn't have this job without it. You unintentionally give the most amazing advice."

Olivia smiled from behind her soup spoon. "Like I said, where would you be without me?"

Grinning at her friend, Crystal continued. "By the time I was done, my résumé came across as if I were a rugged woman who could guide a group of city slickers through the perils of an African jungle. I sent it off and hoped for the best." Crystal stood to carry their dishes into the kitchen. Elf followed, pawing at her feet, and meowing insistently. Crystal groaned. "It's not time yet, you little monster."

In response, Elf jumped to his eating spot on the counter. Crystal dodged a lazy swipe of his claws on her way to the sink.

"Just feed him. We won't get a moment's peace until he's had his meal now that he's started." Olivia grinned at the cat's antics.

"Now he's going to want to be fed this time every day." Crystal groaned and pulled a can of ocean feast from under the counter. Cracking it open, she spooned some into his bowl. As usual, she ignored the queasy stomach induced by the noxious seafood odor. Elf plunged his face and began making smacking noises before she could pull back her spoon. "Before we were so rudely interrupted, I was going to tell you about the next morning. I woke up and turned on my phone to find no less than three voice mails and sixteen text messages. My phone was dinging so loudly, it sounded like I had won the jackpot."

"In all fairness, what did you expect? You did put on quite a spectacle the day before."

"Several of the texts were from you, but then I opened the ones from my mother." Crystal tapped her phone and showed them to her friend.

—*Olivia called and said you quit your job yesterday. What happened?* The next one had been sent one minute after the first.—*How are you going to pay your bills? Do you need to move back in with us? It seems to me like you're having an early mid-life crisis. I assume it's because you're twenty-seven and don't have a boyfriend.*

"By the way, thanks for spilling the beans to my mom." Crystal threw an eye roll at her friend.

"If you ignore my texts in the future, I'll have no option other than to go straight to your mother." Olivia pronounced the threat as she sat up straight and gave her friend a sanctimonious look.

Crystal laughed at the prim look on her friend's face and assured her it wouldn't happen again. "Anyway, how did my mother come to the conclusion that I quit my job because I was having a mid-life crisis? And it's not like I haven't had any boyfriends."

Olivia jumped to her defense. "Todd was a nice guy with a great job. He smelled like a sewer, but we can't all be perfect. Oh, there was that guitarist who slept on your couch for a little while. Whatever happened to him?"

"His band went on tour. I never heard from him again."

"That sucks. Anyone else?"

"Nobody worth mentioning. It doesn't help that my younger sister, Heather, married her college sweetheart at twenty-two. She's already gone and delivered two grandchildren into the eager hands of my parents. She even managed to have both a boy and a girl. I love my sister with all of my heart, but just because things worked out for her so early in life, it makes me feel like a failure in comparison." Crystal hated being jealous of Heather, but her negative emotion was exacerbated by her mother's constant advice on how to improve her life while continually holding her up to the almighty standard of her sister. "I didn't need to deal with any of that, so I ignored her texts as well as her three voice mails. I was looking forward to a new chapter of life and didn't need the old baggage weighing me down." Crystal put Elf's bowl in the sink next to the dirty dishes and went to sit on the couch.

Olivia sat at the opposite end. "What happened with the job, though?"

Crystal explained to her best friend about the interview the following day, the now funny meet-up with Conner prior to her first snowshoe hike, and the mysterious death of Philip Calvert. She ended by telling her about dinner at Conner's and what his cousin Holly revealed. When she finished, the frustration and hopelessness of the situation gnawed on her already frazzled nerves.

"Well, now you know everything. I found a new job, but it's in jeopardy already. What am I going to do, Olivia?" Crystal moaned from the couch. She flopped on her back and covered her face with a pillow.

"Hmmm...." Olivia pondered. "I guess you're

going to have to shack up with this handsome Conner guy. Better not blow the first date if you decide to go with that plan, though."

Crystal plucked the pillow from her face to glare at her friend. "You're not helping. Now, I'm worried I'm going to lose my condo and screw up my first date with Conner."

"Just don't be weird," Olivia advised her. "Or be weird. He seems to like you the way you are, so maybe you should keep being weird."

"*Still* not helping."

"Maybe you can figure out what happened…"

"What do you mean?"

"I mean with the murder case. Oh my god, this is such a good idea. First thing we need to start with is a little research." Olivia stood up, glancing around. She grabbed Crystal's nearby laptop and opened the browser. "What was the dead guy's company called again?"

"Calvert and Associates. I don't know how any of this is going to help," she complained as Olivia typed in the name.

"Hmmm…here's the company page. Wow, would you look at some of the stuff they've designed," she turned the computer to face Crystal.

The new science building on the UW campus filled the screen. It was a large brick structure with a gorgeous circular stained glass window at the top and a series of arched breezeways on the outside.

"That's not all," Olivia checked several other links. "Sear, the new restaurant overlooking Lake Union; it takes six months to get a reservation there. And check this out. This hotel looks straight from the Travel

Channel."

"Wow, those are amazing." Crystal leaned in closer to examine the pictures. "For as dysfunctional as they act among each other, they've managed to design some spectacular buildings."

"I know." Olivia clicked again, "Do these people look familiar?"

Crystal stood and peered over her friend's shoulder, recognizing snapshots of faces from the snowshoe trip above short bios. A picture of Philip, taken at least ten years earlier judging by the hair on his head, was listed first as the principal. Madeleine's photo was to the right of his, with the titles business development and outreach coordinator. Below them were the associates; Ryan and Alice Byrne, Gary Wembley and Justin Watts posing in front of buildings with hard hats and rolled up architectural schematics tucked under their arms. Further down the page, Georgia Patterson, smiling at her desk, was listed as the office manager followed by Bree Pierce, the intern, typing at a computer. "This is everybody I met last weekend."

Olivia squinted at the page as she studied it. "This may not be cool of me to say since he's dead and all, but if Philip was as much of a jerk as he looks in this picture, I'm starting to sympathize with whomever offed him."

Crystal laughed at Olivia's never ending stream of consciousness. "He was worse in person, if you can believe it."

"I find that hard to believe. I'm glad I never met him. These people, other than Bree, have worked for this guy between ten to thirty years according to their bios. It must be a pretty prestigious job for them to put up with him for so long. I wonder what may have changed to drive one of them over the edge. Let's see if this has any answers," Olivia opened a link titled "Recent Business News."

A list of headlines appeared; "Calvert and Associates selected for UW general science building," "Calvert and Associates winner of prestigious AIA award," and "Philip Calvert to retire after amazing career."

"Read the last one," Crystal urged.

Olivia selected the headline and the full article from the Seattle Times appeared. Crystal read the first few sentences.

Philip Calvert, the founder and genius behind Calvert and Associates, is planning to retire this year after the completion of the firm's latest landmark building, the University of Washington's general science building. His wife and business partner, Madeleine Heusley-Calvert, are in the initial stages of selecting an individual to carry on their legacy. The Calverts are rumored to be choosing from among the company's associates, as well as considering several individuals from other firms.

The rest of the article amounted to Philip's résumé of impressive work.

"Now, this is interesting," Olivia said. "If all of the associates are in line to inherit the business, any one of them could be a suspect."

"True," Crystal agreed.

"Hmm…What do you remember happening the night when things started getting out of hand?"

"Ryan, Gary, and Madeleine were all gone from

the chalet when Conner and I made our way upstairs. It could have been one of them."

"What are their motives?" Olivia asked.

"Nobody liked him. In fact, Alice and Ryan loathed him, and Justin and Madeleine didn't care for the way he kept ogling Bree. Gary was called out as a kiss-up by the others, but I get the impression he didn't like Philip either. Even the guy's wife hated him, for crying out loud."

"Hatred, greed and jealousy are the three best motives. Now we're getting somewhere." Olivia cupped her chin in the palm of her hand while tapping her index finger against her cheek.

"I don't know if you can say we are getting anywhere. I don't think we've eliminated anyone but the office manager Georgia as a suspect so far. Bree doesn't seem to have an obvious motive other than Philip's unwanted attention, but something funny happened in her room."

Crystal and Olivia wracked their brains for a couple of minutes.

"What you need to do is question them," Olivia pointed out. "Do a little old-fashioned detective work."

At first, Crystal disregarded the possibility, but the more she considered it, optimism lightened her spirit for the first time regarding the case. She might not have police forensics and training at her disposal, but the sleuths in the hundreds of mystery novels she had read did it with sheer nerve and pluck. The stories weren't real life, but why couldn't she do the same? She had also been gifted with an unusual amount of free time due to the unexpected cutback to a part time job.

"Google their names and see if you can find their

addresses or phone numbers." Crystal was getting into this idea. Playing the role of amateur detective gave her at least something tangible to do, rather than sit back and watch her bank account dwindle.

While Olivia typed away on the computer, Crystal walked to the kitchen and opened the Tupperware Conner had given her the night of the snowshoe trip. Inside was still half of the enormous piece of pecan pie. She transferred it onto a plate and cut it into two, the buttery crust flaking apart. She slid one half onto a separate plate and walked back to the living room. She handed one of the servings to Olivia, who took it from her without glancing up from the screen.

Olivia frowned. "I couldn't find anything. You could go to the firm's office. It's only a few miles from here, a little north of Green Lake."

"Can you imagine me trying to barge into their office asking questions? I'd be tossed out five minutes after I got there. What I need to do is surprise them at home. Catch them alone and off guard, try to get them talking. Wait a second," Crystal thumped her forehead with her palm. "I have all the information I need, or rather Emerald City Outfitters does. They filled out release forms with their contact information prior to the hike. It has to be filed somewhere."

Olivia took a bite of the pie and her eyes widened. "Holy cow, Crys. Did you make this?"

"The chef at the chalet, Roxie, made it."

Olivia forked another bite into her mouth. "I need to meet this Roxie and become her new best friend."

"Aren't I your best friend?"

"You've been a great best friend until now, but you can't bake like this," Olivia teased. Crystal laughed and started into her own piece.

"Now back to business. Are you going to see what you can find out tomorrow?" Olivia urged.

Crystal had no desire to be found prying into company files during her first shift in the store. On the other hand, she didn't want to risk losing her new job, condo, or the chance to get to know Conner. There was too much at stake not to take the chance.

Chapter Nine

Crystal walked into Emerald City Outfitters fifteen minutes before her shift began. Her mother had taught her you only get one opportunity to make a good impression and had pegged Amelia as a person who appreciated punctuality.

She walked through the store and waved at Lisa, who was helping a young girl try on a pair of snow boots.

She arrived at Amelia's office and knocked.

"Come in," Amelia's familiar stern tone rang out. "You're early. I approve."

"I'm excited to start in the store." Crystal had practiced the enthusiasm in her voice.

"I'm not positive you're sincere, but I do appreciate the good attitude. Most guides don't like the tame life of working in the store, but it's a good way for you to see different types of equipment, and to meet the people who use it. It's also a good way to familiarize yourself with new activities by talking to your fellow guides. The greater the variety of outdoor knowledge you have, the more valuable you are to the company."

"I'm excited to learn all I can, but I should warn you, I don't have any retail experience," Crystal confessed.

"I know from your résumé that you don't, but we are happy to train you," Amelia waved away the concern. "I'm going to get you started reading our policy manual and watching training videos. It might be a little dry, but it will give you a good foundation."

Amelia led her down the hall to the break area where everything was laid out. Sitting on the table was a large three ring binder and a laptop.

Amelia showed her the folder on the computer containing the videos and instructed her to start working her way through everything in front of her.

"What if I have any questions?" Crystal asked.

"Write anything you want to ask down. If you feel the need to stretch your legs, come find Lisa or me. She's my senior employee and knows all of this, front to back," Amelia said, tapping the binder.

Amelia left the room and Crystal opened the policy manual. Several hours ticked by, and she forced herself to focus as she read through the documents on vacation policies, stocking procedures, and inventory systems.

"How's it going?" Crystal's eyes flashed open. Had she been drifting off? A smiling Lisa had entered the room and grabbed a brown paper bag out of the refrigerator.

"It's a little boring," Crystal admitted. Lisa produced a yogurt from her lunch bag and a spoon from a drawer.

"I fell asleep reading this stuff my first day," Lisa confessed. "Amelia caught me, if you can believe it. I figured she was going to fire me on the spot, but she only said, 'No rest for the weary.' It's one of her catch phrases. I guarantee you'll hear, 'No rest for the weary' at least once a week."

"She seems like a good boss," Crystal ventured.

"The best. You always know where you stand, and

she listens to reason."

"What a relief. My last boss was a narcissistic know-it-all who took out her anger on the staff. When I met Amelia, I figured she was different, but you never know."

Lisa grinned, "Not to worry. Tough but fair, is our Amelia." She finished her yogurt and started on a banana.

It was time to implement the beginning of the plan she and Olivia had cooked up the previous night. Crystal hated deceiving Lisa, but this was for a good cause.

"I was wondering where the tour group contact information is? I loaned a pair of gloves to one of the guests last weekend, and in all of the chaos I forgot to get them back."

"Ask Amelia. It's in one of the filing cabinets in her office."

"Thanks. I'll ask for it when I get a chance."

Crystal was disheartened to hear where the information was stored. She had hoped it was on the company's computer system, or at least a common area where she could get access. She had considered using the glove story on Amelia, but disregarded the plan. Amelia was the type of manager who would take the initiative and call the fictitious glove borrower, rather than hand out private information. When the person denied borrowing anything from Crystal, the story would unravel, raising uncomfortable questions.

Lisa finished her banana and wished Crystal good luck with the rest of the training.

Crystal thanked her and started the first video, "How to deal with a difficult customer." It was mere background noise, however, as her mind churned over this new problem. She needed to find a way into Amelia's office. The irony of getting caught going through Amelia's cabinets and losing her job, all in an attempt to solve a murder to keep her job, was not lost on her. However, if she didn't try, she didn't see how she could keep working here on half of a paycheck.

Several other employees appeared, introducing themselves with a quick greeting as they passed through the break room until her fellow guide, Suzy, popped in.

"I see they have you reading all the boring crap. Blink twice if you want to be put out of your misery," Suzy said with a grin.

Crystal blinked twice, and they shared a laugh. Checking the time, she was shocked to see half of her shift was over. She grabbed her lunch out of the fridge and enjoyed her meal with the irascible Suzy, but Crystal couldn't help pondering ways to get into Amelia's office.

After Suzy left, Amelia checked on Crystal as she opened a video on returns and exchanges. Amelia asked how the training was going as she warmed her lunch in the microwave.

"Pretty good," Crystal answered. "I had a question…"

They were interrupted by a hastening Lisa entering the room. "Amelia, we have an unhappy customer who wants to speak to the manager."

Without hesitation, Amelia left her food cooling in the microwave and followed Lisa out of the room.

This was her chance. Crystal peeked down the hallway and waited for the two women to disappear around a corner. Seizing the opportunity, she darted the several steps to Amelia's office, eased the door open, and shut it softly behind her.

She studied the three large filing cabinets behind Amelia's organized desk. There were no labels on the outside of the cabinets, so she tugged open the top drawer of the leftmost one. Crystal was ecstatic to find the files inside clearly marked.

The first drawer was full of work schedules. They were identified by two week time blocks and extended back over the last year. Despite her best efforts to be quiet, the drawer clicked shut and Crystal was sure the noise reverberated throughout the store. She winced, but tugged open the next few drawers.

They contained materials labeled "marketing" and "product recalls". Crystal switched to the next cabinet, yanking open the first drawer. It contained information on subcontractors and vendors.

Voices echoed in the hallway, and Crystal froze. They passed by the office and she shut the drawer with a careful hand, but panic was starting to set in. The next drawer consisted of folders containing receipts. "Damn it! Where are you?" she hissed.

She was moving to the last cabinet, when Amelia's voice rose up, coming from outside the office door.

With no real idea of what to do, she flung herself into the chair she had sat in during her interview. She winced as her shoes skidded on the polished concrete floor.

"Thank you, Lisa." Amelia's voice projected down the hall.

Amelia, holding her lunch in one hand and clutching a piece of paper in another, backed into the office and spotted Crystal. "Crystal, what are you doing in here?"

Her mind raced and latched on to the first thing it could come up with, "I was watching the video on returns and exchanges."

"Yes?" Amelia prodded.

"Umm…What if…" *Think, Crystal, think.* "What if a customer wants to exchange an item for an item of different value, rather than a simple exchange?"

Amelia crossed the room to her chair and sat down, gazing at Crystal. "If you had continued watching, you would have discovered the video answered your question near the end."

"Oh, it does? I'm sorry to waste your time." Crystal stood up, trying to beat a hasty retreat.

"Are you feeling ok? You look a little flushed," Amelia asked with concern.

"Oh, I'm fine. It's a lot to take in, is all. There is so much to learn," Crystal was babbling, but couldn't seem to shut up. The disappointment of not finding the information she needed, as well as the panic of almost getting caught, were leaving her flustered.

"I keep forgetting you guides have a hard time sitting still," Amelia chided herself. "I do have a little clerical work you can do. It's not whitewater rafting, but at least you can get on your feet. Why don't we head to the service area and I'll show you what I need done?"

"Sounds great. I could stand to move a little. A rolling stone gathers no moss," she cringed. She was still babbling.

Amelia nodded and the two wended their way past the shoppers to the service area. Two guys in oil-spattered Emerald City Outfitters shirts nodded to her before returning to their work. They were both listening to music on headphones, and the odor of grease permeated the room. Amelia pointed to two boxes sitting on a work table.

"This first box is our quarterly flyer. The second box contains address labels. Stick a label on each flyer and, when you're finished, take them one block north to the post office."

A rush of excitement overtook Crystal. Could it be this easy? As Amelia left the room, Crystal ripped off the packing tape covering the address label box. They were printed in alphabetical order with thirty stickers to a sheet. She lifted a handful of labels and her eyes started scanning as the service guy next to her began waxing a pair of skis with vigorous sweeps of his hands.

The second page of labels had the names, "Byrne, Ryan and Alice," with an address listed below it. When she was most in need, the universe had provided. She peeked out the corner of her eye at the service guys, but one was focused on the skis in front of him as well as the music in his ears while his coworker was across the room oiling a bike chain. She peeled the address from the backing, eased up her shirt sleeve and stuck it to her forearm. She tugged her sleeve back over the label and scanned for the next name she needed.

****

Standing in her kitchen, Crystal peeled the address labels from her arm, sticking them to a piece of paper. She may not have their phone numbers, but this was even better. Not wanting to lose the information after the trouble she took to procure it, she snapped a picture of the addresses with her cell phone.

She and Olivia had devised a plan the previous night in case she managed to find the contact information. After a lot of planning and scheming, they determined the first person Crystal should approach was Georgia Patterson. Georgia didn't seem to have a motive for killing Philip, and hadn't been out of the house when he disappeared. More importantly, she had come across as a bit of a gossip when Crystal spoke to her in the chalet. If Crystal could get her chatting, she might uncover some clues which could help solve the case. Looking at the address on her phone, she could tell Georgia lived only a few miles from her parents' home.

Crystal mulled it over and determined this needed to be as non-confrontational as possible. If she showed up at night, it would feel more like an ambush rather than a social call, and would end in the door being shut in her face. Therefore, despite her impatience, Crystal would have to wait until Saturday. She had checked the business hours of Calvert and Associates and noted they were open Monday through Friday, so at this time of year, weekends were the only daylight to be had. She had given some consideration that the firm might be closed with the tragic death of Philip, but after seeing how much everyone detested him, she thought they wouldn't give a second thought to going back to work.

She sighed and headed to her kitchen to start dinner. She was draining spaghetti and brainstorming questions she wanted to ask Georgia when her phone chimed.

—*What are you doing Saturday night?*—It was Conner.

—*Am I going on a date with you?*—She texted

back.

—*Well, since you asked, I can make some free time.*—Conner stuck a smiling emoji at the end.

—*I'll pick you up at 6:00 p.m., dress warm.*—

Dress warm? Where was he taking her?

—*How warm?*—She sent back. She hoped he would give her a clue as to where they were going.

—*Very warm.*—His answer only made her more curious. They were going to be outside, but given how much he knew about outdoor activities, it didn't narrow it down much.

If she was going to be a wilderness guide and date a wilderness guide, she supposed this was the type of thing she should expect. She sent her address to Conner and flopped down on her couch with her plate of pasta, exhausted from the day's events. Once she finished her dinner, Elf crawled into her lap and curled up for a nap. She stroked his head (not his ears, never his ears), and spent half her time mulling over how to get the information she needed from Georgia, and the other half imagining what Conner had planned for their first date.

Chapter Ten

Saturday arrived, after several restless days. The intentional delay to question Georgia grated against Crystal's proactive nature, but her logical side kept reminding the rest of her it was the best way to handle the situation.

In the time between, Crystal had worked two short shifts at the store and was surprised to find she enjoyed this facet of the job. The customers were enthusiastic and the feeling was contagious. It made her want to guide them through their adventures. She also learned as an employee she received half off everything in the store, of which she was going to take full advantage as soon as she returned to working full time and full pay. In her mind, she had switched from "if she returned to full time" to "when she returned to full time". This was something she wanted in the fibers of her core, and she was beginning to resent all of the Calvert and Associates employees for ruining her first steps to a better future.

Conner had called to tell her he had talked to the Sheriff. He, too, was skeptical after his questioning and had asked his cousin her thoughts. Holly hadn't been willing to come out and criticize the interrogation, but Conner confirmed she was not impressed by the Sheriff's lack of questions. Conner's opinion only reinforced Crystal's conviction that she was doing the right thing by pursuing the leads on her own.

To meet Georgia, Crystal dressed in a knit turquoise sweater and black jeans with a touch of makeup. She was trying to come across as friendly and chatty, not aggressive and nosy, and was confident her outfit hit the mark.

She paced around her apartment until late morning before making the twenty-minute drive to Georgia's home. Her house was located on a corner lot in the Queen Anne neighborhood and was built in the craftsman style. It was small, but classy, with a large open porch covered by rafters. The simple elegance of the home was what she would expect from someone who worked at an architectural firm.

Crystal climbed out of her old car and into the bracing air. Crossing the street, she knocked on the front door. As soon as her knuckles hit, a deafening bark responded, and Georgia's voice called out, "Bear, be quiet!"

The scrabbling of claws and a few more deep barks rang out before the front door opened, and a large Newfoundland bounded out to greet her.

"Hi, big guy." Crystal thumped the side of the excited dog.

"Oh, hello. Crystal, wasn't it?" The tone of Georgia's question made it clear she was unsure what Crystal was doing on her front porch.

"You remember me. I think your place is gorgeous, by the way. It's so fitting for the Pacific Northwest."

A little buttering up would not hurt the situation, all the easier to pull off because it was true.

In preparation for the interview with Georgia, Crystal had looked up how to make a hostile person answer questions. The internet had been a fount of information. The first thing her search turned up was to start getting the person answering questions, however innocuous.

"How long have you owned it?" Crystal asked as she stroked Bear's head.

"Almost a decade, now. Can I ask what you're doing here?" Georgia asked.

The other part of her research made it clear to establish who was asking the questions, and who was doing the answering. Instead of giving a direct response, Crystal responded with another question, "Last weekend was pretty crazy, and I was wondering if you and I could talk?"

Georgia hesitated, but gave a reluctant nod and held open the door. Bear led Crystal, wagging his bushy tail.

Georgia's home was as delightful inside as it was outside. A slate stone entryway with an umbrella stand and coat rack greeted her. The house had an open concept, with the living room and a modern kitchen laid out before her. Hardwood floors, matching walnut cabinetry and granite counters gave the home a natural and sturdy feel. All of the finishes were high end and must have cost a fortune.

"It's stunning in here. I feel like I'm in a five star bed and breakfast. Everything is so cozy. Who was your remodeler?" *Keep the questions going.*

Georgia led her through the living room to a small seating area in front of a large picture window overlooking the front lawn. "My son did it for me," she answered with enthusiasm. "He's starting up his own contracting company. He said he wanted to remodel a house so he would have pictures to show prospective clients, but I think he wanted to do something nice for me."

This conversation was turning in the right direction. "Can you give me his card or his number? I would like to have some remodeling done on my condo someday."

"I'd be happy to. He would welcome any business opportunity." Georgia disappeared and reappeared a minute later with a card emblazoned with "Patterson and Son."

"I have a new grandson. He's only a year old, but my son, George, already imagines him taking over a successful contracting company." She beamed at the thought.

"Georgia and George?" Crystal asked.

"Ha! The name George is a family name handed down every generation. I didn't have any brothers, so I was named Georgia by my father."

Crystal thanked her lucky stars for the research she had done. She had half expected to have a door slammed in her face, but here she was chatting away with the person she was going to interrogate.

"My parents were a tad new age," Crystal confided. "Hippie lite, if you will. I'm Crystal and my sister is Heather."

They talked for a while about the cold weather and the rare possibility of snow in the forecast, Georgia's new grandson (also named George), and her Newfie, Bear, who gave off deep rumbling snores as he sprawled beside Georgia's feet.

During the conversation, Georgia had brewed a pot of Earl Gray tea while chatting to her over the kitchen peninsula. She produced homemade chocolate chip cookies from a cookie jar and laid them out on a plate next to the tea.

Eventually, there was a slight lull in their pleasantries, and Crystal steered the conversation back to the reason she was there.

"Do you remember what happened in the chalet?" Crystal kept her tone conversational and happy. She also kept words like death and murder out of the questioning. No reason to put Georgia's guard up at this point.

"Oh, I could hear a little arguing from my room," Georgia evaded.

"Both Bree and Madeleine fought with Philip," Crystal prodded. "Any idea what it was about?"

"Different things...or maybe the same thing," Georgia answered.

"What do you mean?"

Sighing, Georgia clarified, "Philip was not always a likable man. I hate to speak ill of the dead, but he had a lot of awful traits to go with his admirable ones."

"Such as...?"

"Well, for starters, he had a wandering eye. He and Madeleine started the company years ago, and I believe at the time they were madly in love. She had the business brains and he was the architectural genius. She won the contracts and he produced some of the most iconic buildings in Seattle. Soon, the firm thrived and instead of bidding on work, people were begging Philip to design for them. He hired the best talent out there, the company flourished, and everyone made a fortune. He paid me well, even though I wasn't an architect. I could never have afforded this darling home if not for his generosity."

"What went wrong?"

"Fifteen years ago, Philip hired an intern, fresh out of college. She was a beautiful young woman, bright and promising, but she decided the best way to the top would be to sleep with the boss. She flirted with Philip every time Madeleine was out of the office, and we could all tell where it was headed. I'll attest that Philip didn't exactly dislike the attention. He strutted around like a bantam rooster. Eventually, an affair started. When it was discovered, Madeleine and Philip almost divorced, and the entire company came close to dissolving along with their marriage. Everyone's livelihood was threatened and thus began the resentment. All of the associates blamed Philip for how close the company had come to disaster, while Philip declared they were all ungrateful leeches who had hitched themselves to his star. He kept hiring attractive college interns and began seducing them, more out of spite than any sense of lust, I think."

"I find it hard to believe looking at him."

"This may surprise you, but back in the day he was a looker. Tall, built, with curly golden hair fit for Adonis. It wasn't difficult for him. As time took its toll on his body and personality, it became less seduction and more assault. Several of our last interns have quit in outrage, and I know at least one of them leveled a lawsuit."

"Did he try and seduce Bree?"

"Oh heavens, yes. However this time was different," Georgia confided. "She and Justin had started dating. They attempted to keep it under wraps, but I figured it out. They are frightfully obvious."

"What did Madeleine do during all of this?"

"Her heart was broken the first time it happened. She was such a lively woman, but the past years have left her bitter and angry. Not only was she less important in her marriage, she was also less important to Calvert and Associates. It was now Philip's reputation luring in the work, not her business acumen. For a period of time, I believe she stopped caring what Philip did with the interns. Personally, I think the only reason Madeleine kept showing up at the office was because it was the only thing giving her life meaning. She filled her time with volunteer work, but eventually started drinking. Now, she's inebriated most of the time and doesn't always seem aware of reality. I think she's slipped a cog. She fluctuated between threatening divorce in arguments they had in the office, and acting like she and Philip were still in love. One day she changed her name to include her hyphenated maiden name, and the next she had gossiped about renewing her marriage vows. I had no idea what was going to happen to their marriage if they ever chose to retire and turn over the firm to someone else."

"Did they have a plan for the company in place?"

"They didn't share it with me. I imagined it was going to one of the associates; Ryan, Alice, Justin, or Gary. Another option was to sell it to an outside investor. Philip liked to threaten that course of action when he argued with any of them."

"Didn't his threats create even more animosity?"

"Oh, lord, yes. Gary became insufferable. He spent half his time sucking up to Philip and the other half bad-mouthing the others. Ryan, Alice and Justin have been trying to impress Philip by landing jobs and producing dramatic designs, but none of them have Philip's panache or brilliance."

"So, what happened the night in the chalet?" Crystal asked again.

"We have drifted a little far afield, haven't we? I'm not sure what occurred, because everything happened after I retired for the evening. I had just switched off my light when I overheard Madeleine and Philip arguing across the hall. This was nothing new to me, since they shout at each other in the office, so I didn't pay it much mind. After ten minutes of carrying on, Madeleine threw open their door and ordered Philip to sleep on the couch."

"They act like this in the office, too?"

Sighing, Georgia continued, "I guess I must have worked there too long if I think this behavior is normal for the workplace."

"I think Calvert and Associates sounds like an awful place to work and you're talking to a person whose last boss was borderline abusive." Georgia gave a grim nod at the words. Not wanting to get sidetracked into complaining about their jobs, Crystal returned the conversation to the night in question, "What else do you remember?"

"If I had known what was going to happen, I would have stayed glued to my door, listening. As it was, I fell asleep until more shouting woke me up. This time it was down the hall and harder to hear, but I'm pretty sure it was Bree and Philip. As the night progressed, I think everyone joined in one by one. I kept fading in and out of sleep. The wine I drank with dinner didn't help my memory, either."

"So what do you think happened?"

"I can't say for sure. The staff at this company have always been combative, but this particular night they raised hell. I laid low and waited for the storm to pass."

"I know it was a whirlwind, but did you hear anything to explain what happened to Philip?"

"I wish I could say I did, but I have no good answer. There was a lot of yelling and a lot of noise. I was half asleep and I don't remember most of it."

"Did you go out and see what they were fighting about?"

"Not on your life was I going out there. I didn't have a horse in that particular race. I had no desire to rock the boat when Philip, Madeleine, and people who could be signing my paycheck in the future were mixing it up. I didn't poke my head out until the cacophony stopped and they started leaving out the front door."

"If they all hated Philip so much, why do you think they risked going into a snowstorm when he left the chalet?"

"I'm sure they meant to try and rescue him. I can't imagine any of them would wish him physical harm. They're architects, not criminals," Georgia was emphatic.

"Don't you think the years of animosity could inspire one of them to murder?" Crystal delved.

"If I didn't know these people, I'd say yes, but I don't believe that they have it in their souls to do this sort of thing."

Chapter Eleven

Crystal left Georgia's after a little more small talk and promises to call her son if she did any remodeling. Checking the time on her phone as she climbed in her car, she was shocked to see it was already getting on in the day. She was running late and needed to get home to get ready for her date with Conner. She twisted the key to start her car, which gave a nasty rattle and died. That was new. A second attempt ended with the same result. *Ugh.* The third time, the car kept running. She needed to take it to the shop before her car left her well and truly stranded, but mechanic's bills were off the table until she solved this case and started collecting reliable paychecks. Mulling over everything she had learned from Georgia during her drive, no insights came to her as to who might have killed Philip.

Back in her apartment, she dished out some seafood feast for Elf to enjoy and hopped into a hot bath.

After she toweled off, she debated her outfit for another hour, trying various combinations of clothes and jewelry. She settled on her favorite pair of stretchy black pants, a blue button down shirt with a tan cardigan sweater. She opted for her pair of brown knee-high boots and set it all off with a floral print scarf. A pair of topaz earrings completed the outfit. The effect was somewhat ruined as she donned a long winter coat over the whole ensemble, but at least her boots and scarf were visible and she wouldn't freeze in the night's weather.

Conner buzzed her condo at exactly six. Grabbing her purse, she patted Elf on the head, and trotted down the stairs.

Conner greeted her at the front door. His dark blue jeans and long gray wool coat made for a classy ensemble for their date, and it also didn't hurt it showed off his toned physique. His breath coalesced in the frigid air and he grinned as he took her in, "You look lovely."

"You're looking quite handsome yourself."

"If you follow me, your chariot awaits." He waved his hand in grand fashion at his SUV parked in front of the condo. He held open her door, and she slid into the passenger seat, glancing around. The careful patch of a tear on the driver's seat and the faded black of the dashboard belied the car's age, but overall it gleamed in immaculate condition. The carpet by her feet still showed the lines of having been vacuumed and the interior smelled of cleaner. Outside, Conner circled the car and slung himself into the driver's seat.

"I'm dying of curiosity. Where are you taking us tonight?" Crystal had been pondering this since he'd asked her and still had no idea what was in store.

"We're going to a Seattle classic, Green Lake, but with a little twist," Conner checked his mirror and eased into traffic.

"I adore Green Lake." Green Lake was a park situated in the northern residential part of the city. A three mile paved path encircled the lake, turning to follow the shore line. Soccer fields, trees, and expanses of grass formed a barrier between the path and the rest of the city to create a peaceful urban oasis. Crystal had walked around it several times in her life, but never at night. "What's the twist?"

"I'm going to save that as a surprise until later. You can't expect me to tip all of my first date cards right away, can you? So, I'm going to distract you with a different topic. How have you liked working in the store?"

Crystal laughed, "It's nice. I'd prefer to be guiding, but I'm surprised how much I enjoy it."

"It isn't a bad job at all. I couldn't agree with you more regarding the guiding, though. I've been able to pick up a few extra hours at Alpine Zone, but if this goes on much longer, it's going to start eating into my houseboat savings."

Crystal couldn't stand the vulnerability of telling him of her situation. With the condo as expensive as it was, she had never been able to build her savings like the financial experts advised.

Conner found an open spot on the western side of the park and they climbed out. Crystal shivered a little in the night air as they followed a small gravel path leading to the larger paved lakeside walkway. The sounds of the city faded into the distance only to be replaced by the crunch of gravel under their feet. A few intrepid joggers loped by them as they merged onto the paved path, and Conner steered her toward the southern edge of the lake.

Reaching out, he laced his fingers through hers in a comfortable gesture. Holding hands hadn't thrilled Crystal like this since high school, and her heart started beating faster. Turning his head to look at her, Conner broke the silence of the evening air, "You learned most of my story at dinner with Holly, but I still don't know a whole lot about you, yet."

"There isn't a whole lot of mystery to me. I've lived in Seattle my whole life. My parents still own the same house on Queen Anne where I grew up with my sister, Heather. I attended U-Dub and studied English. My degree landed me a series of clerical jobs, which I quit to become a wilderness guide."

"You wrapped up your whole life pretty succinctly," he remarked.

"That is probably the single most important reason I quit my office job. My life was way too succinct. If you can fit an entire person's life on a tombstone, maybe they aren't living enough."

"A bit of a macabre way to look at it," Conner joked.

"Well, I did go through a goth phase in high school for a year. Some of it must have stuck." Crystal's lips turned up at the memories of her all black wardrobe.

"See, there's more to your life than your first explanation. One year of being a goth-girl."

"I hope to make being a wilderness guide a permanent part. You have to go back all the way to college to when I was this excited about where my life is headed."

"We'll get back out there soon," Conner reassured her with forced joviality.

"I'm not so sure. Based on what Holly said, and how inexperienced the sergeant in charge of the investigation seems to be, I'm not feeling optimistic in the least."

Conner squeezed her hand. "I can't force the

insurance company to let us back out into the wilderness, but I can help you forget all of it for one night. We're almost to the first stop of the evening." He gestured in front of them.

Twinkle lights hung from the trees and a swell of pedestrians were leading them to a stately brick building. Nestled right up to the edge of the lake, it had a large set of red double doors in the front with a grand arched window over the entryway. A marquee at the pediment declared "The Tell-Tale Heart" by Edgar Allen Poe was playing tonight.

"I didn't know this was a theater," she exclaimed.

"Most people don't. It used to be a bathhouse to change in before swimming in the lake, but the building was converted to a playhouse in the seventies."

Conner produced a couple of tickets from his pocket, and they made their way into the crowded theater. A hundred seats were packed close to the stage. Glancing at their stubs, the usher pointed to a vacant pair of seats only two rows back. Side-stepping past the already seated patrons, they took their seats. As she made herself comfortable, Crystal delighted in the excited whispers filling the room as the crowd waited for the play to begin.

Conner slung his arm around Crystal's shoulder and she snuggled up. The warmth after the cold stroll around the lake was fantastic, and even better since Conner's solid presence was doing the warming.

The lights dimmed, and the room fell silent. Ever so slightly, the stage lights rose, casting the room in gray shadows.

A tall gaunt man in a worn Victorian suit and tattered top hat strode out under the lights. He gazed at the crowd for a few long seconds, judging them. After a moment's inspection, he must have found them trustworthy, for he opened in melancholy tones. "True—nervous—very, very dreadfully nervous. I had been and am; but why will you say that I am mad?" He paced the stage, casting furious glances at the audience.

Even though Crystal had read the story, she sympathized with the man. He begged forgiveness from the audience before explaining what had delivered him to such an anxious state, but at the end of the opening monologue he pronounced what he had done, "I was never kinder to the old man than during the whole week...before I killed him." The crowd gasped, and Crystal found her hand clenching Conner's arm at the callous manner it was delivered.

Crystal was fascinated being so close to the stage. Peering into the actor's troubled visage as he pleaded for understanding as to why he had to do this was fascinating. With an abrupt toss of his head, the actor gave up explaining his motive, as if their acceptance was no longer important. Instead, with eerie fascination, they stared as he bragged of when he hid the old man's body under the floor. "I have replaced the boards so cleverly, so cunningly that no human eye could detect anything wrong!" The madness and ego shocked the audience as the actor twisted his face throughout his expositions. Oohing and aahing, the crowd reacted as his own guilt conjured up the beating of the old man's heart in his mind. He broke down, confessed his crimes, and the play wound down as two policemen hauled the man off stage. The actor had taken the old story, delivered it a new life, and received a standing ovation when he trotted back onto the stage for a bow.

Applauding with the rest of the crowd, Crystal's only regret was it was over after a mere thirty minutes. Even though it was a short play, the whole date had been terrific. Filing out of the theater, Crystal expected Conner to lead her to his car, but instead he guided her the long way around toward the northern edge of the lake.

"Our night is only beginning." Conner said. "I made a dinner reservation at a great little place a short walk from here."

A smile sprang onto Crystal's face. Leaning into his shoulder, she hooked her arm under his. They strolled through the frigid night, breath puffing as they recounted the play. She spotted several businesses as the width of the park narrowed. Conner steered their steps off the main path and toward a blue neon sign in the distance.

"The play brings me back to what I said a few days ago. We need for whoever killed Philip to have the same feeling of overwhelming guilt and confess their crimes."

"A confession would help us out a lot. I wonder if any of them have a guilty conscience?"

"I don't know. Georgia and Bree maybe, but the others seem to be hard as nails."

"I couldn't agree more. I talked to Georgia, and I'm convinced she didn't have anything to do with it," Crystal said without preamble.

"Wait, what? You talked to Georgia?"

"Sure," Crystal powered on with confidence. "We chatted earlier today."

"Did you bump into her somewhere? How did that happen?"

"I drove to her house," Crystal said with all of the nonchalance she could muster. "I learned a lot of dirt on Philip and Calvert and Associates by talking with her. More importantly, I have some theories on who might have wanted him dead."

"Visiting murder suspects seems risky, Crystal. Holly hinted that one of these people killed Philip. Do you think you're being safe? What did she say?" Crystal found both his concern and curiosity endearing.

Before she could answer, they arrived outside Sushi Hashimoto.

"I've never had the guts to try sushi before. My friend Olivia keeps badgering me to, but I haven't found the courage to try it."

"Olivia was right to badger you, because sushi is a culinary experience which shouldn't be missed. I'll show you what to do, and I know just what to order since you've never tried it before," Conner assured her.

Confirming the reservation with the hostess, they were shown through the packed restaurant. Next to their table, a large tank of exotically colored fish darted among bright coral, enchanting Crystal. They had only settled in their seats for a minute when a waiter arrived with menus, asking what they would like to drink.

Conner ordered them hot tea and saké, and they poured through the menu together. Pictures were shown next to each variety, and Conner pointed out the different types he would recommend for a sushi novice.

Daunted by the Japanese names, she shrugged. "I'm in over my head, so I'm trusting your opinion. Get us whatever you think is best."

The waiter returned with a pot of green tea, poured them each a cup, and took the order from Conner. Still chilled from the winter night, they both sipped the earthy steaming liquid.

"Circling back to our earlier discussion, I want to get the story straight. You tracked down one of the suspects of a murder investigation—still not sure how you did that—and questioned her in her own home?"

"Pretty much. However, I figured Georgia wasn't a threat or a suspect," Crystal answered.

"I guess that's true," he conceded. "You are a gutsy dame, though."

"Dame? Is this the twenties?" She teased him.

"I guess I feel like I'm talking to an Agatha Christie character, so I might as well speak like I'm in the era," he gave a wry smile and Crystal giggled.

"I'm hardly Miss Marple. I simply asked a couple of questions." It took a few minutes, but she recounted what she had learned from Georgia.

Conner wore an astonished expression. "Wow, they are one messed up bunch," was all he could say when she finished.

He didn't get a chance to add anything more as a large plate of sushi was placed in the middle of the table, and two smaller plates were set in front of each of them. Two ceramic cups of saké were followed by a tray of condiments with a weird pile of green mush in the center.

"It's wasabi," Conner could see her staring at the mush. "It's delicious, but it has a potent kick, similar to horseradish, so use it sparingly."

Conner re-identified each piece of fish on the plate as well as the little balls of rice called California rolls. She remembered they were stuffed with cucumber, avocado and crab meat from the menu. They both unrolled the napkins wrapped around their chopsticks. Crystal had used chopsticks a few times before on a lark, but had never mastered the knack of eating with them. However, she wanted to fit in with Conner, and they both pinched a piece and lifted it to their mouths. She gave a snort of laughter as the sushi in Conner's chopsticks fell onto the table seconds before the sushi in her own chopsticks tumbled to the floor. Conner joined in her laughter, and they agreed to switch to using forks. Finally able to maneuver a piece of tuna to her mouth, she found it not the least bit fishy. To the contrary, it was tender and refreshing. Emboldened, she tried a dab of the wasabi on her tongue. The intense punch of flavor hit her sinuses a split second before her eyes began watering. She grabbed her saké to wash it down and was surprised to find the crisp taste reminded her of a dry white wine as it quenched the heat. Maybe she'd give the wasabi a pass for now.

"I've been thinking," Conner said in between bites. "Who would benefit the most from Philip's death?"

This angle was not something she had considered before. "They all have motives as far as I can tell, so I never bothered to think who would benefit the most."

"I feel like the person with the most to gain may be the person opting to commit murder," Conner reflected.

"Who do you think has the most to gain?"

"From your discussion with Georgia, it sounds like Madeleine would assume control of the company if he were out of the picture. I also feel like Gary might be the first in line to take over if Philip were gone, and Madeleine handed it off."

"Interesting," Crystal said. "My first choices were Justin in a murderous rage, or maybe Madeleine in a fit of jealousy. It seems you like your murder motives in cold blood, while I like mine in hot."

Conner smiled. "If you like your murders in hot blood, Ryan was pretty steamed after Philip insulted him during the hike. Maybe it was the straw that broke the camel's back."

Crystal laughed. "This is the most interesting first date conversation I have ever had. It's like a real life game of clue. I've never investigated a murder—other than police detectives, who has?—and I'm loving every minute of it."

"I still can't believe you were crazy enough to question Georgia." A twitch tugged at his lips.

"Well, I'm going to visit the others, too. I know it might sound risky, but I'll be safe. I suspect I'll have doors shut in my face, but I have to try something."

"Is it that bad?" he asked with a flash of insight.

"It's pretty bad. Before this fiasco, I was living paycheck to paycheck. I don't want to lose my condo, or give up on my new career. I could try and get yet another job somewhere else. However, for the first time, I feel like I'm doing something worth engraving on my tombstone."

Crystal was startled to realize that while her brief experience of being a wilderness guide made her feel fulfilled, being a sleuth excited all of her senses. Everything happening in her life right now both exhilarated and terrified her. It had taken twenty-seven years, but she was excited about waking up and experiencing what each new day held.

Conner nodded, stretching out his hand to cover hers. "I've been an outdoorsman my whole life, so I can't imagine living any other way. I can see in your eyes what this means to you. Promise me you'll be careful, though."

The earnestness of the moment was ruined when the waiter delivered the check and Conner handed off his credit card. After Conner signed the receipt, they zipped up their winter jackets, and strolled back into the night arm-in-arm. The temperature had dipped below freezing and the grass of the park now glistened with a sparkling coat of frost under the light of the street lamps.

"I can only think of one thing missing from this night. We need dessert. Do you like chocolate?" Conner asked.

"You might as well ask me if fish like water. *Like* is not the word I'd use to describe my feelings regarding chocolate. It's more like I *need* chocolate."

"Then I know the perfect place for us." He grabbed her hand and led her down the block to a small building with an artistic chalk drawn sign declaring itself "Rain City Confections." Conner held open the door for her, and she stepped out of the cold.

Inside the cramped store, the place bustled, as patrons selected from a vast array of options. After her first breath, Crystal couldn't help herself. She closed her eyes and drew in a slow lungful, taking in the heavenly aroma. The warm building luxuriated in the sweet odors of sugar and cacao, reminding Crystal of making cookies with her mother and sister. Opening her eyes, she nodded to a bemused Conner, and they stepped to the back of the line to discuss the options sketched on the chalkboard above the counter. When they made it to the register, she had settled on a dark chocolate truffle, a mint truffle, and a hot cocoa.

Conner also ordered cocoa, but selected a hunk of toffee.

Leaving the comfort of the cozy shop, they ventured back into the cold night. Splitting their chocolates, they laughed as they placed the half pieces in each other's mouths. They debated which was the best as they continued to stroll around the lake. After what seemed too soon, they made it back to where Conner had parked. Finding a nearby bench, they sat to finish their hot cocoa and savor the night.

"I've had such a wonderful time, Conner," she said and rested her head on his shoulder. Stretching his arm around her, he squeezed her even closer.

"Me, too, Crystal. I can't remember ever enjoying a night this much."

"I also have to give credit where credit is due. You planned a perfect first date."

She lifted her head to look up and he was already gazing down into her eyes. Then he kissed her.

It was gentle and loving as he cradled her head in his hands. Her heart bounded and she returned his affection. As the kiss carried blissfully on, a cold drop settled on her cheek. Peeking between her eyelashes, she was shocked to spot snowflakes settling around them.

She broke the kiss and blurted, "It's snowing!" Conner began laughing and Crystal blushed. "Well, it doesn't snow often in Seattle."

"No, it doesn't." He smiled. "I need to work on my kissing if you're distracted so easily."

"The kiss was amazing. The whole night has been amazing. The walk, the play—which the goth girl in me couldn't get enough of, by the way—the sushi, the chocolate, the kiss, and now the snow!" Crystal gushed. "This night has been magic." Then she leaned forward and kissed him again.

Chapter Twelve

Several pillows propping her up, Crystal lay on her bed with a quilt over her legs, sipping coffee, and struggling to respond to Olivia's text. After deleting her typed words before sending them, she gave up and fired back—*The date with Conner was too perfect for mere texting. Let's meet for lunch and I'll tell all.* The giddiness from the memories made her want to share everything with her best friend. However, after years of commiserating over horror stories from the dating scene, it was the end of a tradition to have something wonderful to share.

Her mind drifted back to solving Philip's murder. After pondering who to talk to next, Crystal settled on Madeleine. Philip's wife had come up in both Conner's theory of financial gain, and her own of a jealous wife exacting revenge. Madeleine appeared to be a bitter and unapproachable woman, but this case wasn't going to be solved by shying away from difficult situations. She was going to have to crack a few tough nuts if she wanted her life back. She only hoped it was as fruitful as it had been with Georgia.

Mind made up, she lengthened her legs and arms into an epic stretch, when needle sharp teeth latched onto her toe. Elf must have crawled under the quilt. It had been a warning bite, but it was enough to launch Crystal out of bed, knowing worse was on the way.

Elf wiggled out from where he was hiding, jumped to the ground, and began twining between her legs and purring. As soon as Crystal stretched down to pet him, he bolted to his feeding area, meowing the entire time.

Crystal scooped a little wet food out to placate him, and proceeded to shower and dress. An hour later she was ready to go but, after a moment's pause, determined it was best to wait until at least ten o'clock on a Sunday morning.

To keep her mind busy, she tackled a chore she had been avoiding. She logged onto her bank's website, paid her bills, and was distressed at the balance of her account when she was done. She had received her next week's schedule at the store, and thanks to one of the other staff taking a few vacation days, Crystal now had twenty-two hours of pay to help keep the wolves at bay. This time next month, the chore of paying bills was going to include picking who didn't receive money.

She retrieved Madeleine's address from where she had saved it on her phone, and mapped it. The house was on Mercer Island, an affluent suburb of Seattle. It was home to many Microsoft millionaires who had built their mansions there after making it big.

As she drove out of her condo's parking garage, Crystal was happy to see that the snow from the night before had melted. She loved when it snowed, but her car wasn't made to handle bad driving conditions.

The clear roads still didn't stop her poor car stalling at the first intersection. It staggered to life with the first turn of the key, and she puttered across I-90 to Mercer Island, crossing over one of the longest floating bridges in America. She weaved around the island's densely wooded roads, passing by dazzling houses, before arriving at a stunning home cantilevered into the side of a hill with floor to ceiling windows promising expansive views of Lake Washington.

Before she left her car, she leaned into the power of positive thinking. The questioning of Madeleine would be as successful as it had been with Georgia. She was going to come in hard with questions, not answer any directed at her, and have Madeleine singing out her story.

Her mental pep talk completed, Crystal climbed out of her car and approached an imposing front entrance. Two seven foot redwood doors, with large silver handles meeting in the middle, loomed over her. A decorative hammered dark iron pattern crossed at eye level and two massive sidelight windows finished the intimidating effect.

Crystal straightened her shoulders and refused to be daunted by the entry. She didn't see a doorbell, so instead knocked on the heavy wood.

The click of heels on a hard surface approached and both doors were flung open.

Madeleine stood there swaying a little as she held herself up by the door handle. In spite of the fact she was in an obvious state of inebriation this early on a Sunday morning, she was dressed in a stylish light gray pants suit, looking ready to head out to a business function. Her blazer was buttoned at the waist, a black silk camisole showed through the top, and her right wrist sported a glinting diamond tennis bracelet. Her make-up was a little lopsided, but overall she was ready to seize the day.

"Christine, so nice of you to come by to pay your condolences. You are such a lovely young woman,"

Madeleine gushed.

Madeleine's greeting took Crystal aback. This was not how she had planned this questioning to go, but rolled with it to get in the door.

"Of course I did, Madeleine," she answered. "How could I not? By the way, my name is Crystal."

"Isn't that what I said? Come in, come in. Make yourself at home. Poor Philip designed this for us when we were in our twenties. We couldn't afford to build it until twenty-five years later, but isn't it amazing?" Madeleine swept her arm around the main entrance hall.

Crystal had to admit it was a gorgeous home. However unlikable Philip had been, there was no disputing that he had been a visionary. A grand chandelier loomed over a patterned exotic hardwood floor stretching to the back of the house. From her vantage at the entrance, she could see the house was built to give a clear view of Lake Washington and Mount Rainier out the back windows.

They passed a mammoth cook's kitchen outfitted with marble countertops, hickory cabinetry, and stainless steel appliances. An empty bottle of chardonnay sat on the countertop beside a matching empty wine glass.

"Have a seat, dear." Madeleine gestured to an arm chair in front of the grand windows overlooking the Lake. Crystal thanked her and sat, taking in the room. A large framed photo of vibrant tulips in neat rows, centered before an old red barn, graced the wall behind the opposite chair.

Madeleine followed her gaze and asked, "Do you like it?" Without waiting for Crystal to answer, she continued. "I took this photo last April at the Tulip Festival in Mount Vernon with Philip. It was such an enchanting time." Madeleine stared at the picture for several uncomfortable seconds, lost in memory, before spinning on her heel and disappearing into the kitchen. Crystal couldn't see what was happening from her vantage, but a cork popped and her hostess returned bearing two glasses brimming with red wine.

"Thanks, Madeleine." Crystal didn't feel like drinking red wine this early on a Sunday morning, but didn't want to ruffle Madeleine's feathers by turning it down.

She took a delicate sip and found it was excellent. While she wasn't a wine aficionado, she had gone taste-testing at the local wineries with her friends enough to know high quality when she tasted it.

"I can't say how much I appreciate you stopping by, Christine," Madeleine reiterated. "I've received all sorts of flowers, letters and phone calls. The president of the university and the mayor himself called last night to express their deepest regrets at Philip's passing."

Ignoring Madeleine getting her name wrong again, she said, "I was saddened to see him go, too. I've been admiring his work. He was such a gifted architect who added so much beauty to our city." Her own sense of propriety warned her she might be laying it on a little thick. She prepared to back off, but Madeleine ate it up.

"I'm so glad to hear your kind words. Not many young people have come forward to express their sadness, but it gives me hope to see you here."

"I was wondering if you would share a few stories about you and your late husband. Together, you've changed the skyline of Seattle, and I know you must have led interesting lives." Madeleine was in such an expressive mood, she was hoping to turn the talk to the night of his murder.

Madeleine finished her wine, left, and returned with the bottle. She refilled her glass and topped off what little Crystal had drunk from hers. "Stories of Philip and me? What an amazing idea. We'll split this bottle of Zinfandel and remember Philip together."

Madeleine began regaling Crystal with tales of them dating at the University of Washington. How she with her business degree, and he with a masters in architecture, had planned to begin their firm and change Seattle's landscape. Her recounting meandered throughout their lives and spoke of the difficulties when they first opened their doors, the early successes, and the eventual legendary status of Calvert and Associates. She spoke with pride of their program to feed the homeless, and of Philip's many prestigious awards.

As she ended one of her more lengthy stories, Crystal directed the conversation where she wanted it to go. "On our snowshoe hike, it appeared not all of his employees understood him the way you did."

Madeleine gave a dramatic sigh. "You are correct. We try to hide it from outsiders, but we aren't always the most civil bunch."

If the behavior she had witnessed was them restraining themselves, Crystal couldn't imagine what it would be like if they stopped pulling punches.

"What issues did they have with Philip?" Crystal probed.

"Jealousy, mostly. Jealous of his abilities, jealous of his success, and jealous of our relationship." Madeleine stared at Crystal as if willing her to believe all of it.

"Surely, they are great architects in their own right," Crystal chose to keep stirring this pot.

"Oh, they may be competent, but none of them have Philip's flair. Maybe someday Gary will be as good as he thinks he is, but the rest are only good as support staff. They design the smaller features of our projects. It's why I've selected Gary as the new lead architect of the firm. He's the only one who appreciated Philip and me."

"Are you sure he's the right choice?" Crystal asked the question before she considered it. What did she care who took over the firm? However, she couldn't take her words back.

"I don't need to justify my choice to you or to any of them." Madeleine took a huge swig from her wine glass.

Crystal didn't want to lose Madeleine to anger, so she tried placating her, "I have no idea who is qualified. I'm sure you know best and picked him for the good of the firm."

"Damn straight I did." Madeleine was agitated by the line of questioning and growled out the statement.

"What do you remember of last Saturday night? Everything was so chaotic."

"Oh, you were there. I'm sure you remember," Madeleine demurred. Her words were starting to come out a little slurred at this point.

"I was downstairs sleeping and don't know for sure what happened," Crystal filled in a few details to keep Madeleine from dissembling. "I couldn't help but overhear you two having an argument, and later, it sounded as if he mixed it up with several other people.

Was it in regard to handing over the firm?"

"I don't know what the other arguments entailed, but Philip and I had words over his intern. That shameless tart, Bree, kept giving Philip sultry glances, so I told him he needed to fire her. Young women have always been throwing themselves at great men like Philip, and I've had enough." Anger and resentment burst out as she snapped the last few words. "Philip wouldn't fire her, so I made him sleep on the couch to mull over what was important in his life. If he wasn't willing to keep away from these trollops...er..." she stammered, confused in the middle of her rant. "I *mean*, if he wasn't willing to keep those girls away from him, then he needed to rethink our marriage," she finished.

"Aside from Bree's intentions toward your husband, do you think any of the others meant Philip any harm?" Crystal didn't believe Bree had any designs on Philip. If anything, Bree was intimidated and disgusted by the man, but she wasn't going to argue the point with Madeleine.

"They have all been praying for this day to happen, but I don't think any of them have the guts to do anything to hurt him."

"You don't think they are made of stern enough stuff?" Crystal asked.

"Oh, I think they might have tried something if they thought they could get away with it, but Philip and I have several of the best lawyers in the city on retainer. I hired them to protect us from lawsuits and attempted take overs, but I'm sure our staff is aware if they try anything nefarious they'll regret it," she slugged the last half of her wine glass down for emphasis.

"I assumed since the Sheriff was asking questions,

something criminal had happened."

"The Sheriff assured me they were only routine questions," Madeleine pointed out as she topped off her wine glass again. "I'm sure they follow up on any death with at least a minimal investigation."

"You didn't think it was weird how everyone raced out into the night?" Crystal asked.

"Not at all. Gary and I searched together, and he'd never do anything to hurt Philip. Philip was like a second father to him." Madeleine faltered and lost her train of thought.

"Justin and Ryan were out there too, though."

"I'm sure they were out trying to save their meal ticket. They know without Philip, the firm might be doomed. Anyone would go out to search in that situation," Madeleine finished.

"But if Philip was retiring soon, their meal ticket was going anyway," Crystal pointed out. This made Madeleine pause, and she sipped her refilled wine glass, gazing out over the lake. "What do you think happened after you kicked Philip out to sleep on the couch?"

"I'd had a couple glasses of wine and I was sound asleep. I think they all wanted to fight with Philip, like usual. Maybe that floozy Bree made a move on him, and he rejected her. My husband was a man of passion. I'm sure if the others were attacking his character, he would have opted to take the snowmobile and leave. An action like that was the epitome of Philip."

Crystal had to remind herself, that while she had knowledge of Philip being hit on the head before his demise from her talk with Conner's cousin, it was not known by the woman before her. Furthermore, the Sheriff had not hinted at there being any foul play during his questioning.

A grandfather clock in the corner chimed eleven times, the sound echoing in the spacious room.

"Oh my gosh, I'm going to be late." Madeleine shot up. She stumbled over her chair leg, tumbling to the hard floor.

Crystal jumped to her feet and helped Madeleine stand. "Are you ok?"

Tugging her clothes into order, Madeleine straightened her back and lifted her head with as much dignity as she could muster. "I'm fine. Only a few bruises. I'm supposed to be at the mission in a half-hour. They need food." She waved her arms in the air to express her urgency.

Crystal was confused, "Do you have food for them?"

"I do. I take it down every Sunday."

Crystal couldn't stand by and let a person this intoxicated drive. Madeleine could kill herself and anyone unfortunate enough to get in her way. "Can I call you a cab or maybe an Uber?"

"There's no time. They'll be so disappointed," she was on the verge of tears. "I usually don't indulge like this, especially during the day, but it's been so hard without Philip." She lurched out of Crystal's grasp. Staggering in the direction of the kitchen, she muttered "Where did I put my keys?"

"I'll drive you to the mission," Crystal said in desperation. This was not how she planned on spending her Sunday, but didn't see any other option.

"You would do that for me? You are such a good person, Christine." The tears welling in Madeleine's eyes started streaming down her face and she let out a choking wail.

Despite the awkwardness of the scene, Crystal wrapped the sobbing woman in a hug, and made the same soothing sounds she used when trying to calm her niece or nephew.

After a few minutes, Madeleine composed herself as she drew back from Crystal. "Most of the time, I'm not such a wreck," she avowed, "but I've never been under this much stress either."

"Of course not. I'm sure it's been overwhelming," Crystal agreed, though she knew the statement to be a lie. Both times Crystal had been around Madeleine, she had been both inebriated and manic.

"It has been *so* overwhelming, my dear. Were you serious when you said you would drive me to the mission?"

"Yes. It's the least I can do. I'm parked out front. Where's the food?"

"All of the food is already loaded in my car, so we'll just take it." She tracked down her keys on a small table by the entryway and passed them to Crystal. "I'm parked in the garage." Madeleine set off deeper into the house, leading Crystal down a hallway.

Crystal was amazed by the beautiful home. Thick exposed beams, elegant wainscoting and views from virtually every room they passed awed her. At the end of the hall, Madeleine opened a door to the garage. A Maserati convertible sat next to a Porsche SUV.

"The Cayenne is mine. Philip's is the Gran Turismo."

Crystal hesitated, "I think the seat of your car is worth more than my entire vehicle. I'm scared I'm going to wreck it if I drive."

"Don't be silly. It's a car. You point it in the direction you want to go and step on the gas. You can guide us there," Madeleine started giggling. "Get it? You're a guide and now you're guiding me."

Crystal gave a weak grin as Madeleine laughed so hard she complained her stomach hurt.

Easing into the car, Crystal tapped the button on the dash marked "start" and the car purred to life. The clock was even working. This vehicle was already more impressive than her own, and they hadn't left the garage.

Madeleine stretched a hand above Crystal's head to the visor and punched a garage door opener. The door rolled open and Crystal stepped on the gas.

Chapter Thirteen

Twenty minutes later, they arrived at the mission in downtown Seattle. The entire drive had overwhelmed Crystal. The remote possibility of crashing anything with the word Porsche emblazoned on the back had terrified her to the core, and she hadn't been able to enjoy one minute of the trip. To add to her dismay, Madeleine had insisted on blaring the Beatles the entire way, slurring along to "Yellow Submarine" and "Hey Jude" as if she were the star of a karaoke bar. She had urged Crystal to sing along the entire ride, which had only stressed her out even more.

"Thanks for driving, dear. I'm sure by the time we head back to my place, I'll have sobered up enough to take over."

"Aren't we dropping the food off and leaving?" Crystal felt a sinking feeling in the pit of her stomach. What had she gotten herself into?

"Oh, we do way more. We prepare and serve the food, too."

"Only the two of us? For the whole mission?"

Madeleine laughed, "Don't be silly. Of course not. I coordinate with the local Catholic church. Volunteers come here after mass to help out." She threw open the door and staggered as she misjudged the distance to the ground.

"I think I'm going to have to text my friend and let

her know I'm going to be a little late," Crystal called after Madeleine. She didn't want to miss her meeting with Olivia, but her friend would understand.

—At the mission downtown. Will be late. Keep you posted. She unbuckled her seat belt and joined Madeleine at the back of the Porsche.

Her phone chimed and she checked Olivia's reply—*you must really not want to move back in with your parents if you checked into the mission.*

—Ha, ha. This day is out of my control.

She tucked her phone back in her pocket. Looking up, she saw several people approaching to help unload the car.

Crystal was taken aback when she recognized two of them. Ryan and Alice were among the group closing in on her. Alice did her own double-take when she spotted Crystal, and strode up with a frown.

"What are you doing here?"

Crystal's mouth opened, but no words came out. Alice's question had caught her off guard, and she did not know how to begin coming up with a plausible excuse for being there.

"She was offering her condolences," Madeleine jumped in and saved her. From the assertiveness in her tone, she was used to handling Alice this way. With resolute dignity, Madeleine added, "She also offered to join us today."

Madeleine ruined her facade of poise by hoisting a box of ground beef and staggering backward. Crystal caught her arm and steadied the tipsy woman. Madeleine straightened, threw back her shoulders, and proceeded with a stately walk to the back door of the mission.

Madeleine's stagger gave Crystal an idea. She caught Alice's eye as the others all grabbed a box and whispered, "When I witnessed the state she was in, I couldn't let her drive here. She's had more than her fair share of wine."

Alice nodded, mollified. "That, I can believe. Did she tell you she usually doesn't indulge this much, and certainly not during the day?"

Crystal nodded.

Alice snorted and shook her head. "Figures. Well, come on then. It looks like you'll be helping today."

Crystal grabbed a box filled with packs of shredded cheese, Alice grabbed another with taco shells, and they followed the others.

Inside the mission, homeless men and women sat at cafeteria tables as a few children ran around playing tag. They all wore dirty clothing and could use more access to showers, but otherwise it was like any other social event. Crowds gathered around different tables, patting backs, and swapping stories. One group of four had broken out a deck of cards and was playing gin rummy.

They passed through the main area on the way to the kitchen when one man shouted, "What's for lunch today, Alice?"

"Tacos, Joe."

A cheer roared from the crowd, and a happy buzz of chatter filled the room.

"Tacos are always popular. Instead of being handed something and told to eat it, they get to assemble it themselves," Alice confided to Crystal. "Last taco night, our friend Joe over there confessed that it's their favorite. He said that it's because they don't have a lot of control over their lives, and small things, like picking what toppings they like, is something to treasure."

"I can understand," Crystal said, and found she did grasp it. Her own life had recently had a mind of its own, and she was willing to do whatever she could to put it back on the path she wanted. To accomplish this, she needed information from this woman and her husband.

After looking at Alice's stern face in her peripheral vision, she opted to see if she could get anything from Ryan first. She put the cheese down on a stainless-steel countertop and walked over to the dual sink where Ryan was busy rinsing lettuce. Washing her hands in the unoccupied sink, she grabbed the first head of washed lettuce from a colander. Spotting a nearby knife and cutting board, she set herself up on the table behind him.

"Thanks for coming down today," Ryan said with a grunt. "And thanks for taking care of…" He nodded in the direction of Madeleine who was busy unpacking cans of olives and jalapeños.

"I was happy to," Crystal said. "How long have you been doing this?"

"A couple of years. Our church volunteered to cover Sunday lunch, so Alice and I have been helping most weekends. Ever since Madeleine found out, our company has been funding the meals as part of its outreach program."

"This is awfully nice of you," Crystal said as she chopped. "I didn't mean to intrude on your day, but once I saw the condition Madeleine was in, I couldn't let her drive anywhere. When I mentioned it to your wife, she hinted Madeleine gets herself in this state often. Is that true?"

Ryan sighed, "Unfortunately, yes. She's always been a heavy drinker, but this last week.... Let's just say, I don't think she's had a sober moment."

"How are you handling Philip's passing?"

"Ok. I'm guessing this isn't a news flash to you, but Philip was not a pleasant human being to work for. Don't get me wrong. He was a great architect, and I appreciated the opportunity to work under him, but you got a glimpse of what he can be like."

Crystal slid the head of lettuce she had finished chopping into a large stainless steel bowl and grabbed another. "He was pretty rude to everyone, including us guides."

"Being an ass was his way. He was an egomaniac who took credit for the entire company's work. He never did wrong. No one else could do right. I think he got used to treating those around him like garbage, whether they worked for him or not."

"Except Gary?"

"He liked Gary like Mr. Burns likes Smithers on *The Simpsons*. It's nice to have a sycophant tell you you're the best thing since sliced bread whenever you open your mouth. However, he never considered Gary much of an architect."

"Madeleine confessed she was handing over the firm to Gary. She said he was the only one who appreciated Philip and her." Time to see if she could get a reaction. Crystal studied the target of her questioning.

Ryan's cheeks flushed a splotchy red and his knuckles tightened. "She did, did she? Well, she always did have a soft spot for the idiot. Philip may have seen

Gary for what he was, but Madeleine must have finally killed enough brain cells to believe the lies coming out of his mouth."

Crystal could see Ryan stewing in anger over this last subject as he finished with the final head of lettuce. Snatching up the knife where Crystal had lain it, he attacked the lettuce he'd just washed, whacking the blade with loud thunks into the cutting board below. Watching him, Crystal chose her next words with care.

"I was questioned by a Sheriff regarding Philip's death. I figured the whole situation was weird, since he died in an accident."

Ryan did not even lift his gaze. He sped up his knife work, intent on turning the lettuce into confetti.

"I shared everything I remembered from the night. What do you remember?" Crystal asked him.

"I think you should mind your own business," Alice slid in next to her husband.

"Excuse me?" Crystal acted befuddled.

"You've agitated my husband and are asking questions we already discussed with the Sheriff in charge of the investigation." Ice radiated from her, and she took a step closer to Crystal. "We're upset by the whole sad event, and now you come in here and reopen fresh wounds."

"I didn't mean anything," Crystal defended. "I was only talking to Ryan."

"Well, let's talk about the rain or the football game, shall we? This tragedy is hard enough to cope with. We don't need to mull over Philip's death."

"She said Madeleine plans on giving the firm to Gary," Ryan blurted.

"Who takes over the company is her choice."

Alice's tones were back to calculating as she pondered her husband's words. "We can, however, try to talk her out of it. Why don't you go help her before she slices her thumb off chopping onions?" Alice pointed over at Madeleine who was struggling with a monstrous chef's knife. Ryan nodded and left, leaving Crystal alone with a frosty faced Alice.

Crystal attempted to regain some control of the situation, "I didn't mean to upset your husband or you. I was passing the time while we worked."

"You meant to pass the time by asking leading questions regarding the possibility of us being implicated in Philip's murder? You meant to pass the time by ambushing a drunk woman and weaseling your way into her good graces? You meant to pass the time by angering my husband by telling him the goal we've worked so hard for our whole lives is going to be handed to an inferior colleague with an uncanny ability to kiss the ass of his superiors? You need better conversation topics to pass the time, Crystal."

Silence fell between the two women as they stared at each other. Crystal was the first to break her gaze. Alice gave her one last stern look and carried the lettuce bowls to the serving area.

"Are you ready for the crowd?" A wizened man in a mission apron walked up behind Crystal. "I haven't seen you here before. I'd be happy to show you what to do."

Crystal had been thinking of how to excuse herself from the whole situation, but couldn't think of a reason to turn down his helpful countenance. Instead, she thanked him and followed his lead to the service line.

"I'm going to place you here at the beginning.

Your pretty, smiling face is more welcoming than my wrinkled, old mug. Hand each person a plate and greet them. In the short time before we start, I'm going to have you wrap utensils in napkins that will get picked up at the end of the line." Crystal smiled at the compliment and set to preparing the silverware, placing each roll on a nearby stainless steel platter.

She had finished a large stack, when the same grandfatherly man walked into the middle of the room.

"Dinner is ready, everyone. Let us thank our servers and Calvert and Associates for the food today. Before we enjoy our bounty, I will ask you all to join me in saying grace."

Everyone fell quiet as the man led the room in a quick prayer. As he came to a close, the eager crowd began lining up. Another volunteer swept by her, scooped up the tray with her wrapped bundles and bustled it to the end of the line. Crystal stationed herself at the start, and thought of what to say. The first person approaching Crystal was a middle aged woman, towing two young boys by their hands.

"Hi everyone, how are you doing today?" Crystal asked.

"We're doing fine," the lady responded. "Dinner smells delicious."

"Thank you," the children chorused.

She handed them each a plate and they took the next step down the line. In the background, Alice and Ryan flanked Madeleine, talking to her simultaneously. Madeleine's face alternated between confused and irritated. She kept trying to speak, but every time she opened her mouth, Ryan and Alice talked over her.

The next person was a young man who mumbled a

quick thanks, wouldn't meet her eyes and shuffled down the line. However, the next three people all greeted her, and asked her name. On the whole, almost seventy people passed through the line. After everyone had their first serving, a few returned for seconds. The entire time, Ryan and Alice maintained their verbal assault on Madeleine, who became more red-faced and flustered as the meal went on.

After the last homeless man walked through a final time, the lead volunteer indicated they should haul the extra food to the back. Crystal grabbed a platter with a few broken taco shells remaining and carried it to the kitchen. The rest of the volunteers each followed her lead, carrying the remnants of the meal back to the prep area.

Like finches at a feeder, Ryan and Alice still clustered around Madeleine, keeping up a continuous chatter. Leaving her tray on a table, Crystal crept closer in an attempt to overhear.

"Remember the Polinsky account? That award-winning design was all Alice's," Ryan said.

"And do you remember the disaster at the Green Valley Academy? Gary's work. We had to redo the entire facade."

Madeleine hit her breaking point. With a quick heave, she lifted the serving container of diced tomatoes in her hands and slammed it down on the stainless-steel countertop. The loud crash silenced the room, including Ryan and Alice.

"Enough," Madeleine growled. "I don't need you two horseflies following me around and annoying me like this." She waved her hands in the air as if she were waving away imaginary buzzing insects.

"We want what's best for Calvert and Associates after Philip's untimely death," Alice soothed.

"You want what's best for you!" Madeleine's shouts echoed in the kitchen. "I'm beginning to think Crystal was right. Maybe you two did have something to do with Philip's death."

Alice and Ryan both whirled on Crystal, who was standing mere feet behind them. What an inopportune time for Madeleine to finally get her name correct.

"I didn't say you had anything to do with Philip's death," Crystal protested while the entire room stared.

Madeleine continued her rant, "First you kill him, and now you're attempting to bully me into giving you the company."

"Maybe you should leave us all alone," Alice said in a soft, angry tone to Crystal. "This isn't any of your affair."

"We didn't kill Philip," Ryan protested. "Sure we had a rocky relationship with the guy, but we aren't murderers."

"Methinks thou doth protest too much," Madeleine fired back. She plunged her hand into the leftover tomatoes in front of her and flung a fistful at Ryan and Alice. Crystal stepped out of the way, but some of the tomato flew over the intended targets and splattered her shoulder.

As Ryan and Alice wiped the mess from their faces, Madeleine started speaking in fierce and strident tones. "You are going to pay for what you did. I'm going to call the Sheriff's Office and then my lawyers. I'm going to tell them everything I know and make sure you both go to prison for a very, very long time."

Alice flicked tomato from her hands and glared at

Madeleine.

"Even if this wasn't all some horrible accident, who do you think has the most to gain from Philip's death?" Alice's voice remained the same level of calm, which was a sight to behold, considering she had tomato dripping from her cheek. Her eyes, however, burned with fury.

Crystal stopped brushing the chunks of tomato from her shirt as Alice let loose on Madeleine. "Gary knows he's your pet. With Philip out of the way, he was all but assured of getting the company."

"But he was with me looking for Philip," Madeleine protested.

"You were on your third bottle of wine, Madeleine. Gary was the one who woke you up. Not a single person knows what he was doing prior. Seems to me, he woke you up to establish an alibi."

Madeleine burst into tears. She started sobbing into her tomato covered hands as a dozen people stared on at the uncomfortable scene.

Ryan hesitated and took a step forward as if to comfort her, when Madeleine dropped her hands and let out a shriek of rage. She seized the stainless-steel pan holding the remnants of taco shells, and flung it at Alice with all of her might. The pan struck Alice's head with a thunderous clang, sending her sprawling onto the ground with the platter on top of her.

Several volunteers ran to restrain Madeleine as she grabbed for the metal bowl with the last of the shredded cheese. Ryan was on his knee next to Alice in an instant, inspecting the blood streaming from her temple. Grabbing a roll of paper towels from a nearby countertop, he shouted at the volunteers holding

Madeleine. "Get this drunk a cab and get her out of here." He yanked several towels from the roll and pressed it to his wife's forehead.

Madeleine let herself be led from the room, tears still streaming from her face. The fight had fled from her.

Crystal could tell this was an opportune time for her to leave, as well. This day had given her a lot to ponder, but there wasn't anything else to be learned, and she was most certainly not welcome.

With as much stealth as she could manage, she grabbed her coat and slipped out the back door. Everyone was focused on Alice and Madeleine and not paying any attention to her.

She caught herself looking for her car when she spotted the Porsche Cayenne. She had handed the keys back to Madeleine when they arrived, and now was stuck downtown with her car on Mercer Island.

Sighing, she called Olivia.

"Hey, Crys," her friend greeted. "I headed over to my mom's to help her take down her Christmas lights after you texted me. Mom has to leave for water aerobics soon, so your timing is impeccable. Are you ready to get together?"

"In a manner of speaking. Can you pick me up in front of the aquarium on the waterfront?" Crystal spotted Ryan poking his head out of the mission to look around. She ducked into a doorway.

"Aquarium? Aren't you at the mission?"

Ryan, not seeing anything, gave up and turned back inside.

"It's been another weird day. I'm walking there now."

"I can't wait to hear everything. Your life is so much more interesting since you quit your job. You're like my own personal soap opera. I'll be there in ten minutes."

Crystal made her way down the hill to the waterfront. She weaved her way through the crowd of families streaming in the direction of the aquarium and spotted an unoccupied bench. Weary, she sat down and composed herself after the day's excitement.

Several minutes later, Olivia's Volkswagen Beetle pulled up in front of her. Crystal climbed in, thrilled to see a friendly face.

"Do you have blood on your neck?" Olivia asked.

Crystal glanced in the visor mirror, "It's tomato. There was an incident at the mission."

"It must have been quite an incident if you had to look in a mirror to check whether it's tomato or blood." Olivia's cheekiness was already lightening her mood. After a quick glance over her shoulder, her friend slipped into traffic.

"It was eventful, but I typically don't go wandering around with blood on me."

"Well, the last time you were in a place I wasn't expecting you, someone ended up dead. You can't blame me for jumping to conclusions."

Crystal laughed. "You're right about one thing. My life has become a lot more interesting in the last couple of weeks. Can you drive us to Mercer Island?"

"Mercer Island? Why are we going there?"

Crystal took in a deep breath and exhaled. "My car is there. I'll explain on the way."

****

By the time they made it to Madeleine's house,

Crystal had broken down the day's events to Olivia.

"Park out on the street. I don't know if her cab beat us back here, and I am *not* interested in dealing with any more of her crazy today."

"I'll wait here so you can follow me to a place I know. There is so much more I want to ask you."

Crystal hopped out of the Beetle and trotted to her Honda. Several lights were on in the house, but she couldn't remember if they had been on when Madeleine and she had left.

Jumping in her car, she winced at the high pitched whine which now accompanied every turn of the key in the ignition. Not waiting to see if anyone was peeking out of the windows, Crystal shot from the driveway and followed Olivia's flower taillight covers through the twisting streets of Mercer Island. Bare maple trees and evergreens crowded the road, making her feel as if she were back in the forest.

Ten minutes later, Olivia stopped in front of what appeared to be an old hotel. A weathered hand carved oval sign declared it to be the Roanoke Inn and Tavern.

Parking beside her friend, she climbed out of her car. "What is this place?"

"It's the Roanoke Inn. It's famous." Olivia flourished a hand at the building.

"Why?" Crystal asked as they passed under the awning covered entryway. A large porch in the front, hidden by shrubs, had a dozen people gathered around tables, chattering and laughing. Half drunk beers and plates of food sat in front of them as space heaters kept back the worst of the winter's chill. The place gave off a comfortable vibe, and the nervousness constantly keeping her on edge eased as they crossed through the front door.

Inside was dim, but the cheerful buzz and the feel of time and history permeated the room. A fireplace crackled in the center of it all, and a bar lined the right side of the room.

Two men were just leaving the table in front of the fire and Olivia pounced on the opportunity. Crystal sat opposite her and the ambient warmth of the fire further eased the tension from her knotted muscles better than any masseuse ever could.

Having secured a table, Olivia continued. "This place started as an inn in the 1910s. A ferry used to dock somewhere over there, before the floating bridge." She pointed over Crystal's shoulder in the direction of the freeway.

Now, since Olivia had brought it to her attention, the place did have the feel of an inn. A hallway led away from the main room that they were sitting in, and Crystal could spot small rooms full of tables where people gathered for a Sunday dinner.

"The business struggled, since there was no real reason to come to Mercer Island back in the day. Rumors say it became a whore house and a speakeasy during the roaring 20s." Olivia leaned forward, enjoying retelling the salacious history. "It has morphed into this place, the local tavern for Mercer Islanders and an awesome place for us non-locals who have discovered it."

"Well, I think it's great," Crystal declared, looking around.

"Enough of the history lesson. You've spilled on today's zaniness, but what the heck happened with Georgia? And Conner?" She wiggled her eyebrows at

Crystal.

"May I get you something to drink?" a smooth masculine voice caused Crystal to turn around. Tall and lanky, a dark haired waiter stepped up to their table. He gave a perfunctory smile at Crystal's smudged face and tomato stained outfit. However, when his eyes fastened on Olivia his grin brightened by a thousand watts.

"Can I get an IPA?" Crystal asked with as much dignity as she could salvage. She wasn't this unkempt as a general rule, but didn't know how to convey it without saying, "I don't usually spend my day rolling around in taco fixings."

"Of course, and for you?" he asked Olivia.

"Same for me, please," she answered with a look to match their waiter's.

"My name is Luke. If you need anything else, please don't hesitate to ask. I'll be back with your drinks and to take your order, shortly." He grinned at Olivia again and headed back to the bar to place their order.

"Anyway, like the state's nickname, Georgia is a peach," Crystal said. "Once I got her talking, she was happy to chat. We had tea and cookies, and she revealed all sorts of Calvert and Associates gossip. She tries to get along with everyone and avoid trouble, but it isn't the easiest thing to do when you have as much drama in your workplace as she does."

"I must say the drama factor is pretty darned high. They're worse than Smith, Axford, and Devry. First, Georgia's boss was murdered. Now her other boss hit one of the employees in the head with a metal tray. I can't believe they behave this way in front of strangers. I wonder what it's like in their offices Monday through

Friday."

"I can't imagine," Crystal answered. "I'm still no closer to figuring out who did this, though. Georgia seems to be out of the mix, and Madeleine seems upset to the core with her husband's death. Ryan and Alice might have had something to do with it, but I don't know anything for sure."

"It seems like you need to keep investigating," Olivia said.

"I do. I think Gary is the next person I need to talk to. Alice was right when she said he has the best motive. He was Madeleine's obvious choice when Philip died to take over the company. It gives him a strong incentive to eliminate his boss."

"Is this company even worth it? The buildings they design are spectacular, but does it merit murder, misery, and working with people you hate? Why not join another firm, or start your own?" Olivia asked.

Luke returned, placed their beers in front of them, and took their matching orders for cheeseburgers and fries. In college, Crystal had never liked the taste of the beer served at the parties she had attended. Over time, she had learned to appreciate many of Seattle's quality microbrews. When she indulged in a drink, she preferred wine, but somedays a beer was simply necessary. She took a sip and the crisp citrus bite of the hops hit the spot. After today's craziness, she needed a drink. "They all seem to think it's worth it. Their firm has an amazing reputation. They don't have to look for work. It's delivered to them by people with majestic dreams and piles of money. They get all of the elite projects in the city, and none of them seem the least inclined to give it up."

"We did see multiple awards on their web site for the buildings they've designed. I guess prestige beats happiness for them," Olivia took a sip of her beer. "But enough murdering architects and vengeful wife gossip. Spill on your date with Conner. I've waited long enough to hear the details." Luke laid two burgers in front of them as they continued to chat.

"It was incredible." Shoving all further consideration of Calvert and Associates to the back of her mind, Crystal recounted for her friend the walk around Green Lake, the play, the dinner, and of course, the grand finale, the kiss in the snow. The happy memories helped Crystal forget the crisis in her life revolving around the murder of Philip Calvert.

Luke sauntered back and asked how they were doing.

"My friend here just got a new job as a wilderness guide, but some jerk died on her first snowshoe hike, so she might have to quit to pay her bills. If she can even find another job. Other than that, we're good." Olivia delivered the saga of Crystal's life with her unending cheerfulness.

"Oh, hey, that's rough," Luke agreed, taking the seat next to Olivia. "I've been trying to get a new job for several months, now. I'm a graphic designer."

"Really?" Olivia asked. "Graphic design is so cool. Have you done anything I would know?"

"Not unless you follow my friend's band, The Geoducks. I designed their logo and album covers. I'm still looking for my first job in the field. I finished school a few months ago and have been working here to pay the bills."

An older waiter waved at Luke from across the

room to get his attention. Luke held out his finger to signify he would be one more second.

"I've got to get back to work. The guy waving at me is my boss, and he doesn't believe in chit-chatting with the customers," Luke said with a slight smile. He jotted a few things down on his pad and placed it face down in front of Olivia. He wished them a good night and walked to the front of the restaurant to greet a couple who had walked in.

Olivia turned the check over.

On me, (202) 555-0165 ~Luke

Olivia grinned. "Who do you think he meant this for?"

"You, dummy." Crystal smiled, happy to focus on something as normal as her friend getting a guy's number. "I'm a complete mess, and he's been checking you out since we sat down at our table."

Olivia's smile broadened, and she tucked the note into her purse. "I might call him," she gave a demure grin, but her eyes twinkled.

"You better. You have to admit, it was nice of him to pick up the check, and not a bad move." Crystal winked. "He's the most normal guy to give you the time of day in months."

Despite their dinner ending on a high note, Crystal felt the pressure of her investigation jumping back to the forefront of her mind. The employees of Calvert and Associates knew something that they weren't sharing. If she were lucky, Gary would be the one to talk.

Chapter Fourteen

Crystal had the early shift and helped open the store for the first time. She spent her day doing her best to stock shelves and help customers, but her mind was on how to approach Gary.

At a loss, she used her phone to search for him on her lunch break, and found he had a Facebook page. Among the hundreds of selfies he had taken with friends, various vacation photos, and pictures of buildings he had designed, were religious check-ins at Atlas Fitness every evening. Her sister, Heather, had a membership there and Crystal sent her a quick text asking if she could use her club number.

Heather's text back explained that she had a friend, Abby, who worked at the counter, and Crystal could ask her for a day pass to check out the gym.

With the beginnings of her plan in mind, Crystal was able to better focus on work. She had Gary's home address, but approaching a single man who happened to be a suspected murderer, in his house without witnesses, was way too reckless, even in her book.

When her shift ended at three o'clock, she waved goodbye to her co-workers and raced home. Changing into her workout clothes, she drove her car to Atlas Fitness. As she walked through the front door, a man and woman greeted her from behind the counter.

She approached the woman. "Abby?"

"You must be Crystal. Heather said you would be stopping by, and that you wanted to check the place out." The guy lost interest and started fiddling with his phone while Abby gave Crystal a tour of the gym. Wishing her a good workout, Abby left her among a sea of elliptical machines and sweating people. Crystal made her way back toward the entrance of the gym, climbed on an exercise bike and began pedaling.

Checking a clock on the wall, she noted it was half past four. According to his Facebook page, Gary should be there anytime within the next hour. She paced herself with a low resistance and put in ear buds to blend in. Thirty minutes passed, and no sign of Gary. She kept peddling and looking. The clock on the wall struck half past five. She hadn't seen any time later than this on his Facebook page, but she wasn't ready to give up, yet. However, even with her slow pace, Crystal could feel her muscles tiring. She knocked the resistance down to the easiest level and marshaled herself to keep peddling. After thirty more minutes, Crystal was defeated. It was time to give up and try again tomorrow. She wasn't sure how she could manage to get in the gym again without buying a membership, but maybe Heather could appeal to her friend, Abby. She began to extract her foot from the pedal strap, when Gary strode in through the front door. She shoved her foot back in the pedal and began pumping her legs. A woman, ready to jump on Crystal's exercise bike, gave a disgusted snort and wandered off to find a free machine.

He checked in at the front desk, and then on his phone's Facebook page. Crystal sat up straight to get him to notice her. It would be best if he spotted her first, and not vice versa. The meeting would seem more natural if it were a chance encounter in Gary's eyes.

Unfortunately, he was looking down at his phone while simultaneously struggling to untangle his head phones. He walked right by Crystal without even glancing up. He untangled the cords and situated himself on a stair master overlooking the weight lifting area.

Crystal climbed off her bike, her legs wobbling. Making her way to the weight section, she set herself up in front of Gary. She had never lifted weights in her life, so she glanced around to see what to do. Spotting another woman her age, Crystal observed as she hefted two hand weights up and over her head.

Grabbing a similar set of weights, she positioned herself in Gary's direct line of vision, and began lifting. After almost dropping the weights with the first lift, she realized she had grossly overestimated her strength in relation to the woman she was imitating. She swapped her weights for lighter ones, all the while doing her best to stand out. She did a few shoulder presses, and then windmilled her arms in imitation of a stretch. She sneaked a peek, but Gary was fixated on his phone's screen as he churned away at the stairs.

Crystal was getting annoyed, and the workout flushing her face was compounded by embarrassment at her foolishness. After fifteen minutes of trying to catch his attention, a curvy blonde strode into the weight area, clad only in a sports bra and leggings. She did one stretch and Gary's beady eyes shot up from the screen he had been staring at. He ogled the woman doing lunges for a second, before his eyes drifted to Crystal and widened in recognition.

"Whatever works," she muttered under her breath. She was a little upset he hadn't been checking her out and also a little disgusted that he was the type of creep staring at girls in the gym while they exercised. Rather than go too deep down that mental rabbit hole, Crystal gave a little wave. She headed to the area near the front, set aside for stretching. A smoothie bar was adjacent to the space, where the guy from the front counter was now running a blender.

Sure enough, Gary followed her back.

"Crystal, right?"

"Gary," she said with false enthusiasm. "How are you doing? How have you been handling your recent loss?"

"Loss? Oh, yeah. Philip. Very sad." He dropped his expression into one of solemnity for a second before brightening. "Your name was mentioned at the office today, by Alice, and not in a flattering way. I asked myself, why would my coworker be talking about our guide from the other weekend? And then voilá, here you are."

"I know, right? Kismet. Did you ask Alice why she was talking about me?" She needed to probe a little to determine if her cover had been blown.

"Alice and I don't talk to each other, if we can help it. Professional differences, personality differences…if there is a difference, we have it."

Crystal wasn't sure if Gary was hiding anything he had overheard, so she sketched a bare bones version of the truth. "I headed over to pay my condolences to Madeleine on Sunday and ended up driving her to the mission."

"Where you, of course, would have run into Ryan

and Alice. Those two goodie two-shoes have been volunteering there for years. What caused Alice to speak your name in vain?" he leaned forward, falling into a stretch to get closer.

Crystal crossed her own arm in front of her, stretching her shoulder. "I shared with her the same thing Madeleine told me earlier. The company was going to be handed over to you."

"I knew it! There was no way Alice and Ryan were getting the company. I'm sure Alice was fit to be tied. No wonder she was pissed off at you, shooting the messenger and all." Gary had a huge grin on his face. He waved at the guy working the smoothie bar counter, "Two banana-acai with protein boost. I'm buying." He turned his attention back to Crystal. "Tell me everything. What did they do after they got that bit of news to choke on?"

"They followed Madeleine around the entire time, trying to persuade her they deserved to be the ones to take over the firm, not you."

"I bet they did. Losers."

"Then they tried to convince Madeleine you had the most to gain from Philip's death and were therefore the most likely suspect in his murder."

Gary drew back in surprise. "Murder? He drove a snowmobile off a cliff."

"A Sheriff wouldn't be asking questions if it weren't a little bit suspicious," Crystal remarked.

Gary would have been a terrible poker player. His face fluctuated from gleeful to worried. "Alice must be desperate," he said after regaining his composure.

"Madeleine seems to think so, too. In fact, she hinted they may have had something to do with Philip's death. She threatened to expose Alice and Ryan to the Sheriff, and planned to turn her lawyers loose on them."

"Yes!" Gary punched his fist in the air. "I knew I could count on her."

"Do you think they could have had anything to do with it?" Crystal asked. She acted distracted, falling into a runner's lunge, but listened with keen anticipation.

"Totally. Philip despised Ryan and Alice. When he got into some trouble years ago, they testified against him in court. I testified on his behalf. Anyway, after the trial, he couldn't legally fire them since they fell under some sort of whistle-blower protection law, so they continued to tolerate each other for years."

"Did they have it in them to kill him, though?"

"Probably not. They have always been a pair of wimps when the going got rough."

"Do you remember anything from the night Philip died?" Crystal asked, stretching for her toes.

"Not much. I drank with Madeleine for quite a while, called it a night, and crashed in my room. I swear the woman drinks more than my frat brothers did twenty years ago. I must have fallen asleep. Well, if I'm being honest, I passed out. The next thing I remember hearing was the sound of a snowmobile taking off. I thought it was weird, so I got up to see what was happening. Everyone was racing in and out of rooms, carrying on about Philip leaving. I woke Madeleine, and we headed out to go look for him."

"Ryan and Alice seem to have a motive for killing him. Do you think Justin, Bree, or Georgia could have had anything to do with it?"

"Georgia? No way. She had nothing to gain, and

she was wallpaper to Philip. He thought of her as much as he thought of his copy machine. Necessary to make the office run efficiently. Justin wouldn't have done it, either. He's a lot younger and joined the firm long after the court case. Bree's our next dumb, pretty intern, which were the only qualifications Philip looked for when he selected them."

Their two smoothies were delivered to the bar, and Gary fetched them, breaking the line of questioning. Returning to Crystal, he had already dismissed the notion of Philip perishing at the hands of a coworker. "Tell me what happened yesterday afternoon at the mission. I want to hear everything." With a wolfish grin, he handed her one of the two smoothies.

Crystal regaled him with a detailed account. Gary hung on every word, all pretense of stretching gone. When she recounted the tomatoes and the serving pan being flung at Alice, Gary chortled.

"Do you think you'll get the firm?" Crystal asked after her story. Gary was a clear attention seeker, and needed to have his ego stroked to keep him talking. This question was sure to do it.

"I can't see why not. It's all in Madeleine's hands now, and she'll support me. She hates Ryan and Alice, now more than ever, and Justin is too new. I'm the only choice."

"What was the issue you testified about on Philip's behalf, long ago?"

"Nothing big. One of his bimbo interns accused him of sexual assault. I testified I had seen no such behavior, but that I had seen the intern flirt with Philip. I said she was trying to get a permanent position with the company and when Philip shot her down, she must have made up the charges for a payday."

"Ryan and Alice testified against him?" Crystal did her best to put incredulity into her voice. However, having seen how creepy Philip had acted toward Bree, it was tough to muster up the correct tone.

Gary sipped at his smoothie and smirked, savoring the memory. "They sure did testify against him. They fabricated a bunch of stuff, saying Philip harassed the girl. Philip's lawyers were amazing. They got it all thrown out on some technicality. Philip was exonerated, the intern left, and Ryan and Alice ended up in Philip's doghouse."

Crystal tasted her smoothie, too, and was pleased by the simultaneous tart and sweet flavors that were surprisingly refreshing after her workout.

"So Madeleine believed her husband." Crystal sipped her drink with nonchalance, doing her utmost to appear interested, but not too interested.

"I don't know if that is true in the strictest sense. She couldn't deny the affairs. Several interns slept with Philip over the years and were found out. I think they even had to pay one off. The time and stress of it all began to break her. In public, she always blamed the interns and not her husband. It worked out well for Philip. He sleeps with young hotties, his wife accuses them and fires them. Love is so damned blind."

"She never blamed Philip?"

"I think she did deep down, but she slipped into a state of denial she couldn't get out of. She drank more booze and more often. After a decade of marinating her brain, I don't think she can tell reality from her imagination anymore."

"It's sad." Crystal's heart ached for the widowed

woman.

"Sure is, but it's worked out great for me. I'm going to make millions. I can see my face on Architectural Digest already." He framed an imaginary magazine in the air by forming a box with his thumbs and index fingers.

"What are your thoughts on Alice's theory that you had the most to gain from Philip's death? Based on my understanding, she wasn't far off the mark."

Gary clenched his fists. "First, I had nothing to do with it. Second, let's see her prove it."

"Do you think Philip approached Bree like he did the other interns?"

"On the record, I say she approached him. Off the record, he was all over her like he was with all of the other interns. I'm sure he planned the retreat as a way to land her before retiring." Gary snorted at the thought. "I think he liked the challenge of doing it right under his wife's nose."

"It sounds like a pretty awful place to work." Crystal was aghast.

"Not at all. Calvert and Associates is where careers are made. You put this company on your résumé and you get your foot in the door of every architectural firm in America. Employers will fight for you to come work for them. As an intern, you had to put up with Philip's grabby hands and constant stares, but you were set for life."

"Do you think Justin and Bree have something going on?"

"Huh, I never noticed. Maybe."

Crystal didn't see a way to get any more information from Gary, so she started the process of extricating herself from the conversation.

"It was nice seeing you again, Gary. I hope this whole horrible situation is laid to rest soon, for all of you."

"Yeah, me too," he said in a distracted tone. "What do you think of Wembly and Associates?"

"Excuse me?"

"I wouldn't change the name of the company right away. I don't want to be gauche. I'd wait an appropriate amount of time. Maybe a year."

"Don't get too ahead of yourself. Madeleine doesn't seem stable, and Ryan and Alice have filled her head with conspiracy theories."

"Good point, but now I know what's going on, so I can control it. I'll talk to Ryan and Alice at work tomorrow and get them to shut up."

"Try not to bring me up. I don't need Alice hating me any more than she already does." In truth, Crystal didn't want her suspects talking to each other. If they started comparing notes regarding her snooping, it would make it harder to keep questioning them.

"Sure, sure," he said, once again not paying attention. "Hey, if you want to go out, give me a ring sometime. I'm going to be a wealthy man, soon. We'll have a great time. Hand me your phone and I'll add my name to your contacts."

"My boyfriend wouldn't like it if I went out with you," Crystal demurred.

She had used a fictitious boyfriend in the past to turn down unwanted advances, but now she envisioned Conner in the role.

This statement didn't slow Gary down, "Of course you shouldn't tell your boyfriend. Him knowing would ruin the fun."

"I'll keep it in mind," Crystal attempted a smile, but inside she was gagging. She typed in her password and handed her phone over. He punched in his digits and handed it back with a leer.

"Don't forget to give me a ring," Gary called out as Crystal left the gym.

Chapter Fifteen

Shuffling across her kitchen, Crystal was reminded of how much she had overdone it at the gym the previous evening. Her aching shoulders protested that she was not a weightlifter, and were giving her fair warning they were going to rebel if she continued lifting heavy objects anytime soon.

Grabbing her phone after pressing the start button on the coffee maker, Crystal groaned at a text from her mother.

—*I talked to my friend Linda, since the guide thing isn't working out. Her company is hiring an accountant. Isn't that wonderful news?*

There were so many things wrong with this text, she didn't know where to begin. Determined not to start any drama with her mother by sending back an indignant reply, Crystal opted to ignore the text. The fact that her own mother didn't have an inkling as to what her former job had entailed confirmed to Crystal how right she had been to switch her career. She meant well, but had always advised her daughters to take the path most traveled.

Her mood buoyed when she saw another text, this one from Conner.

—*How's the investigation going, Nancy Drew?*

—*Almost cracked, smart guy. We'll be out guiding before you know it.* This wasn't true, but being flippant was better than saying she still had no idea what had happened.

Her coffee finished brewing, and she made herself two pieces of toast to go with it.

Nibbling on breakfast, Crystal pondered her next step. She couldn't think of a way to approach Justin in a safe manner. She tried the Facebook trick like she'd done with Gary, but hadn't been able to locate a page for him. Either he didn't have one, or kept it private. Which left Bree. Bree had been shy and peaceful the entire trip to the chalet, so it appeared safe to approach her. Crystal checked the address she had for her, an apartment building in the U-district, an area of Seattle which took its name from its proximity to the University of Washington.

Since it was a Tuesday, she had to bide her time until after the workday ended. Waiting for the light of day on the weekend, like she had done with Georgia, seemed prudent, but twenty year old women didn't often hang out at their apartments waiting for social calls on weekends and Crystal didn't have forever to get to the bottom of Philip's murder, so tonight was the night. To keep her mind occupied, she opened Bree's Facebook page to see if there was anything useful for her upcoming questioning.

Bree's page was public, and Crystal browsed through the posts. It consisted of pictures she would expect from someone recently graduated from college. Selfies in front of the famous cherry blossom trees on campus and with her friends out on the town. Pictures of her family, but only one with Justin, pressed cheek to cheek, from the snowshoe hike. Crystal was startled to remember she had taken this particular photo of them.

Bree had also set her relationship status on Facebook to "It's complicated." Crystal didn't need to be Sherlock Holmes to solve that mystery.

It also showed Bree volunteering at the U-district PAWS cat adoption center and singing in a church choir. This made Crystal feel a lot better approaching her. A cat-saving, church-choir attending individual shouldn't be a threat to her safety, even if Crystal showed up unannounced at her apartment.

Crystal whiled away the day running a few errands to get cat food and restock her own pantry. Conscious of her budget, she had to harken back to her college days to remember some of the cheap eats she had made back then. Macaroni and cheese, spaghetti, and Top Ramen now graced her pantry. If she was going to eke out another month's mortgage payment, every dollar was going to be needed.

Six o'clock rolled around, and Crystal left her condo, heading out into the standard seasonal cold rain.

She weaved her way through rush hour traffic and parked outside a small apartment complex with a dozen units. The address she had swiped from Emerald City Outfitters told her Bree lived in unit 204. She dashed through the rain and leaned on the buzzer on the outside of the building. She waited thirty-seconds, and tried once more. Again, no answer.

Crystal retreated to a nearby coffee shop, ordered a chai tea, and nursed it for an hour, while the rain continued its relentless onslaught outside. Finally, she left the warmth of the coffee shop and dashed back through the storm to try the buzzer again. Still, no answer. A young man in a UW baseball cap with a laptop bag slung over his shoulder flung open the front door on his way out. Spotting her, he held the door open saying, "I'm not supposed to let strangers in, but you look trustworthy."

Crystal slipped inside the door, thanked him, and made her way up to Bree's apartment. She banged on the door, called out Bree's name and waited. No answer.

Deflated, Crystal gave up. She made her way back through the downpour and unlocked her car. Climbing in, helplessness overwhelmed her. She was scheduled to work the next two evening shifts with the closing crew, so she couldn't talk to Bree until Friday night. The probability of Bree sitting alone in her apartment as the weekend began, didn't seem likely.

Crystal sighed, feeling defeated. She turned the ignition, but nothing happened. A clicking noise from under the hood responded, but the engine refused to turn over. Her anger boiling, she kept cranking the key, over and over. After a couple of tries, her car choked to life.

She merged into traffic and turned toward home. Her investigation was going nowhere. She hadn't eliminated anyone from suspicion except Georgia, the kind, elderly office manager. Maybe, it was time to give up on this dream and start looking for another job.

In the midst of contemplating a new future, Crystal was surprised when hot tears began rolling down her face. She dabbed at them with furious swipes of her sleeves. Between the rain and her crying, she was finding it hard to see the road. She attempted to compose herself, but couldn't help feeling like a life she hadn't even had a chance to live was being stolen from her. With a quick yank of the steering wheel, she steered her car into a fast food parking lot, and let the sorrow of it all wash over her. She wanted to leave the dead end office life behind, but it was the only thing for which she was qualified. How hard was it to fake being an accountant? She had faked being a guide, after all. She sighed. Math had never been her strong suit. She had received several Cs in her mandatory classes, and had been an English major for a reason. It left her feeling useless and trapped. Her skills weren't worth much in the job market, and she didn't know where to turn to make herself happy. Her own mother couldn't even specify what she'd done her whole life, because it was so boring, monotonous, and mundane.

For the brief moment she had been a wilderness guide, her self-esteem had skyrocketed. She had shared with her friends and family what she did, and they understood. Her father was proud of her. Olivia was happy for her. Her mother may not be supportive of her new career, but at least she knew what Crystal did on a daily basis. She was no longer a pointless cog in a corporate machine.

Then, there was Conner. She liked him and was confident he liked her in turn. However, if she returned to the office world, he wouldn't be happy with that listless version of her. The old Crystal was unhappy, angry, and miserable with the life choices that had landed her in a mundane job. Inevitably, he would drift away, and the nicest guy she had ever gone on a date with would fade from her life.

Crystal sobbed in her car as her new fulfilling life left her grasp. Anger and resentment boiled in her stomach, and an amazing amount of fury swelled inside her for the entirety of Calvert and Associates as she considered each of them. Horrible Philip, who had been so detestable one of his coworkers had killed him. Madeleine, the manic drunk, who couldn't control herself, much less her awful husband. Calculating Alice, with her frosty glares and cold shoulders. Bumbling and angry Ryan, who couldn't seem to do anything right. Obnoxious and misogynistic Gary, the next Philip in the making, in both position and attitude. Stupid Bree, who wasn't home tonight. And Justin, who she didn't know how to confront. It was because of them she would be losing her job, her new way of life, and her new boyfriend.

Her sobbing eased and she tugged her sleeve over the heel of her hand to dab at the tears. The heartache refused to let go of its grip on her lungs and her inhale shuddered as she forced herself to take deep and calming breaths. Leaning back against the headrest, she closed her eyes, attempting to come to grips with the pain. She embraced the reality of the situation. Being a wilderness guide wasn't meant to be. She would have to quit her new job and go back to being an office assistant. This would lead to her losing her condo as she struggled to get her feet under her. Conner and her worlds would drift apart. This was setting her life back six years to when she had been a recent college graduate, unemployed and living with her parents

She was startled by a new feeling welling deep inside. A sizzling spark seized hold and her spirit fanned it to a flame; keep digging, keep fighting. She wasn't willing to accept any of these failures. Crystal's tears dried in the heat of her resolve, and her mind centered around the one person who had information regarding the fateful night, but she hadn't had the courage to face. Justin. It wasn't safe to visit him alone in his home, but she wasn't willing to resign herself to her old life. She had one stone left to turn, and she had to do it. Letting fear rule her now would cause her to wander through the rest of her life wondering "What if?"

She opened up her phone to where she had Justin's address. Her GPS app informed her he lived fifteen minutes away on Beacon Hill. She found some leftover napkins in her glove box, dabbed her remaining tears, and blew her nose.

With new resolve, Crystal merged back into traffic and worked her way across town to Beacon Hill. She drove by Justin's small home, parked half a block away in the first open spot, and admired the expansive views of downtown. Even through the rainstorm, the lights of Seattle filled her vision and she took a moment to drink them all in. She gnawed on her lower lip, second-guessing the wisdom of this plan as Conner's warning to be careful rang in her mind. After a second of contemplation, she stopped doubting. The safe avenues to get her life back on track had all turned out to be dead-ends. This last path was more dangerous than the others, but it was all there was left to try. If this risk wasn't taken, she was on a crash course to failure. As a precaution, she sent a quick text to Olivia—*I'm at 312 Beacon Ave. If I don't text back in an hour, send help.* It wasn't much, but at least it was something. She could imagine her mother saying, "At least we'll know where to find your body" in response to her foolhardiness and smiled to herself.

Crystal flipped the hood of her jacket over her head and dashed out of her car. She stepped through the beating rain, passing in and out of the light cast by several street lamps, making her way down the block to Justin's place.

An older Toyota parked in the driveway told her he must be home.

A black wrought iron fence, and no outdoor lighting, made the house forbidding and dangerous. She undid the latch of the gate and walked over a cracked concrete walkway to the front door.

In the daylight, Crystal could tell Justin's home would appear cozy and comfortable. However, in the dark and rain, her paranoia told her eyes could be watching from every shadowed corner.

Taking a deep breath, she stepped up to the front door and knocked.

The door was flung open and Crystal was stunned to see Bree. The two women stared at each other, both startled.

"I was expecting Chinese food," Bree said, shuffling her feet.

"Umm, I don't have any," Crystal said. "Can I come in?"

A car slid to a halt in the wet street with a decal stating it was from "Khoi's Chinese Garden". The car's flashers began blinking and a young Asian man bolted from the car, two white bags in his hands.

"Hello, did you order from Khoi's?"

"I did," Bree answered.

He handed the food to Crystal and the bill to Bree. He took Bree's credit card and swiped it through a small reader fastened to his phone. He spun the phone for Bree to sign then dashed back through the downpour to his car.

Bree looked at Crystal holding her dinner and waved her inside.

Crystal spoke first. "I was looking to talk to Justin as well. Is he here?"

"Not yet. He's working late tonight," Bree answered.

Crystal placed the bags on the table and Bree called back from the kitchen. "Are you hungry? I ordered Kung Pao chicken for myself, but they always send way too much. There is plenty to share."

Crystal had been trying to ignore the scents wafting from the bags she had been carrying. She hadn't eaten dinner, and her stomach rumbled at the prospect of a meal.

"That would be nice," Crystal said. She didn't remember reading any tips on the internet about how to interrogate people over dinner, but her hunger insisted she wing it.

Bree returned with a couple of plates and forks and set them on the table. She also handed a cup of hot tea to Crystal.

"I always make some tea when I order Chinese takeout. They give it to you when you sit down in the restaurant, and I can't imagine not having the two together."

Crystal thanked her. This was not going as she had envisioned, at all. She was having a hard time establishing an upper hand in this interrogation situation, when her suspect was handing her hot tea and Kung Pao chicken with impeccable hospitality. Still, she needed to get the ball rolling if she were to learn anything from this meeting.

"Are you and Justin dating?" she asked.

Bree dumped the chicken and a side of rice onto each plate before answering. "We are, but we're trying to keep it from our co-workers."

"Hiding how you feel has to be awkward."

"Totally. It's hard to have a relationship and hide it forty hours a week. Only talking business at work, driving separate cars, and no social media updates. Are you seeing anyone?"

Crystal was a little taken aback. Bree was acting like they were two girlfriends chatting over dinner. She chose to gloss over the question and hit her back with another.

"I'm starting to see someone. Why do you have to hide it from people at work?"

"Do you work with the guy you're dating?"

"I do."

"Do *you* hide it?" Bree answered in turn.

"It's only been one date, and I suppose we're not hiding it. We haven't considered the pitfalls of mixing dating and work together."

"Justin and I have to keep it a secret. It's not against company policy or anything, but Justin keeps saying it's for the best."

"I'm pretty sure everyone knows," Crystal informed her. "I figured it out during our short snowshoe hike."

"Good," Bree snapped. "I hope everyone does."

"Why do you have to cover up that you are seeing each other?" Crystal asked again.

"Office politics, or so Justin says. You wouldn't understand," Bree waved her hand.

"Try me," Crystal gave a knowing look. "Does it have something to do with Philip?"

Startled by her knowledge, Bree sat up and nodded. "Justin warned me when I started. He said Philip likes to go after the interns. If he and I were openly dating, he was positive Philip would fire me so he could hire a more available girl."

"You stuck around after you learned the boss was so awful?" Crystal was aghast.

"This was my big chance. All I had to do was keep my boss's hands off of me, and I would have a résumé giving me a crack at any job opportunity I wanted. As an architect, it's easy to find yourself unemployed if the economy turns ugly, or end up designing piddly little jobs with bad pay."

"How did keeping Philip's hands off of you work out?"

"Umm...ok." She peered down at her hands.

"I know he was a monster. From what I've gathered, it sounds like he passed lecherous looks and inappropriate touching long ago. There was even a court case and a settlement based on sexual assault by at least one previous intern."

Bree was taken aback by Crystal's grasp of Philip's darker side.

"Justin warned me, but I didn't believe him. I figured Philip was a run-of-the-mill dirty old man. He gave me a lot of looks, and there was the occasional inappropriate comment, but nothing I couldn't handle."

"Was Justin right? Did it turn into something worse?" Crystal hated turning the screws on someone as likable as this, but she could tell Bree was holding back information.

"No, never." Bree's voice trembled.

"Do you want to get into what happened the night

Philip died?" Crystal tried a different avenue.

"I guess," Bree whispered. She sat motionless at the table, staring at her fingers intertwined before her. Their dinner laid on the plates, forgotten and growing cold. A thrill of excitement coursed through Crystal. Bree was holding something back, and if Crystal could play this right, she could get Bree to spill everything.

Taking a moment to compose herself, Bree spoke. "After you headed downstairs, we all had a toast to the completion of the new university building. We ate dinner together and the whole company was civil with one another, if you can believe it. Everyone even laughed some. It was the happiest I've ever seen them together."

"Philip, too?" Crystal interjected.

"Oh, yeah," Bree answered. "Philip most of all. He was enjoying the whole night, telling stories about starting out and cracking jokes at everyone's expense. He kept staring at me, though. Every time he did, Madeleine would glare at both of us. She would have tossed me out in the snow if she could have gotten away with it."

"What did you do?" Crystal asked.

"After dinner, I pretended to be tired, and retreated to my room to get away from the whole situation."

"Is this when the arguing started?" Crystal asked.

"Yeah, it was Madeleine who started it. She kept yelling at Philip."

"Were you the topic of their argument?"

"Yes. She wanted Philip to fire me because I kept flirting with him. Can you believe her?" Bree clenched her fists as she flared up. "I've never once made any sort of move on Philip. Ever. The woman is off of her rocker if she thinks otherwise."

Bree was more correct on Madeleine's mental health than she realized. Madeleine might not be ready for a padded room and a straitjacket, but the woman would reap quite a benefit from a few sessions with a psychiatrist. "He stared at you the entire time we were traveling to the chalet, and I can verify I never once witnessed you say one word to the man or get closer than absolutely necessary." Crystal took the chance to reassure Bree.

"Thank you! Maybe you can tell the crazy lady I didn't want anything to do with her disgusting husband." Bree's eyes smoldered at the memory of the false accusation. She picked up her fork and stabbed a few pieces of chicken. "She accused all of the interns of the same thing. You'll notice we were all women. Philip did the hiring and she did the firing. I'm sure a succession of women kept trying to get into Philip's size fifty-two pants, and he wasn't to blame at all," she snarled.

Bree was on a roll now, but not in a helpful direction. Time to redirect her.

"What happened after?" Crystal nudged her self-righteousness.

"Madeleine ordered him to sleep on the couch. He found Ryan and Alice enjoying the ambiance of the main room. At least that's what Alice said when Philip asked her what they were doing. Of course, they had been eavesdropping on the conversation. However, it's not like they had to be in the main room. Unless you were hard of hearing, you could hear the two argue halfway to Timbuktu."

"Why would they be snooping, do you think?"

Crystal asked.

"Justin thinks they were trying to get dirt on Philip, something juicy enough to leverage him into giving them the company."

"You mean blackmail." This was new to her, but it made a lot of sense with what little she had learned of Alice and Ryan.

"That's what Philip called it in the ensuing argument. Afterward, Madeleine and Gary showed up and joined in the yelling."

"Where was Justin in all of this?" Crystal asked.

"Keeping out of the middle of it, like me. He's the junior associate, and was never given any serious consideration for taking over the firm. He weathered the storm in his room like I did. Georgia, too."

"What did the others squabble about?"

"Old grudges, mostly. There was the court case a while back involving Philip. Alice and Ryan testified against him, and Gary testified on Philip's behalf. They trotted out their dirty laundry, brandishing it for anyone to hear. Why do you want to know all of this, anyway?" Bree narrowed her eyes in sudden suspicion.

"I guess I'm just morbidly curious as to what happened. I mean, it's not just anyone who gets questioned by the police about a death." Crystal danced around the accusation.

The trusting woman nodded in satisfaction. "I guess that makes sense."

"What happened after the argument?" Crystal asked.

"The fight broke up after it had run its course. Philip slept on the couch like he'd been ordered. Justin snuck over to my room, and we gossiped about the huge meltdown we had overheard."

"And?" Crystal urged her to continue.

"Nothing else happened," Bree lowered her gaze and stared at her hands stacked on top of each other. "Philip must have left at some point and took off on the snowmobile."

Crystal mulled this over for a bit. Bree's version didn't add up from what she remembered. "I remember another argument right before the snowmobile took off. And I swore some glasses broke."

"I don't know what you're referring to. I'm sure the glass breaking was the wine table. Philip must have tipped it over on his way out." Bree shrugged.

"I remember hearing shouting before Philip left. What was it about?"

"I don't know. I must have been asleep by then," Bree gnawed on a thumbnail before glancing in the direction of the front door.

"You said you were talking to Justin," Crystal argued.

"Not all night," Bree protested.

"What happened to your room? A shelf was knocked over and debris was scattered everywhere."

"An accident. Justin must have bumped it on his way out to help find Philip."

Their conversation was interrupted by a flash of headlights through the front windows.

"Justin's home." She shot out of her chair, turning away from Crystal.

Before Bree could reach it, the front door opened and Justin announced himself, "Hey, babe. Did you order my General Tso's chicken?"

"We have company," Bree called out.

Justin stepped into the dining room and spotted Crystal. His eyes widened before he narrowed them and frowned. "Well, I guess I shouldn't be too surprised to find you here. I had a little talk with Alice today and it seems you have been asking some questions."

"A few," Crystal admitted.

"Why? What's in it for you?" Justin studied Crystal, more curious than angry. He stripped his wet jacket from his lean frame, and draped it over a dining room chair.

"Curiosity. I want to know what happened to the man who died when I was supposed to make sure he got home safe and sound." Crystal said, trying to act casual.

"Why aren't you letting the police investigate?" Justin said. "You aren't going to find anything out that they can't."

"I'm only asking a few questions to see if the stories all add up."

He gave her a condescending smirk as he pulled a chair out from the table and sat down. "Seriously? You think you can do a better job than a trained detective? What were you two discussing, anyway?"

Crystal had a flash of inspiration. "We were discussing the confrontation with Philip in Bree's room."

"Nothing to say, since nothing happened. Philip opened the door, was surprised to see me there, and left on the snowmobile," he said off-handedly. Bree had been trying to interject but hadn't been able to get any words in edgewise.

"Is this what actually happened, Bree?" Crystal queried.

"That's what happened." Her robotic answer told it all.

"Why did you lie, then?"

"What did you tell her?" Justin asked, voice rising in anger.

"I said he was never in my room. We heard arguing until he left on the snowmobile," Bree answered. She lowered her head down to stare at the table.

Justin swore. There was an arrogance in his attitude Crystal could exploit. He acted as if he had all of the answers and was confident he had control of the situation. Crystal was ready to dispel this and dug in again. "Why would you lie? Is there something I should know?"

"No, nothing," Bree stared at her hands clasped in her lap, and her body start to tremble.

"I'm sure it's embarrassing is all," Justin explained. "It's not everyone who is willing to talk to a stranger regarding an attempted sexual assault by their boss."

"A man ended up dead." Crystal tried for shock. "The Sheriff's department believes he was hit on the head, taken out to a cliff, and dumped over the edge to die." The words had the desired effect as Bree's tender nature betrayed her, and tears welled in her eyes as Crystal recounted the murder. "What happened to Philip? How did he end up dumped in the snow? I know you know something." Crystal was close to uncovering an important fact and couldn't help but pressure these two with everything she had.

Tears were now streaming down Bree's face, but Justin's mouth twisted in an angry snarl.

"We never meant…" Bree began.

"We never meant to talk to you," Justin grated. "I think it's high time you left, Crystal."

"Justin..." Bree began.

He cut her off with a large chopping motion of his hand and a glare. The same glare landed on Crystal. "You need to leave, now, or I'm calling the police."

"You should tell the Sheriff what you know. I'm sure if you come forward, anything you help with will mean leniency in the case." Crystal didn't know this for sure, but it sounded good. She was desperate and was going for long shots.

Justin fished his phone out of his pocket and tapped it three times. He turned the display toward Crystal to show her the numbers 911. His thumb hovered above call while he glared daggers at Crystal.

Crystal stood up, defeated. Bree stared at the drama unfolding before her, tears still running down her face, and her eyes red-rimmed.

Without another word, Crystal left the table and trudged toward the front door. A small part of her hoped Bree would call her back, or shout out a confession, but nothing happened. Justin walked behind her like a security guard escorting a suspicious teenager out of a department store. Reaching around her, he flung the front door open.

"Goodbye, Crystal," he said icily. "Keep your nose out of our business and you won't get hurt." With his threat lingering in the air, Crystal stepped through the front door and back into the rain.

Chapter Sixteen

Crystal stood on Justin's front doorstep, frustrated. She had stumbled onto something big tonight, but had no real information to show for all of her work. Conjecture by a wilderness guide would not close the case to the satisfaction of the Sheriff's Office or an insurance company. She made her way down the block toward her car, thinking to herself as raindrops pattered her jacket. The best she could do was call the Sheriff tomorrow and tell him everything she had learned. Even though she didn't have a lot of confidence in his abilities as a detective, maybe he would surprise everyone by solving the crime.

Climbing into her car, she thought of other angles she could take and mulled over the prospect of ambushing Ryan and Alice at their home to question them regarding their blackmailing attempts. She was imagining the cold reception she would get from them as she turned her car key.

The lights on her dash lit up for a second, followed by a weak click underneath the hood, but her car didn't even turn over. She tried again with the same result. She tried a few more times, but her car didn't give any indication that it was inclined to start.

Great. She was positive Miss Marple never had to deal with indignities like broken down cars in January rainstorms. Had she ridden around in cars or were they after her time? Crystal's mind wandered as she sat, this time thwarted by her temperamental vehicle.

She sent a quick text to Olivia to let her know she hadn't been murdered by Justin, and then called her dad.

"Hi pumpkin," he answered in his typical jovial tone. "This is a pleasant surprise. What are you up to? How's work at ECO Adventures going?"

"It's going good, Dad. I like the store a lot, but I hope to be out guiding again, soon."

"Happy to hear it. Is there any news on the case?"

"They've made some headway, but I don't know if they're going to solve it," she could hear the irony in her own voice as well as the sadness.

"What's wrong, Crystal?" he asked. "Is everything ok?"

Crystal was not going to unload on her father regarding her failed questioning of murder suspects, so she said, "My car won't start. I think it's my battery, and I was wondering if you can come give me a jump?"

"Of course, are you at your condo?"

"No, I'm on Beacon Hill," she gave him the address of the house she was parked in front of.

"What are you doing there?" he asked.

Preoccupied by mulling over her grilling of Justin and Bree, Crystal hadn't considered making up a reason to be there. Her silence stretched a few seconds before she blurted, "Visiting a friend."

She could hear her father in the garage collecting a few items.

"Would this friend be a boy? Maybe your coworker, Conner?"

"No, he lives in Georgetown. This is a different

friend. Another guide, but a girl." Her excuse sounded lame to her own ears.

"Oh, oh," her father chortled. "So, you know where Conner lives? Anything else your mother and I should know?" He was only curious, and she found herself grinning at his playful questioning.

"I think I get my inquisitive nature from you. Did it ever get you into trouble?"

"All the time. I'll be there in ten minutes," and he hung up.

Rather than sit doing nothing, Crystal popped open the hood of her car and glared at the battery. She wiggled the cables and turned the ignition again with no luck. She was getting ready to try again when her father's car appeared around the corner.

He parked in front of her, and walked out in the rain with a multi-meter in his hand.

"Wonderful Seattle January night," he deadpanned. He touched the multi-meter leads to the battery terminals. "Your battery is in pretty bad shape," he confirmed. "I might be able to jump it, but you need to go directly to the auto parts store and have them replace it for you."

"Thanks so much for coming out, Dad. I can't say how much I appreciate it," Crystal said. "Especially, in this weather."

Digging out his jumper cables, he said, "Anything for you, pumpkin. Promise me you'll get a new battery, or you and I are going to be spending more quality time together tomorrow morning." He squeezed the jumper cable clamps like crab claws a few times to emphasize what he meant by quality time.

"I will." How was it her parents could still reduce

her to a young child with a few well worded sentences?

He hooked the batteries together and started his car. A few minutes later, he motioned out of his window at Crystal. Cranking the ignition, her car sprang to life and she waved back at her father. He climbed out, unhooked the cables, and shut her hood. She joined him outside in the rain.

"Thanks, Dad. I don't know what I'd do without you."

"Happy to do it." He wound the jumper cables and gave her a warm smile. "Not as though I wouldn't ever be there for you, but try calling Conner next time. Knights in shining armor love to rescue fair maidens in distress."

"You're worse than Mom," she groaned.

"I'm just sharing a few tips from a guy's perspective. Besides, giving unsolicited advice is a parent's prerogative."

She hugged him goodbye and he drove away with a wave. Getting back in her car, she was startled by Justin's front porch light flicking on.

She dared not turn her car back off, so she spied on him through her rain spotted windshield as best she could. Justin advanced out of the house holding a large black garbage bag. It was only a quarter full, and he spun it around with a flick of his wrist and tied it closed. He walked to his gleaming silver Lexus sedan, parked behind what Crystal now realized was Bree's older Toyota. With a click of his key fob, the trunk hatch popped open and he slung the bag into the back. Slamming the trunk, he glanced up and down the street before climbing into the driver's seat. Crystal was too far away to make out his facial expression, but his darting eyes and twitchy reactions screamed more alertness than was warranted for an evening errand.

He backed out of the driveway and drove down the hill. Filled with curiosity, Crystal merged behind him and followed. He took a few turns, meandering through the streets, and Crystal did her best to stay far enough behind to not be spotted, but close enough to not lose him in the darkness and weather.

They crossed under an overpass and a sign declared they had entered the International District. Most of the buildings were old brick affairs in this part of town, and Crystal spotted Chinese, Japanese, and several other languages she couldn't identify on the storefronts. Patrons willing to brave the awful night's weather could be seen through restaurant windows as she drove by.

Justin took a sharp left turn down a tight alley. Crystal halted at the mouth of the passageway, and peered out her driver's side window through the rain smeared glass. Several sooty brick buildings flanked either side, and she spotted dumpsters in shadowed niches down its length. The narrow gloom of the alley only had enough width for one vehicle. Justin's Lexus was parked thirty yards away under a dim light mounted above the back door to one of the businesses. Why would a successful architect be parked down a dingy alley by a dumpster in a rainstorm? This whole situation was out of the ordinary, so she scooped up her phone and started recording. She didn't know how well a video would turn out through the nighttime weather, but she had to try something. The brake lights to Justin's car flickered off and the trunk sprung open.

Justin hastened out of the driver's door, trying in

vain to cover his head from the falling rain with one hand and retrieving the garbage bag from the trunk with the other. He darted furtive looks up and down the alley, squinting in the light cast by the lone lamp above him, before lifting open the lid of a nearby dumpster. He flung the bag in, and let the lid slam shut. With one last glance around, he jumped in his car and drove off. Crystal hit the stop button on her phone to halt the recording.

Turning down the alley, she parked in front of the dumpster. Leaving her car running, she climbed out and searched in her trunk. In an emergency repair kit her father had given her years ago, she found a flashlight. The light mounted on the wall was enough for her to see the alley but did not illuminate the alcove the dumpster sat in. She couldn't see either end of the alley and took comfort that the overhead light spoiled not only her night vision, but that of Justin, who wouldn't have been able to spot her recording him. With a disgusted grimace, she focused her attention back on the dumpster. Even in the cold January night, it smelled wretched. Dumpsters were supposed to have terrible odors, but this one was the worst she had ever had the displeasure to be around. Training her flashlight on the back exit of the business, she wasn't surprised to see Chinese characters were stenciled on the top of the door. Underneath, in English, it read, "Han's Fine Meats."

This explained the awful odor. Justin had flung the bag into a butcher's dumpster. She lifted the lid with one finger and played her flashlight inside. Leaning against the back wall, and three quarters of the way down, the half-full black garbage sack rested atop a small mound of much fuller bags.

A new wave of stench wafted out, and smacked Crystal in the face. She gagged and retreated, waving one hand in front of her nose and wiping her watering eyes with the sleeve of the other. She needed to get the bag, but she didn't know how to do it without throwing up.

Putting her hands on her knees, she steeled herself. Once the air cleared, she breathed in deeply, once, twice...

"Do you want a hand?" a raspy voice called out from behind her.

Crystal let out a yelp and backed up against her car. What she had assumed was a pile of junk in another shadowed alcove, stood and shook off a dark green tarp, as well as a couple of blankets. Memories of her self-defense class flashed in her mind as the tall homeless man unlimbered himself from where he had been sleeping. She recalled her instructor explaining that punching people with her keys poking through her fingers was a good way to fight, but they were hanging from the ignition of her running car.

"Hey, I remember you," the man continued in his gruff voice. "You were there on Sunday."

This was bad. The man was touched in the head and thought he remembered Crystal from somewhere. She edged toward her car door, keeping her eyes on him. As she studied his face to gauge his intentions, it struck her. He did look familiar.

"Joe?" Crystal ventured.

"Hey, you remembered my name," he said. "You've got a good memory."

"Why aren't you in the mission on a night like

tonight?" Crystal now remembered where she had seen him.

"I like my independence. They have a lot of rules there, and I prefer to live my life how I choose."

"Why here?" Crystal gestured at the alleyway.

"Why not?" he said with a toothy smile. "No one bothers me." He gestured at the dumpster.

"I can see why not. How can you stand it?" She was abashed as soon as the words left her mouth. This was the man's home after a fashion.

"You get used to it." He held his palms up in a what-can-you-do-about-it motion. "Are you trying to get the bag the tall guy tossed in there?"

"Yes."

A crafty look crossed Joe's face. "I'll get it out for twenty bucks."

The whole scene was surreal to Crystal. She was bargaining with a homeless man to retrieve a bag of garbage from a dumpster in a dark alley in the middle of a downpour where a potential murderer had tossed it. Maybe her life had become a little *too* interesting.

Crystal was happy to fork over a hundred dollars to not dive into this particular dumpster, but she was intimately aware of the contents of her wallet these days. "I only have five bucks," she apologized.

"Well, five will do. We'll call it a discount for helping at the mission." Joe stepped over to the dumpster, pushed his palm in a back-away motion, and paused. "You might want to give me some space. This isn't going to be pleasant."

Crystal heeded his warning and walked down the alley several paces from the dumpster. Joe waited until she had retreated, nodded, and flung open the lid. Even at a distance, the noxious smell of rank garbage rolled over her.

"You should smell it in the summer," Joe said in a conversational tone. "This is nothing."

He stepped onto a small metal ridge lining the bottom of the dumpster and with a grunt, threw his leg over the edge. The filth of the dumpster, not to mention the lingering odor, caused Crystal to gag again, and she retreated a few extra paces.

"Which one is it?" Joe asked, his voice echoing from inside.

"The small...urk...the small one in the back." Crystal forced her voice to keep steady.

"Got it." The bag was flipped out of the dumpster to splat on the narrow, paved lane. Joe clambered out after, easing himself to the ground.

Crystal skipped forward and grabbed the bag. "Thank you, Joe," she cried. She popped open her trunk and tossed it in the back. Slamming the trunk shut, she grabbed her wallet from her purse on the passenger seat. Inside, she was delighted to find eight dollars, all of which she pressed into Joe's hands.

"We agreed on five," he said, handing her back three dollars.

"Consider it a tip for a job well done, Joe. I don't think I could have done what you did for me. You don't know what this means." In truth, Crystal had no idea what this meant at all. Not until she got a chance to get a look in Justin's garbage bag.

"Well, if it's a tip, then it's a tip," Joe tucked the extra ones in his pocket. "Pleasure doing business with you."

Crystal's car shuddered, almost died, and with a

loud whine returned to a rough idle.

"If you don't mind my saying, your car is a real piece of junk," Joe offered, "and I've owned bad cars in my life. You should have it checked by a good mechanic."

Indignation flared in Crystal. A man who lived in an alley next to a dumpster had called her car a piece of junk.

"I'm off to the auto store for a new battery right now."

"Good," he said. "Have them check your starter and alternator, too, if they can. I was a mechanic a long time ago, and I didn't like the sound of your car's hesitation."

"Thanks for the help and the advice," Crystal said, "but if I'm going to make it in time before the auto parts store closes, I've got to run."

"Good night, then, and good luck with whatever is in the bag. Hope to see you at the mission sometime, and maybe you'll tell me what you're up to. I'm burning with curiosity, but I can tell you got places to go and things to do."

"I hope to see you at the mission, too." Crystal found herself meaning it. She couldn't imagine she would volunteer to work on Sunday afternoon with Madeleine, Ryan and Alice, but maybe a different day would be nice.

****

Crystal arrived back at her condo at nine o'clock. The guys at the auto parts store had replaced her battery for a hundred dollars and checked her alternator. They recommended she have a mechanic replace it, too, but it would set her back three hundred additional bucks.

Crystal had paid for the battery with her credit card without any knowledge of how to pay for it, much less an additional three hundred dollars to a mechanic. She resigned herself to calling her dad the next day, asking for his advice and maybe his help swapping in a new alternator.

Crystal laid out a few plastic bags to protect her table and plunked the one Joe had retrieved from the dumpster on top of them. Burning with curiosity, she used a pair of scissors to cut open the top of the bag. She frowned when all it revealed was a wadded-up bundle of towels.

She sliced the side of the bag open to get a better look and discovered they were covered in brown stains. She dumped the towels out onto the other garbage bags. A cursive "B" logo was stitched into the corner. After a moment's reflection, Crystal recognized the logo. It had been monogramed on all of the towels in the chalet. These must be the stolen towels Roxie had complained about.

She poked at the towels with her fingers to see if anything was hidden in them before it struck her what the brown stains were. Blood.

"Ewww!" She cried out loud and ran to the kitchen sink. She pumped some soap onto her hands and turned the faucet to the hottest water she could stand. She scoured her hands and then repeated her hand washing a second time. Elf, curious about the strange items in his territory, hopped on the table, sniffing the towels.

"Shoo!" Crystal shouted at her cat. Elf glanced at her with feline contempt and plopped down on the table, tail twitching. Crystal flicked her wet fingers at the cat, and he scrambled off, fleeing for the bedroom.

"I'm going to pay for that later," Crystal muttered as she dried her hands. She would have to be extra vigilant of her vengeful cat. He had a long memory and liked to get even, pouncing when she least expected it.

She had overcome her initial disgust at the idea of towels covered in dried blood sitting on her kitchen table, and a grin started tugging at her lips. She had discovered what she had been looking for all along. These towels must be soaked in Philip's blood and Justin had been trying to destroy the evidence. She admired his cleverness in picking a butcher's dumpster. If someone found blood-soaked towels in any other dumpster, it was cause for alarm. However, in this particular dumpster, it was business as usual.

Crystal grabbed her dishwashing gloves from underneath the sink, pulled them on, and started shoving the towels into yet another garbage bag from her pantry. With a loud clunk, something rolled out of the last towel and tumbled across the floor.

"Ew! Ew! Ew!" Whatever it was, she was sure she did not want it rolling through her condo. Purple crystals glinted back at her from the inside of the stone as it came to a halt. Recognizing it as a geode, Crystal spotted blood stains covering it as well. *Was a chunk of hair stuck to it?* Thrusting the geode far away from her body, a fresh wave of revulsion made her skin crawl. She placed the glittering rock on top of the towels in the new garbage bag.

She crammed the original bag in with the towels, and used a twist tie to seal it shut. The rest of the garbage bags on her table were shoved into yet another bag, as well as her dish gloves. There was no way those were ever going to be used again.

Crystal caught another whiff of the dumpster, and wrinkled her nose. She double bagged the bloody towels and geode and hauled the other bag to the garbage chute in the hallway. Returning to her condo, she smelled the room again. The stench still lingered, and after a few exploratory sniffs, she realized the odor was emanating from her. Horrified, she stripped off her clothes in a frenzy, threw them on the hot cycle in her washing machine, and jumped into the shower.

Twenty minutes later, her skin was pink from scalding water and hard scrubbing, and she was dressed in her pajamas. As she switched her clothes from the washer to the dryer, she mulled over her course of action. She considered contacting the Sheriff, but worried the wheels of justice might not move fast enough to get her back to work in time to save her condo and job. She wasn't sure if this was the case, but the most certain thing to do was coerce an admission from Justin or Bree as to what had happened the fateful night Philip died.

She tossed around several different ideas in her head and came up with the beginnings of a plan. It was late, but she gave Suzy a call.

She answered on the second ring. "Hey, Crystal, what's up?"

"Hey, Suzy. Sorry to call so late, but I need to ask a favor."

"I'm happy to help if I can. What do you need?"

"I noticed you were working the morning shift tomorrow. Do you mind swapping with my closing shift?"

"You mean sleep in as late as I want and work the night shift like I'd prefer? You're doing me the favor.

I'll even email Amelia to say it was my idea since you're new and all."

"You're awesome. I owe you one."

"No, you don't. We guides look out for one another. Talk to you later, Crystal." Suzy hung up.

Happy, and confident everything was falling into place, Crystal relaxed for the first time in days. Rubbing her eyes in exhaustion, she made her way to her bedroom, where Elf shot out from the closet, pounced on her toes with his claws, and scampered to the living room, confident his form of kitty justice had been served. Crystal sighed, staunched the blood from the scratch on her toe with a tissue, and lay down for a night of well-earned rest.

Chapter Seventeen

The next morning, Crystal got ready and headed downstairs to the parking garage with the bag of bloody evidence in tow.

She locked it in her trunk, grateful that she didn't have the type of car she had to worry about being stolen. Her "real piece of junk," as Joe had called it, coughed to life and she drove to work. She helped Lisa get the store ready and unlocked the front door at opening time. Today, Crystal was stationed in the snowshoe department and had a wonderful time showing customers everything she had learned a little over a week ago as they picked out their own snowshoes. One lady asked Crystal about guided tours appropriate for her first-grade students.

"We offer tours for all levels of experience," Crystal said, "but we are on temporary hiatus. Check back soon, though, because I'm pretty sure we're going to resume any day now." The cheekiness of declaring this to a complete stranger was unlike Crystal, but it was a little inside joke to amuse herself. The woman thanked her and promised she would keep in touch.

The rest of the day crept by at an agonizing pace. Crystal was eager to get on with her plan, and excited with the prospect of getting her job, and life, back. After dragging out for an eternity, her shift ended and her plan began. She sent a quick text to Conner, and positioned her car by the entrance to the parking garage.

Fifteen minutes later, Conner's SUV made its appearance. She got out to meet him.

His usual grin greeted her. "Crystal, why the mysterious text?"

"I was wondering if you would help me with something?"

"Anything. What do you need me to do?"

"I think I've Miss-Marpled this case closed," she proclaimed.

"Are you serious? How?"

She opened her trunk and handed the garbage bag to Conner. "Will you give this to Holly, and make sure they compare the blood inside to Philip's DNA? Also, I am pretty sure the geode in there was the murder weapon."

As Conner stared at her, open-mouthed, she produced her phone and forwarded him the video from the previous night. "Send her this, too. It's Justin dumping the bag in Han's Fine Meat's dumpster in the International District. You can't make out it's him, but you can see his license plate when he parks under the light. If she needs an eyewitness, Joe, a homeless guy, lives next to the dumpster. He'll identify Justin, but he might want twenty bucks to do it."

Conner shut his mouth. He tried to say something and closed his mouth again.

"I've had a couple of busy days," Crystal beamed. "If everything goes according to plan, we'll be up and guiding before you know it."

"This is amazing," he said in awe. "How did you do all of this?"

"My natural inquisitive nature, and a little luck,"

she said, remembering her conversation with her dad the previous night.

"I only have a half-shift, but I'm still working until four o'clock. I'll call Holly to meet me afterward, but I won't see her until then."

"Perfect. I need to do some things before this all gets out. I consider this lighting the fuse. I don't want it to go off yet, or everyone will run for cover."

"You're not going to do anything dangerous, are you?" he furrowed his brow with concern as he searched her face for a clue as to what she was planning.

"I'm just going to have a little chat with Bree is all. Thanks for caring." Impulse seized her, and she leaned forward and planted her lips firmly against his.

Conner did his best to respond to the kiss, with a bag full of bloody evidence dangling in one hand.

Crystal pulled away with a wicked grin. "I'm off to go catch bad guys. I'll call you later." She jumped in her car and hardly cared that it took two tries before it whined to life. She peeked in her rearview mirror as she drove off and was amused to see Conner still standing in the same place, watching her car drive away with his eyebrows raised in astonishment.

Now that the first part of her scheme was behind her, Crystal refocused on the second phase of her plan. She swung by her condo, fed Elf, and grabbed her binoculars.

Hoping she wasn't going to be late, she sped as much as traffic allowed toward the office of Calvert and Associates, north of Green Lake where she and Conner had their first date. The memory of it brought a surge of warmth, and gave her courage to see her plan through.

Future dates with Conner were one of the things she was fighting for, and this was symbolic of how much her life had changed for the better since she walked out of her previous job.

Following her phone's GPS, Crystal closed in on Calvert and Associates. She passed an engineering firm, the human resources building of a coffee company, and a few other businesses she didn't recognize. The buildings were all standard affairs, what you would expect to see in any business park. After peering left and right for half a block, she spotted what could only be Calvert and Associates. It stood out from the surrounding structures, clearly meant to showcase their abilities. The office consisted of sheets of glass set at dramatic angles. Crystal couldn't help but take a moment to admire its beauty glinting in the sunlight. As she passed by, she noted the parking lot behind the firm contained Bree's old Toyota.

Crystal parked her car across the street, a block away to avoid being spotted from the company's windows overlooking the neighborhood.

Noticing a convenience store in the rearview mirror, Crystal scampered to purchase some snacks for the stakeout. She returned a few minutes later, arms full of chips, cookies and several bottles of iced tea. Dumping them on the passenger seat, she lifted her binoculars.

It was hard to make out what was happening with the late winter sun shining on the windows, but she could see people moving around the office. She spotted Georgia at the front desk talking on the phone. Shifting her binoculars, Crystal noted Gary in the office facing her, a large slanted desk to the side covered in architectural schematics. He clicked away on the computer before him, attention fixed on the screen.

Ten minutes into the stakeout, Crystal found her mind wandering and her eye sockets aching from the pressure of the binoculars. She set them down next to her snack pile and rubbed her eyes. She couldn't imagine how cops could do this for any length of time. Ripping open a bag of Cheetos and screwing the lid off an iced tea, she sat waiting, munching, sipping, and staring at the office building, barely daring to blink. Her mind drifted to Conner and his part in her plan. She checked the time on her phone. He still had another thirty minutes left on his shift. Soon, he would call Holly and the police would come down on Justin like a ton of bricks. She finished her snack and iced tea, cramming the bottle and bag into a plastic sack she had hung from her car's gear shift. Still, no change in the activity in the office.

After another hour of sitting, the flaw in her plan became evident. She *really* had to use the restroom. Maybe it had not been a good idea to load up on iced tea to while away the time. She wanted to run to the convenience store for a quick bathroom break, but she couldn't risk missing Bree leaving. Steeling herself, she did her best to forget it. Her mind over bladder was only effective for a few minutes, and she repositioned herself over and over to try and remove the discomfort.

Darkness in Seattle arrived early in the winter, and as the sun set and the streetlights flickered on, she found she could see into the windows of the office. Georgia and Gary hadn't budged from their original locations, but now she could make out Justin's office. Like his colleague, he was sitting at his desk, facing a computer. As Crystal trained her binoculars on him, Bree walked in and handed him a manila folder. Justin said a few words to her and Bree responded, taking a seat in a nearby chair.

This was her chance. Bree didn't seem to be going anywhere soon. Crystal flung the binoculars on the passenger seat, jumped out of her car, and waddled back to the convenience store. She had a furious debate with the clerk as to whether she was considered a paying customer, since she had bought food and drinks earlier. Mid-argument she spotted an ad showing the silhouette of a couple walking on the beach with cigarettes in their hands, and inspiration struck her. Thinking ahead, she purchased a pack, shoved them in her pocket, and received the bathroom key in return. A few minutes later, she returned to her stakeout, relieved.

Bree's car was still there. Crystal settled the binoculars back to her eyes and scoured the building. Gary and Justin were still in their offices, Georgia still manned the front desk, but Bree was nowhere to be seen.

As if Crystal's thoughts could conjure her target, the intern popped into view, with a long winter coat buttoned to her throat. She and Georgia exchanged good-byes, and Bree walked out the front door.

Crystal started her car, which let out its characteristic squeal. Frowning, Bree's head swiveled at the noise, forcing Crystal to duck her head to avoid the intern's searching gaze.

A few seconds later, Crystal peeked her head above the dash. Bree was seated in her car, swinging the door shut. A moment later, she turned into traffic and Crystal followed.

Crystal had been counting on Bree and Justin to continue to drive in separate cars, and she also hoped Justin working late was a common occurrence. She followed Bree as best she could in Seattle's crowded rush hour traffic. She managed to put one car between her and Bree, making it several miles before being thwarted by a yellow light the car in front of her had refused to run. However, losing site of Bree wasn't a problem. From the direction she had taken, Bree was going to her place in the U-district.

Crystal eased off the gas the rest of the way to Bree's apartment, parking across the street from the building's front door.

Bree wouldn't let her in if she paged her on the intercom, so Crystal stood in front of the building and produced the pack of cigarettes she had bought at the convenience store. Crystal was thankful the store clerk hassling her had brought this to her attention. She needed a benign reason to be standing outside of a building during a January night. Lighting a cigarette, she put it between her lips, and not thinking, inhaled, which caused her throat to burn and inspired a massive coughing fit. Wiping tears from her eyes, she cautioned herself to avoid making that mistake again and did her best to act casual. She hoped she came across as just another resident taking a quick smoke break outside, and not a person trying to weasel her way into an apartment building where she was unwelcome.

After fifteen minutes of standing in the cold, and having to relight her cigarette several times, Crystal was passed by a young backpack toting co-ed who unlocked the front door to the building.

Crystal flung her cigarette to the ground, stomped

on it, and caught the door as it swung closed.

"Sorry," the young woman apologized. "I didn't know you were coming in."

"It's all right." Crystal gave the girl her best innocent smile.

Turning away, the student headed down a hallway. Crystal walked up the stairs to apartment 204.

Pausing a moment, she opened the voice memo app on her phone, tapped record, and tucked it back in her pocket. She knocked on Bree's door and waited.

A few seconds later, the front door was flung open and a joyous Bree was calling out, "Justin, you're early. Oh, it's you again." Her face fell as Crystal stepped into the apartment without an invitation. "What are you doing here?"

"I thought we could chat some more. We didn't get to finish our conversation yesterday, and I figured now would be a good time to go over a few last details."

"I don't know. Justin will be stopping by soon, and we're going out to dinner at the new seafood place which opened last week. We have reservations."

"I won't be long then." Crystal yanked out a chair and took a seat at Bree's dining room table.

"Ok..." Bree did not have it in her nature to be rude and force her out. "Let me go freshen up first." Bree retreated to the bathroom and Crystal took a moment to position her phone next to her keys on the table. She wanted to get the best recording of this conversation as possible.

Bree returned after a moment and sat across the table from Crystal, watching her with a wary expression.

"When we were talking last night, you were telling

me about the night of Philip's death. He entered your room, and you and Justin scared him off," Crystal summarized.

"That's not what I said happened," Bree protested.

"It's what Justin said," Crystal pointed out. "What has changed since we last talked is I witnessed Justin throw a bag of bloody towels, and the geode I believe was used to hit Philip on the head, into a dumpster last night. Furthermore, I recorded it on my phone."

The blood drained from Bree's face. "Are you blackmailing me? I don't have much money." She glanced around her apartment as if to locate something she could bribe Crystal with to buy her silence.

"I'm not looking for money. The evidence is on its way to the police. What I'm looking for is your testimony as to what happened the night of the murder. If you come forward before the police receive the evidence, it'll go easier on you and Justin." Crystal had used this same tactic the last time she had been with Justin and Bree, but now she had leverage.

Bree believed it, because her mask broke and she took a deep shuddering breath. "I'm not sure where to begin. I've been interning at Calvert and Associates for almost a year, now. From the first day there, I hit it off with Justin, and we started dating within a month. We hid it from the others to protect me from being fired, but it also gave Philip the green light to start harassing me. I did my best to never be alone with him. When he called me into his office, I would leave the door open, stuff like that. Still, he would do things and say things that creeped me out. Justin kept an eye out for me and would try to protect me. He'd step in when Philip cornered me in the break room or would walk into his office to interrupt him to discuss a project if I'd been in there too long. I considered quitting a few times but couldn't force myself to give up on the opportunity. I was at the end of my rope, when Philip announced his impending retirement six months ago. We've all been waiting for him to leave since his announcement, but he kept hanging on. I think he wanted to see this last project through to the finish." Bree conveyed all of this with wide eyes and deep breaths, trying to describe the last year of her stressful life. "The office was in turmoil. Ryan, Alice, Gary, Madeleine and of course Philip mixed it up with regular shouting matches. This wasn't anything new, but it got worse once the future of the company was so uncertain. After the new science building was completed, Philip booked the snowshoe hike as a celebration and a team building exercise. 'A way to put the past behind us,' is what he called it. No one was buying it. Justin was leery of his motives from the outset. He warned me Philip might try something since his time at the company was running out." Bree sighed, "I wish I had pretended to be sick. I was so selfish, because I hoped it would be a fun trip and maybe a romantic night with my boyfriend." She stared off into space, lost in thought.

"What happened then?" Crystal urged her on with a gentle prod.

"We already talked about the night leading up to Philip coming into my room. That was what happened. However, when Philip walked in, Justin wasn't actually there. Ryan and Alice had been talking in the main area, and Justin hadn't been able to sneak over. Philip, on the other hand, didn't care if Alice and Ryan were watching him. He barged in, shut the door, and said if I was grateful for my job, I would show it." Moisture welled in the corners of her eyes. "I jumped out of bed and asked him to leave, but he shoved me against the dresser and grabbed me." Fat tears began pouring down her cheeks and her shuddering breath culminated in a sob. "He was ripping at my clothes. I was terrified, and grabbed for anything I could get my hands on to protect myself. I felt the geode on the shelf above me and seized it. That's when I knocked the shelf off the wall."

Bree buried her face in her hands, and her voice dropped to a whisper. "Then I hit him in the head as hard as I could. I was so scared. I screamed as he fell. Justin ran across the hall, and turned on the light. There was so much blood running from Philip's head, I was positive I had killed him," Bree was sobbing now. Crystal headed to the bathroom, spotted a box of tissues, and set them in front of her.

Nodding her thanks, Bree grabbed a tissue and dried her eyes.

"You didn't know he was alive, did you? Not until I told you last night?"

Bree shook her head. "Ryan and Alice had come running to my room by this time. Alice took his pulse and declared he was dead. I freaked out, sure I was going to jail for murder, but Alice assured me he had this coming. She also said we could make the problem go away."

"It was Alice's idea?"

Bree nodded, continuing to dab at her eyes. "She explained she had a plan. She wanted to drive his body off the cliff on the snowmobile, faking an accident. There wasn't any time to think it through. We all followed her orders, since they made sense at the time.

Ryan and Justin carried him down the hall, knocking over the wine table. I was sure someone would come out of their room at any moment and discover us because of the noise we were making. They loaded Philip on the snowmobile, and Ryan drove off into the night while Alice and Justin mopped up the blood with the towels."

"You're telling me this was all an accident, followed by an actual murder?"

"More than an accident," Bree pleaded. "It was self-defense. He was a horrible man who deserved what happened. Not only for what he did to me, but what he did to other women in the past."

"I'm sure the police would understand self-defense, given his sordid nature. I'm not so sure how well they will accept the actual murder, not to mention the subsequent cover up."

"You have to trust me. Justin and I knew nothing. It's why I'm telling you this. Alice took his pulse. She must have known he was alive."

A key turned in the lock of the front door.

Chapter Eighteen

Justin entered the apartment, tailed by a stormy Alice and Ryan.

"You're here," Bree cried. "What are they doing here?"

"When I got your text, I decided it was best for them to be part of this. For better or worse, we're all in this together." Justin gave Bree a one-armed hug, but kept his eyes fixed on Crystal over his girlfriend's hair.

Crystal couldn't believe she was such an idiot. Of course, Bree had texted her boyfriend from the bathroom.

She slipped her phone in her pocket and stood.

"Thanks for the chat, Bree. Give me a call if you want to talk again." Crystal strode toward the front door.

Ryan grabbed her arm, thrusting her back into the chair.

"What was that for?" Crystal cried.

"Don't play coy with us, dear," Alice growled. Crystal could still see the gash on her forehead where the pan thrown by Madeleine had struck her. Alice had attempted to cover it up with a liberal amount of foundation, but it hadn't completely masked the bruising. "You have been prying into our business and playing us against one another. It's time for it to stop. Let me see your phone."

"My phone?" Crystal played dumb.

"Your phone. The one you have been trying to hide in your pocket since we arrived."

Crystal withdrew her phone from where she had shoved it and reluctantly passed it to Alice. Alice seized it and navigated to the lock screen.

"What's your code?" Alice's tone was businesslike, as if she were asking for a bid on a home renovation project.

"I'm not giving it to you." Crystal lifted her chin in defiance.

Alice gave a quick nod to her husband. Ryan's backhand dashed Crystal from the chair, leaving her dazed and startled to find herself on the floor. A second later, pain flared across her cheek as her senses returned.

"Code?" Alice's tone never wavered.

"What are you doing?" Bree cried. "She didn't do anything to deserve this."

"Do you want your boyfriend and you to go to jail? Would it be nice to see him in fifty years when you both get out? You two can get your marriage license and AARP cards on the same day." Alice was relentless.

"Justin, make her stop," Bree cried.

"We have to know what she has on her phone," Justin grated. "It's for our own good."

Crystal rolled over in time to catch a boot in her ribs from Ryan. She cried out and curled into a ball to protect herself.

"Code, Crystal," Alice commanded.

"4321." Crystal gasped.

"Not very original," Alice chided and entered the

numbers. "Well, well, well, look what we have here," Alice crowed above Crystal, "a recording app."

Silence filled the room as Alice worked the screen. Bree's voice emanated from the phone's speaker. "Alice took his pulse. She must have known he was alive," was repeated into the room.

Alice paused the playback and punched a few more buttons on the screen. "And deleted," she said with finality. "So we have an unwelcome intruder and a squealing snitch working together," she said to her husband.

"Hey," Justin said. "I don't like the tone of your voice."

"Don't worry, Justin." Alice gave a tight smile. "We won't do anything to your precious Barbie snitch. The intruder, though…" she continued. She dropped Crystal's phone on the ground beside her head. A moment later, Alice's heel crashed down, shattering the screen. "Ryan, get this filth on her feet. We need her out of here and taken to someplace quiet, where we can deal with this situation."

Ryan grabbed Crystal under the armpits and yanked her to a standing position. She pretended to comply, but as Ryan's grip loosened, she flung her elbow out behind her as hard as she could. Ryan's nose crunched as she connected. Bellowing, he staggered back from her.

Crystal darted for the door, but Alice hooked her foot with her own, sending Crystal sprawling to the ground. Rolling over, she braced herself to jump up and fight, but froze as Alice drew a dangerous looking, matte-black pistol from her handbag.

She leveled it at Crystal's head, "Hold still. You're

beginning to make me angry."

"No, no, no," Bree moaned from the corner she had retreated to.

"What are you doing, Alice?" Justin asked in a strangled tone. Crystal wished his words hadn't been so shaky when he spoke.

"Taking out the trash." Alice spouted the cheesy line with complete calm.

"I think she broke mah nose," Ryan cursed in nasal tones. Blood streamed down his face, dripping from his chin. Keeping her glare and gun trained on Crystal, Alice stepped into the adjacent kitchen, yanked a hand towel from a rack, and tossed it to her husband.

Alice mentioning trash and the image of a bloody towel reminded Crystal of her ace in the hole. "You can get rid of me, but it won't do any good," she bargained. "I know Justin was trying to hide the bloody towels."

"Ha," he exclaimed. "Even if there was such a thing, you would never find them."

"You threw them in a dumpster last night in the International District." Crystal rushed the words. "The towels, the geode, and a video of you disposing of them are on their way to the police, right now."

The blood drained from Justin's face, and he put a hand on the wall to steady himself.

"Too bad for you Justin," Alice lamented. "I guess you're going to jail after all."

"But I didn't kill him. Neither did Bree. You and Ryan did."

"Good luck proving it. The murder happened in Bree's room. I'm sure the Sheriff's department will find all the trace evidence they need, if we point them in the right direction. Furthermore, you were caught on video destroying evidence. Excuse me, *trying* to destroy evidence," Alice said with a sneer for his incompetence. "The only thing linking us to the crime is her testimony," Alice flicked the barrel of the gun at Crystal.

"And our testimony," Bree proclaimed.

"Your word against ours." Alice was back to being ice cold as she spelled out the situation to Bree. "All of the physical evidence points to you. You can attempt to bring us down with you, or we can testify on your behalf, and tell the court what a terrible human being Philip was, and try to get you off with self-defense."

Bree glared at Alice, but it was the only fight she mustered against the domineering woman.

Crystal had a flash of insight and narrowed her eyes at Ryan. "That's why you were outside the chalet without snowshoes."

"Whad are you talking about?" he growled through his wound, still wiping blood from his face.

"You had taken the snowmobile, but forgot to take snowshoes," Crystal remembered.

"You just won't stop being curious, will you?" Alice sighed. "This is what landed you in this unenvious spot to begin with. It's why we need to make sure you don't tell anyone what you know."

Justin jumped in, "You had so many motives, though. You testified against him in court years ago. Any person who spent time at all with you two and Philip in the same room can vouch that you loathed one another."

"You think this is about petty revenge and not liking each other? If you can't think any deeper than that, I'm not surprised you managed to get yourself recorded destroying evidence. We never cared about him being an appalling human being. We want what is rightfully ours. We've worked our entire lives to help build this company. His predilection for being unfaithful almost ruined all of us these past two decades. He nearly cost us our reputations and our livelihood. If our firm was sunk because of him, the fat commissions we make on our projects would be gone, and no one would be willing to work with us, because his unsavory record would tarnish our good names. We didn't testify because we wanted to do the right thing. We testified to get him thrown in jail. We wanted him out of the way, where he couldn't do any more harm. After we had come off looking like angels protecting an innocent victim in court, we planned to set up our own firm and lure all of his old clients away from him, while he rotted in a cell. Everything was ruined when his team of lawyers cleared him of the charges by making that idiot girl who accused him look like a gold-digging tramp."

"That's why you decided to kill him," Justin whispered in horror. "You plan on doing the same thing, but with him permanently out of the way."

"Now that Madeleine has decided to give the firm to Gary, that's exactly what we're planning to do. It will be harder to steal clients from Madeleine and Gary, with Philip suffering a tragic death rather than doing time for sexual assault, but with him retiring and handing off the company to anyone but us, we decided to make our move when an opportunity presented itself." Halfway through the diatribe, Alice tilted her head back and drew a deep breath in exasperation. "I'm tired of explaining everything to you idiots. The lesson to be learned is that the world is a hard place, and you need to seize what you want, because no one is going to give it to you. Ryan, it's time to go." Alice glanced at her husband, who had managed to staunch the blood flowing from his nose. He nodded to his wife, and shot a hate-filled glare at Crystal as he stalked up to her. He seized her arm, squeezing hard enough to cause her to cry out in pain.

"Goodbye, Justin. Goodbye, Bree. For what it's worth, I do hope you beat the charges. Know, though, if you bring us into it, we'll do everything we can to bury you." Alice motioned to her husband. He flung open the door and forced Crystal through. Alice laid her coat over her arm to cover the handgun and followed.

The apartment door swung shut behind them and Ryan yanked Crystal toward the stairs leading to the first floor.

"Where are you taking me?" Fear twisted inside her, and her mind reeled for a way out. Her cheek and side throbbed where Ryan had backhanded and kicked her. The pain reminded her these people were not bluffing with their threats. She tugged against Ryan's grasp, but he leaned forward and wrenched at her arm, dragging her to the stairs.

"We're going to a place where you can be taught how to stay out of other peoples' business," Alice answered.

Frantic, Crystal again struggled to remember her self-defense lessons. One memory blazed in her mind; in the cases of an abduction, you don't go meekly with your kidnappers, and never get into their car. You fight for your life. She hurt and ached, but she mustered herself for one more attack.

As Ryan took the first step down the stairs, Crystal stopped tugging against his grasp and flung her whole body forward against him. Ryan lost his balance on the steps, falling headfirst down the stairs. Crystal slammed onto his back, driving the wind out of him. They tumbled down, her weight bouncing on top of Ryan.

Crashing together in a heap at the bottom of the stairs, he gasped, and she was flung forward, rolling toward the front door.

"Grab her, you idiot!" Alice's shriek made it obvious she had lost her calm at long last.

Crystal jumped to her feet and almost fell over again. The world spun, but she managed to steady herself on the handle of the door.

Out of the corner of her eye, Ryan struggled to stand. He took one lurching step forward and tumbled over, gasping and holding his chest.

Crystal wrenched the door open and recoiled as a gunshot thundered through the closed confines of the apartment building lobby. The glass front door shattered into thousands of pieces in front of her.

She let go of the handle and lunged through what remained of the door, the glass shards crunching under her boots.

Alice's footsteps thudded down the stairs behind her. There were only a few precious moments, and Crystal staggered across the street as fast as her aching body could manage, dodging an oncoming truck. The headlights and blaring horn dazzled her as she stumbled to the sidewalk and the relative safety of her car.

Yanking out her keys, she crouched down and shoved them in the lock. Peeking through her windows, a furious Alice appeared in the shattered glass doorway, her handgun still tucked under her coat. Alice's eyes darted up and down the street, seeking her quarry.

As careful as possible, Crystal cracked her door and slithered in, keeping a wary eye on Alice, who continued to scan for signs of Crystal.

Plunging the key in the ignition, Crystal gave it a furious crank. The old car gave its characteristic squeal, but in a full-blown mutiny, it refused to start.

Alice wheeled on the noise and spotted Crystal. Her eyes widened in alarm, and she leveled her gun and squeezed the trigger.

Crystal flinched at the muzzle flash and cried out as her passenger window exploded, showering her with glass. She turned the key again, but the car still refused to start. Another bullet smacked into her dash, shattering the speedometer.

Crystal threw open her door and flopped to the ground, keeping her head low as a third bullet cracked into the body of her car. The gunshots ceased, and the sounds of shouting from a nearby building filled her ears. Alice must be coming. Wild thoughts of sprinting as fast as she could kept flashing through her brain, but she was too terrified to break cover. She cast around for any sort of weapon. Her snowshoes and poles lay where they had been tossed in the backseat. Plunging her hand in, she latched onto a pole and yanked it out, clutching it in both hands.

She braced herself, straining to hear the sounds of Alice's footsteps, but her own gasps and the hammering of her heart were making anything as soft as a footfall impossible to hear. She flicked her eyes left and right, trying to see which way Alice was going to come around the car.

A shadow cast by a nearby streetlight gave Alice away as she burst around the back of Crystal's car. In that split second, Crystal reacted. She stood and cracked her pole down on Alice's outstretched arm with every ounce of strength she could muster.

Alice yelled in pain, the pistol flying out of her hand to skitter across the sidewalk. Cradling her arm in shock, Alice glanced up in time to see a desperate Crystal, who, with a powerful swing, smashed the pole over the woman's head.

Alice crumpled to the ground without a sound. Ryan staggered out of the apartment door, one arm wrapped around his waist, and his face twisted in pain. Spotting Crystal standing over his wife with her snowshoe pole, he lurched into the street toward them.

Dropping her makeshift weapon, Crystal ran to where the gun had fallen. Ryan pulled up level to his wife, when Crystal whirled on him, clutching the handgun.

She wasn't sure if she could shoot either of these two terrible people, even if they had meant to murder her. So, she did what she did best. She bluffed.

Pointing the gun at Ryan, she mustered her steeliest voice. "Don't move." Despite the shakiness she could hear in her words, her tone must have been stern enough. Ryan sank to his knees, wincing in pain as he thrust his hands up past his shoulders in surrender. In the distance, Crystal could hear the wail of police sirens.

Epilogue

Crystal stood in the snow, bliss filling her soul as she absorbed the clean air, the gorgeous snow-flocked forest, and the bracing chill. Everything was wonderful, and she had to remind herself she had almost not been alive to enjoy this moment.

Responding to 911 calls sparked by the gunshots, the police, including Holly, had raced to Bree's apartment building. In moments, they had Ryan and Alice in handcuffs, as well as Justin and Bree. True to his word, Conner had shown the video, and transferred the evidence, to Holly earlier in the afternoon. A subpoena was issued for Justin's arrest and the police had begun scouring the city for him.

Returning to the present moment, Crystal faced her captive audience, twenty-four first graders. The teacher she had met in the store had indeed kept checking back, and as soon as the guided tours became available, she had booked her class. As Crystal explained to the children the various ways small mammals survived during the winter, she reflected on how her life had unfolded in a fairy tale fashion.

Holly had received a commendation due to the fact that her informants (Crystal and Joe) had helped solve the murder case of Philip Calvert. After testimony from everyone involved, Justin and Bree were charged with withholding evidence and obstruction of justice, but it appeared they were in the clear on the murder charge. Ryan and Alice, however, faced the full wrath of the law. Not only were they being charged with Philip's murder, they had added attempted murder to their rap sheet by trying to kill Crystal. Blackmail and extortion were being considered by the district attorney, but he assured Crystal the murder charges were enough to keep them locked up for a lengthy amount of time.

As she wrapped up her lesson to the fidgeting audience, Conner took over and led the children on a short hike to an open field surrounded on two sides by a gentle hill. At the top of the hill was a collection of sleds which Conner had placed there earlier. The children were released to their own devices, and with shouts of glee, charged into the snow. They set to building snowmen, throwing snowballs, and rocketing down the hill on the sleds.

"Your black eye is almost faded," Conner informed her as he stepped next to her to help keep watch on their charges. Crystal had spent an evening in the emergency room getting checked out. She had come through relatively unscathed, but was covered in bruises from being slapped, kicked, and from her impromptu ride down a flight of stairs on top of Ryan.

However, she was proud of how well she had defended herself. Ryan and Alice had come out much worse in the exchange. Ryan had suffered a broken nose and rib. Alice, on the other hand, had a broken wrist, as well as a concussion from Crystal's snowshoeing pole. The self-defense classes she had taken had paid off in a big way.

One of the most wonderful things of all was the gratitude and acceptance of the other guides. Amelia had called them all into work for a short meeting to tell them the police had arrested and charged several suspects with the murder of the man who had supposedly died of an accident while under their care. The insurance company had conceded there was no fault with ECO Adventures, and were renewing their coverage. Amelia had distributed the schedule for the upcoming trips and left the room.

As soon as Amelia had departed, Suzy had stood and announced, "Any badass who takes a hit, gets to her feet, and beats the crap out of the psychopaths attacking her is a friend of mine." Ethan and Conner had laughed and applauded, echoing the sentiment. Suzy had then presented Crystal with a new phone to replace the one Alice had destroyed, and proclaimed all of the guides had chipped in to buy it.

Crystal returned her attention to Conner. "It's feeling a lot better. If I didn't see the bruise in the mirror every morning, I would have forgotten it was there."

Conner glanced over at her. "Are we still on for tonight?"

"Dinner at La Travierta? I wouldn't miss it for the world." Crystal laughed with the sheer joy of the moment.

Conner grabbed hold of her hand. Together they kept watch on the children frolicking in the snow. Soon, it would be time to leave, but for now they stood together, surrounded by the beauty of the snow-covered forest.

Thank you for purchasing
this publication of The Wild Rose Press, Inc.

For questions or more information
contact us at
info@thewildrosepress.com.

The Wild Rose Press, Inc.
www.thewildrosepress.com

To visit with authors of
The Wild Rose Press, Inc.
join our yahoo loop at
http://groups.yahoo.com/group/thewildrosepress/